SUNSHINE

TRIDENT AGENCY
BOOK ONE

KIKI CLARK
EM LINDSEY

Cover Designer: Natasha Snow Designs
Editor: Sandra Dee, One Love Editing

There's a fine line between hate and fated mates...

Jeremiah has better things to do than babysit the bratty crown prince of the Sirens. His personal protection agency is the best though and the king and queen won't settle for less.

Being a practically invulnerable Hellhound doesn't hurt either.

Remi's selfish and uncaring attitude drives him crazy and confirms his suspicions about the prince being nothing more than a spoiled man-child. He doesn't care that the more time they spend together, the more possessive his Hellhound becomes of the little princeling.

Or that it turns out first impressions might be misleading…

Falling for a client is the last thing he can let happen. His name and his company's reputation are on the line. He won't be led around by his… instincts.

When things begin to heat up between them though, he can't deny their connection might just be destiny. One thing he knows for sure?

Fire and water will always make steam.

*Sunshine is the first in the new Trident Agency series by co-writing duo, EM Lindsey and Kiki Clark. It features a grumpy Hellhound affectionately known as Sunshine to his teammates, a half-Siren prince who's more interested in sassying than following orders, a size difference a certain bodyguard loves to take advantage of, and truckloads of *chef's kiss* possessiveness and touch him and get unalived vibes.*

1

REMI

"Come on, man. Don't be a fuckin' pussy. If you wait any longer, you're never going to hook up."

Remi dragged both hands through his hair, then glanced over his shoulder. There was the smallest niggle of worry in his gut, but he was getting better at ignoring it. It was just years of training—for the media, for perceived threats against his family, for whatever bullshit excuse his parents used to try and keep him in a bubble.

It had taken him a long time to wear them down about university, and he had spent the last two years proving to both them and the naysayers in his personal guard that nothing was going to happen. Because he didn't live in a damn movie.

Yeah, he was the crown prince, and yeah, there was some… controversy about his parents being fated mates in spite of the fact that they were mixed species. And sure, people yelled horrible things at him sometimes because he was only half Siren.

But he wasn't going to let those assholes stop him from living his life.

Hell, he was two years into his membership with the Kappa Alpha Chi fraternity, which was almost entirely human, and none of his fraternity brothers gave a shit that he was half Siren. His mom had thrown an epic fit about it when he said he was pledging, saying that a house full of frat boys would only exploit his powers, but none of them had ever even hinted about wanting him to take off his ring and use his Voice.

Sometimes, they liked putting him front and center at events and fundraisers, and that made him uncomfortable, but he understood. But for the most part, he was just another one of the guys, and while he was with them, he didn't need to think about his future. He didn't need to feel the weight of being the heir to the Kingdom of Midlona or the pressures of needing to marry well and produce children and all the other responsibilities that made him want to pull his own face off.

A hand dropped on his shoulder, jostling him out of his thoughts, and he looked over at the frat VP and his best friend, who was smiling at him with too-straight teeth. Thaddeus McCornal was the son of some politician that Remi should probably know, but he'd spent a lot of his life deliberately not paying attention to human politics.

It was always war and anger and random laws being passed to try and suppress Supes. And okay, he might be going to school in a human country, but he wasn't going to stay there after graduation. The moment he'd been accepted to Hillsland University, Thad had taken Remi under his wing and promised to show him the ropes.

And he had.

Remi's face stretched into a genuine smile as he met his friend's blue eyes, and he let Thad drag him past the bouncers and into the fray.

The bass was heavy, rumbling through his bones, and he felt a pang in his chest because it had been so long since he'd been able to sing. At home, he could take off his ring and let his power flow as freely as it wanted. Plenty of spells protected Midlona from anyone who might be affected by Siren Song. He was safe there.

Music was part of him, just like breathing, and though he couldn't participate, he could still feel it. He closed his eyes and swayed along to the beat as he hung on to Thad's shirt while they made their way up to the bar, and he shook himself out of his self-imposed trance as Thad started ordering a round of shots for everyone.

"Double for this fucker right here," Thad said, shaking Remi's shoulder. "He finally nutted up and got rid of his freak ex-boyfriend."

Remi winced. "He's not a freak."

And he wasn't. Remi had thought maybe Oz was actually the one—not a fated mate because he was pretty sure he was too human for that—which was all well and good because he didn't even want a mate. But his humanity, in the end, was the problem, and he'd been dumped.

"Dude. He's a fucking Nephilim. I can't believe they even let him near our school. Do you know what those freaks are capable of?" Thad said.

Jori—the president—leaned in and nodded. "Yeah. Relax, man. We know you're not one of them, okay? You're, like, one of the good ones."

Remi took the shot handed to him and let the alcohol burn through his veins. He was more sensitive to it than humans were, so it only took the single drink to have him swaying in his seat and laughing along at nothing. The crowd seemed to get thicker and the air hotter, and he wasn't sure if he wanted to cry or vomit or dance—or maybe all three.

"I gotta get up," he said, pushing off the stool.

Jori whooped loudly and grabbed his arm. "Fuck yeah, baby. Let's dance!"

Remi found himself pulled into the crowd, and in spite of the fact that the world was spinning and he was surrounded by humans, he let himself go. He moved his body the way it wanted to move, and he could feel people staring, but he didn't care. There were hands on his hips, and someone was in front of him, keeping him moving to the beat.

Then there were more hands, dragging him… somewhere. His head was still spinning hard, and he felt a sudden rush of panic because he wasn't on the dance floor anymore, and the person was holding him too tightly.

He tried to pull his hand away, but his limbs felt heavy and weak.

"Stop," he said, slurring the consonants.

He pulled harder, but the shadowed figure in front of him just laughed. "Shut the fuck up."

The stranger kicked out, and Remi realized it was a fire exit, but no alarm was going off. He stumbled over the lip of the doorway and fell to his knees. His thin jeans did nothing to protect his skin, and pain radiated up his thighs, the gravel cutting into his palms as he tried to brace himself.

"Where's the fucking car? We need to get him—"

Before Remi's panic broke through the haze of liquor burning its way through him, there was a shout, then a scuffle. His head spun when two shots were fired, the loud cracking making his ears ring. He couldn't seem to get his balance, but a pair of strong, familiar hands had him.

"Your Royal Highness." It was his personal bodyguard, Greg, and he sounded pissed—which made sense seeing as he was a Demon, and their tempers were legendary. This wasn't the first time Remi had given him the slip this semester, and he knew he was one fuckup away from his parents dragging him back home and forcing him to finish his education through tutors.

"I'm sorry," he said, his tongue still thick. "I don't… I don't know what happened…"

"Come with me, sir," Greg said. His tone was still clipped, but his touch was gentle, and he supported Remi's wobbling steps toward the large SUV.

As the door opened, he froze and started to fight Greg's hold. "Wait! My friends…"

"Remington," Greg said, and the power in his voice had Remi frozen to the ground. "Your friends are fine. The guards have shut the club down, and they're searching for any more suspects."

Remi blinked, his head starting to hurt. "I don't understand."

"You were almost kidnapped, sir. Your parents have already been informed, and they've… requested your presence back at the palace."

Remi tugged his arm away from Greg, but he knew he wasn't about to get far. "I have class," he said weakly.

Greg merely cocked one of his thick eyebrows, making him look very much like a Demon, especially the way his skin seemed to shimmer under the yellow streetlight. "I think your professors will give you extensions if you need them."

"Isn't this kind of an overreaction?" Remi grumbled as he gave in and finally climbed into his seat.

Greg was quick behind him and let out a sigh as he shut the door. "No. Any attempt on your life is taken seriously, sir."

Remi scoffed as he fumbled in the little minifridge for a bottle of water. It was imported from Midlona, and it was one of the few things that could truly quench his thirst. His head started to clear a bit more, and he felt shame curling through him, making his cheeks heat up.

Gods, everyone was going to be talking about the incident. They'd all know it was because he was the stupid, fucking crown prince. They'd all stare at him—blame him for the club shutting down. Blame him for disrupting everything.

And he had to go crawl away like some scolded child because of it.

"This is stupid," he said. "Just take me back to my apartment. It's not a big deal."

Greg gave him a long look, then said, "It is. It wasn't an isolated incident."

When Remi's mouth fell open to ask him what the hell he was talking about, Greg pulled out his phone and showed him the screen. Remi's vision was still screwed, so he had to close one eye, but after a second, he processed the article headline.

Siren Queen Grace and her husband, King James, of Midlona, along with the young prince and princess, were attacked today on a royal walkabout during the opening of a new children's hospital.

If anything could sober Remi, it was that. His parents were overprotective, but he loved them, and they loved him—almost beyond reason. And the fact that his little brother and sister had been involved was like taking a bucket of cold water to the face.

"Are Sadie and Percy…"

"They're fine, Your Highness," Greg said softly, tucking his phone away. "But there's something going on, and until we can get to the bottom of it, your parents feel it would be safer for you at the palace. And," he added when Remi sucked in a breath to argue, "I happen to agree. I'm better at my job with my whole security team. I can't let anything happen to you."

Remi deflated against the seat of the car, pissed as he was because he was tired of his life being disrupted all because of who he was. But he couldn't deny that Greg was right. At least for now. He'd go home and wait a week, and when nothing happened—just like always—he'd annoy his parents into letting him come back.

He'd use all of his charm to get his professors to give him some extensions, and life would go back to the way it was. The way it should be. And who knew? Maybe while he was home, he could finally mourn the loss of… well, maybe not Ozias, but the loss of what he thought Oz was going to be.

His first relationship. His first disappointment. And one more person who thought he was too weak and pathetic to take care of himself.

Remi knew he was behaving like a petulant brat, but the alcohol was wearing off, and he was pissed. All the quiet understanding he'd felt in the car had dissolved with his buzz, and he'd kicked up enough of a fuss that Greg gave in and took him back to his place so he could pack.

The Demon also didn't put up a fight when Thad showed up and Remi proceeded to lock Greg and the small security team out in the hallway. Greg knew Remi didn't have the power to slip away from him, and Thad was just a human, so there was little they could do.

Not that Remi didn't consider it.

"I wish I had, like, a secret bathroom window or an attic or something," he muttered savagely as he tossed more of his shirts into his third case.

Thad watched him with a mild expression and quirked eyebrow. He looked very much like a politician's son, the way he was sitting in Remi's armchair with his ankle resting on his knee, his blond hair perfectly in order in spite of the chaos earlier that night.

After a second, Thad let out a sigh. "I mean, you're the crown prince, man. Why don't you just order them to leave you alone?"

"Because they work for my parents," Remi said, his voice half a growl. He tossed the lid over the third case and moved on to the fourth—his shoes. "And they're unreasonable, overprotective assholes. One tiny kidnapping attempt, and they act like it's the end of the world. It was probably just some dickhead who wanted ransom money, and it's not like we couldn't afford to pay it."

Thad's second eyebrow joined his first as he watched Remi load up his case with pair after pair of shoes. "So, uh, how long are you going to be gone?"

"Not long, if I have anything to say about it," Remi told him. He glanced down, then flushed a bit and offered Thad a sheepish grin. "I don't like to leave my favorite pairs behind."

"Bro. I'm not judging," Thad said, waving his hand. "My dad gets so pissed whenever we take our ski vacation because we need a whole separate car for all me and my sister's crap."

Remi managed a smile in spite of himself and the current situation. But hearing the word *sister* made him think of his own. The twins were barely four and completely helpless. He didn't like the idea of being so far away from them, especially if someone was targeting their family.

He really did feel suffocated by his parents some days. As far as kingdoms across the world went, Midlona was fairly innocuous. They mostly traded in Siren Water, which gave most Supes a feeling of euphoria—nicknaming it love potion. Humans were barely affected, but they still craved the shit, and Midlona's economy was thriving. The only real controversy happened long before Remi was born when his mom fell in love with a scholarly, second-born human prince whose elder brother had nine kids, which effectively removed him from ever taking the throne.

As Remi grew up, his dad had always told him he'd never wanted the crown, and it was only the love he had for his wife that changed his mind about taking on that kind of responsibility.

Remi used to dream about a love like that. Hell, he still did. He wanted to fall head over heels for someone who he'd willingly give up a kingdom for. But he'd only had the one relationship, which had been thrilling at first, considering that Oz was a TA and forbidden fruit.

He was also one of the only Supes on campus, which was why Remi was drawn to him in the first place. Ozias was good-looking and nice, and there was an edge of danger about him, considering he was Nephilim, and they were notorious for being both powerful and unpredictable. Remi assumed there was a hidden, tantalizing darkness under Oz's quiet, nerdy façade.

And maybe there was, but it was obvious after six months that he had no plans to show that side to Remi. Ever. Remi did his best to antagonize him into hate sex, needle him into showing his power—anything he could think of to get Oz to come to bed with a little bit of edge.

Remi fantasized about those big hands taking him by the throat and putting him on his knees and…

Yeah.

Oz had just been… kind. He'd been sweet and careful with Remi, constantly checking in and never moving beyond second base. Remi wanted more though, and it was clear Oz had no interest in that.

Remi let his friends call Oz a freak and whatever boring, banal insults they could come up with only because he was frustrated, but the truth was, he was just afraid that everyone was going to be like Oz. That every person he fell for would see him as some weak, delicate princeling who needed protecting.

He was a Siren, after all—and only half at that. His single ability was a half-potent Siren Voice and Song that he wasn't allowed to use outside of Midlona's borders lest he start an international incident.

"Yo. Are you going to be okay?" Thad asked him, shattering his inner crisis monologue.

Remi looked up and affected a smile, hoping it looked like his usual lazy, smug grin. "I'm fine. Just annoyed, you know?"

Thad gave him a somber nod. "It happens to the best of us. Don't stress about it. One time, my dad got this string of death threats against his entire family, and he made me miss out on homecoming week."

"Shit," Remi said. "Who did he piss off?"

"Oh, you know. The leftist assholes who think that every single being in the world should be able to walk around totally unchecked. But, I mean, you know me. You know I don't have a problem with Supes. You're my best friend."

Remi nodded in spite of the uncomfortable sensation rising in his gut. It was happening a lot more with Thad lately, but he shoved it down because Thad and his fraternity brothers were his only friends and his chance to be fucking normal for once.

"And my dad's just like me. I mean, we have tons of Supes working for our house. He just thinks there should be some legislation passed that protects people who can't protect themselves. I mean, shit, imagine if Dragons were allowed to just walk free. Or Demons? Hellhounds, bro?"

Remi's stomach twisted. He'd never met a Hellhound, but they had Dragons working for their personal security team. And there was no way in hell Thad didn't know that Greg was a Demon after all this time.

"So yeah, those animal rights activists got all up in arms about his vote and started threatening my whole family. Obviously, it blew over," Thad said, waving his hand like he didn't have a care in the world. "Your parents will stop panicking eventually."

Remi blew out a puff of air and glanced around his room. It looked trashed from the way he'd been packing, but whatever. He had a service to take care of it. The only thing that mattered was that he had his favorite things ready to go and that he would follow Thad's advice and just wait until the storm passed.

Then he could get back to his regularly scheduled program of pretending like this wasn't just a pause in his destiny before his role and his title took over and erased every chance he had to be just some guy.

2

SUNSHINE

If someone were to have asked Jeremiah what the biggest downside of being a Hellhound was, they'd probably expect something like being a supernatural pariah, or not having any kind of pack or family, or not being allowed in half the countries in the world because of his hellfire. And those were issues he'd faced most of his life.

The fact that he'd grown up between shelters and living on the streets because of those things should have been enough.

But no. The answer he'd give would be not being able to feel the heat enough to wake up when his goddamn bed was on fire. Of course, he learned his lesson years back when he'd woken up to a spray-down with a fire extinguisher the day the only decent foster family he'd ever had kicked him out. They didn't want to believe him when he swore that he'd never intentionally hurt them.

But it hadn't mattered, and he'd just felt more like a freak —a reject—after losing out on that family, and he'd been pretty sure no one would ever take him in again.

He'd learned to sleep with fire-retardant blankets, and he kept his door closed and locked everywhere he went after that. He could control it now that he was older, wiser, and well trained in defense, but when he slept… sometimes he slipped.

It didn't really bother him as much anymore when the bright, orange glow behind his closed eyelids was fire instead of the morning sun, but it served as a reminder that he'd always be a little off-kilter when he had to deal with powerful politicians. He tried to keep his teams—his family—away from those in power, only because almost all of them were corrupt and not above exploiting the Trident Agency for their own gain—and they'd had everyone from presidents to kings attempt to use them as scapegoats when things didn't go right.

The Trident Agency had set up shop on the border between the kingdoms of Midlona and Averna. Sirens and Gargoyles had formed a strong alliance hundreds of years before Jeremiah was even a thought in the universe, and they were two of the only countries who offered open sanctuary to almost all species. Neither kingdom blinked at the sight of a personal protection agency that employed a melting pot of creatures, in spite of the fact that both sides tended to stick to their own just like everyone else.

So when the queen of the Sirens called for help, he damn well fucking answered. Even if it meant he woke up the morning of the meeting bathed in hellfire.

There was no Hellhound community for Jeremiah to run to, even if he wanted to escape his current situation—not that he would. But it just wasn't something that happened. Hellhounds had never been given a chance to form their own communities. In school, they learned about the one time three thousand years ago when Hellhounds attempted to form their own kingdom near the Angria Desert. They thrived for fifty years before a horde of Demons came in to raze them to the ground, scattering them to the winds.

Now, the few that remained could exist quietly, so long as

they didn't stir up trouble. But for the average Hellhound, a higher education was next to impossible, and getting a job doing anything but the most menial, demeaning tasks in a city was a damn miracle.

Jeremiah himself was a walking, talking contradiction. He was rich, he was powerful, he had contacts in high places, and people didn't fuck with him. But he was still feared, looked at with disgust. It had taken years of working his ass off to get where he was, of expanding the agency into several teams and cultivating favors from high-ranking officials to make sure that if he or any of his people went down, they'd topple governments.

And he still didn't always feel steady.

Taking a few deep breaths, Jeremiah pulled his fire back in, waiting for it to settle as a warm simmer under his skin, then threw back his blankets and rose. What he wanted more than anything was a quiet, lazy morning where he could drink coffee on his balcony and not have to think for a while.

What he had instead was a meeting with the goddamn queen and king of Midlona at eleven that morning because all five members of the family had been the victims of what appeared to be a coordinated attack. The eldest son, Remington, was off at Hillsland University, which was a fucking choice in itself, though Jeremiah told himself he wasn't allowed to judge what the family did.

But Hillsland was also the most notoriously anti-Supe country on the planet, so why they allowed their half-Siren son to attend school there was beyond him.

He would put money on the attacks being orchestrated by some fanatic purist in one of their weird human churches over there, but he knew better than to assume it was the simple answer. Queen Grace and King James had stirred up controversy the day she rejected her arranged marriage to a well-born Siren lord and gave her hand to a human royal with no real fortune, power, or particular good looks.

It had pissed off humans and Sirens alike, so Jeremiah had to consider all angles.

Because when it came to politics, there was always more than one thread that needed to be unraveled.

Taking his time in a cold shower, he soothed his heated skin, then dressed in his usual attire—ripped jeans, a T-shirt, and his leather jacket. He always stood apart from the rest of his Alpha Team in their pressed suits and perfectly combed hair, but he'd long since realized it didn't matter how he dressed or spoke or conducted himself. The moment anyone knew who he was—*what* he was—they wrote him off.

So why bother trying to please anyone?

He finger-combed his waves, not bothering to do much beyond add a little product to keep it from frizzing, thanks to the humid Midlona coast, and then he filled his travel mug with as much coffee as he could fit without it spilling over and snagged a piece of fruit from the bowl before heading out.

His motorcycle wasn't parked far from his building, and he slipped his coffee into the little holder on the side before taking the fruit down in six enormous bites. He could feel eyes watching him. His neighbors hadn't been thrilled when a Hellhound had bought the penthouse of their building, but he didn't give a shit. He just kept his head down and waited for them to stop sending letters to his mortgage company about the risk of the building going up in flames.

It had been five years now, and while they still gave him a wide berth, they'd stopped overbuying fire extinguishers and demanding that the city install a couple of extra hydrants by the street. A few still scurried away if they came across him in the elevator or by the mailboxes, but he preferred the solitude to the endless chatter some of them exhibited with other tenants.

Swinging one leg over his bike, Jeremiah pulled out his phone and checked his messages. He only had two, both from

Priest. He was the unofficial Alpha Team messenger, but only because he never stopped running his mouth.

Priest: *Hope you're all on your way.*

Priest: *The queen is hotter in person than she is on TV. Think she'd let me hear her Siren Song if I asked nicely?*

Sunshine: *Don't get any fucking ideas. This is a big client, and we could use the cash after the last few pro bonos.*

Priest: *Aww. Hellhound's all bark this morning. See you soon?*

Jeremiah decided to ignore him—and the fact that someone had changed his name in the group chat *again*—and shoved his phone into his pocket before revving his engine and tearing off down the street. It was a long ride to the castle, which was just going to set up an even longer day, but he supposed that when it was all over and they uncovered whatever plot was threatening the royals, it would be worth it.

Opening the lid to his coffee, Jeremiah blew a small stream of hellfire to warm the liquid back up. He heard one of the gate guards suck in a breath and the familiar sound of people reaching for weapons. He ignored them, even as Priest stiffened on his right and Knight on his left. Storm brought up the rear, so he was entirely protected if someone decided to get a little… overexcited.

"If we could speed this along," Priest drawled. His tone held a warning that most people took seriously, considering he wasn't just a Demon, but he was an Incubus. Most Demons had the ability to turn their powers on and off at will, but Incubi struggled more than others because they were always, *always* hungry.

The guard to their left swallowed thickly, but the one making a quick approach—a hulking Dragon who looked oddly familiar—just smiled. "Don't mind them. They're still in training."

Before Jeremiah could say anything, he was elbowed out of the way, and Storm was wrapping his massive arms around the guard. They both shared the same dark umber skin and mahogany eyes, though the guard was definitely taller and broader than their team member.

It was obvious they didn't just share the same species, but they were very clearly related.

"This is my asshole big brother," Storm said with a shit-eating grin. He was normally as stone-faced as a damn Gargoyle around outsiders, so it was interesting to see how profoundly his face shifted at having his family near.

Jeremiah fought back the ugly little surge of jealousy and reminded himself he didn't need blood family like that because he had this. He had his team. He had Knight and Priest, who were the sole reason he was there standing there that day. They'd started the Trident Agency with him years ago and stood by him through all the bullshit they'd gone through in the beginning. And now they had Storm and Slate, adding to their team and family.

He didn't need anything else. He had more than most.

He cleared his throat and extended his hand, and it said something about Storm's brother that he didn't hesitate or flinch before shaking it.

"It's a pleasure. I'm Thorne, head guard here at the palace, and I'll be with you during the interview today. My team will be providing any additional security you feel your team might need."

Knight let out a small cough, and Jeremiah could see his eyes wrinkle with a smirk behind his sunglasses. "Assuming we take the contract."

Storm rolled his eyes. "Don't worry about him. He's always a dick. This is—"

"Priest," the Demon said, quickly taking Jeremiah's place

in the handshake line. "That's Knight, but he won't shake your hand. Vampire thing," he added, and no one called him out on the bullshit. Knight didn't shake hands because he couldn't stand being touched by people he didn't trust, but it was easier to just blame it on his condition. "And this is Sunshine, our fearless leader."

"Jeremiah Avril," he said with a glower. The others went by their code names, having adopted them as nicknames years ago, but Jeremiah's was a poke at him being perpetually grumpy, so he used his real name in professional settings, even if he couldn't get the team to call him by it.

Avril was the sole possession he had left from when his parents abandoned him on the streets at the tender age of three. He couldn't remember if it had belonged to his mother or father, but he'd kept it anyway as a reminder that no matter how much he earned or achieved, he couldn't forget where he came from.

Thorne smiled at each of them, then beckoned them along through the main foyer doors. "Easton's told me a lot about you. It's nice to put faces to the names though. I'm sure most of the stories are exaggerations."

Storm shoved his brother good-naturedly. "Shut up."

"I'm sure they're all true," Priest butted in, grinning widely. "Especially all the ones about Storm—sorry, *Easton*—doing late-night flights to get us all tacos after a long day."

Thorne gave his brother an unimpressed look, but the corners of his mouth were twitching.

Jeremiah ignored the banter and took in the surroundings, not really impressed by palaces anymore. Instead, all he could see were little nooks and crannies where an attacker could slip past the royal guard and attack the family. Extravagance always led to a false sense of security, and that was how kingdoms toppled.

He made mental notes as they were led up a staircase, down a massive corridor with mirrors on either side, and through an atrium with a fountain. He could taste the power of the water on the air as it gently hit his heated skin. The euphoria of Siren Water didn't work on him… much. It gave him a few minutes of a high, but it left as quickly as it came, and he always felt a little shitty after.

He caught Knight's eye, and he just shook his head and rolled his eyes. Jeremiah was glad to know they were on the same page about all this… nonsense.

Thorne came to a halt in front of a pair of guarded, massive double doors, intricately carved with some ocean scene featuring Sirens wrapping long tails around each other, holding giant spears. He vaguely knew there had been some war centuries ago between the Sirens and other ocean shifters, but it wasn't something he ever paid close attention to.

Each species had their own origin myths, and for a long while, Sirens had been almost as feared as Hellhounds. After all, it was hard not to worry about a creature who could control you with a single spoken word.

Except Sirens were beautiful, and they had done their part in creating a magical device—often worn as a pendant or ring—that could suppress their Voice. That, and keeping to their own borders, had set most other kingdoms at ease, though he'd heard plenty of whispers from both human and Supes alike that they needed to be further restrained.

It was why the attack hadn't surprised him.

It *was* why he was surprised the human-Siren marriage had lasted for this long.

"Give me one moment to make sure they're ready for you," Thorne said.

The two guards let him slip past, and Priest let out a sigh, sagging against Jeremiah's arm and fluttering his lashes at him. "Gods, Sunshine, you're so warm. Hold me."

"No," Jeremiah said flatly, keeping his attention on the closed door in front of them.

"Spoilsport," Priest muttered, but he kept his head resting on Jeremiah's shoulder, and he made no move to dislodge Priest from where he was comfortable. It reminded him of the early days on the streets when Priest was young, half-starved, and freezing to death during unforgiving winters.

He knew the damp air was hard on the Demon, who didn't come with his own internal furnace like Hellhounds did, and he had to fight the urge to wrap an arm around Priest. The Incubus was always cuddly as hell, but Jeremiah tried to at least appear halfway professional in front of new clients.

"If this is some kind of power trip to keep us waiting…" Knight warned quietly as the minutes dragged on.

Storm scoffed. "My brother wouldn't work for people like that."

Knight turned and cocked an eyebrow at him. "Your brother might be a good person, but even good people debase themselves if they're paid enough."

Storm's eyes flared orange, and the guards at the doors straightened even further, eyes narrowing on Knight. "Say that again."

"No. He won't," Jeremiah said, putting an extra growl in his voice. "I don't know if you two are high from the fucking fountain or what, but get your heads out of your asses. We're about to meet a goddamn queen and king."

Knight rolled his shoulders, likely trying to shake off the effect from the water he hadn't even realized was hitting him. "We don't need this job. I have a bad feeling."

Storm had his eyes closed and was focused on settling his breathing, but he gently extended his arm to brush his forearm against Knight's in apology.

"No, but the more contracts like this we take, the less bullshit we have to deal with if people get upset about any of our… tactics," Jeremiah reminded him, lowering his voice so the guards watching them wouldn't hear. "Once this meeting is over, you and I will head back to HQ."

Knight nodded once, jaw tight. None of them said anything, but it was obvious something about this place was triggering a memory from Knight's past, and when that happened, he tended to shut down. Jeremiah would make sure he was taken care of when they left though.

Just then, the guards shifted, and both doors opened behind them. Thorne was there without his casual smile from before, but he didn't seem tense, so Jeremiah didn't stop his team from following him into the enormous room.

"What do we do again?" Priest hissed to him as they stepped past the threshold. "Do we bow?"

"You fuckin' curtsey," Knight murmured.

"I'm going to fuck you in your dreams if you don't shut your mouth," Priest threatened under his breath.

Storm had to turn a laugh into a cough, his face getting red at the effort to contain it.

"And I'm going to set you all on fire if you don't knock it off," Jeremiah warned them. He stepped ahead and set his gaze on the queen and king, who he expected to be in thrones. Instead, they were seated on a sofa, side by side, holding hands.

They both rose when the team got close enough, and Jeremiah forced his knee to bend just enough to be considered a respectful bow. Out of his periphery, he could see his team doing the same, and the royal pair were either satisfied or they were too stressed to care.

Jeremiah was betting on the latter.

"Your Majesties," Jeremiah said.

The queen offered something that might be considered a smile. She was overwhelmingly beautiful, with hair the color of white opal. Her eyes were an iridescent violet, which might have looked strange on any other being, but it fit her perfectly. When she moved her hand, Jeremiah could see faint scales shining along her skin, a lot like a Dragon's when they half shifted.

To her direct contrast was her husband. He was several inches shorter, stout, with a slight belly and dark hair. He was handsome, though perhaps not classically in the human world, let alone the kingdom of Sirens, but when she turned to look at him, Jeremiah saw genuine love in her eyes behind her worry.

"We're very grateful you could see us," she said, gesturing to the remaining seats in front of them.

Jeremiah waited until the queen and king resumed sitting before he lowered himself to the edge of a chair and folded his hands between his spread knees. "I was forwarded your security team's file yesterday, and I have to confess, it's not a lot to go on. No witness was able to get any kind of positive ID on anyone, and from what I understand, your son was… inebriated."

The king looked disappointed while the queen sighed and rolled her eyes up toward the ceiling. "Yes," she said. "He's at university."

"A human university that's only started recently admitting Supes after a lawsuit forced them," Priest cut in. He always played devil's advocate in these meetings, seeing what kind of reaction he could get out of potential clients. They liked to know what they were getting into before agreeing to a contract. "In a country notorious for their… antiquated views on what people like us should and shouldn't be allowed to do."

"We try to let him make his own choices. Learn from his own mistakes," she defended.

Priest smiled unkindly. "Until those mistakes bring terrorists to your door."

The king started to look angry, but the queen just looked devastated, turning her wet eyes on Jeremiah. "Do you think that's who's behind this?"

"No," Jeremiah said before Priest could continue riling them up. Knowing how hard to push wasn't always the Demon's forte, his self-control pretty much nonexistent. "Not necessarily. It's one option we'd need to explore, but unfortunately, your marriage alone has earned you outspoken enemies."

"We knew that going in," the king said, speaking for the first time. His voice was pleasant—low and even and kind. He seemed quiet and even a little plain, but Jeremiah instantly knew what the queen had seen in him when she'd fallen in love. "We just didn't think it would ever get this far. We thought people would grow to accept us and our children."

"Well, we can get to the bottom of it, and while we can't guarantee that there won't be another attack," Knight said, leaning forward over his knees to meet the royal couple's gaze, "we are the best in this business. Our only real concern is your son. I read the reports last night, and he seems a bit…"

"Reckless," Jeremiah cut in, because it was true, and he had no plans to sugarcoat it. The crown prince had made questionable decisions that put him in a vulnerable position, and from his personal guard's report, it seemed like the prince had put up a fight about returning home.

The queen sighed and shared a look with her husband before she glanced back at Jeremiah. "Yes. He's been a bit… rebellious lately. We were hoping that his time in university would make him understand the importance of his role. I just hope—"

The queen's words were cut off when a door to the side opened. The entire Alpha Team jumped to their feet, but they relaxed a second later when the youngest royals rushed into the room, laughing with a disgruntled nanny at their heels.

"I'm so sorry," the woman was panting, but the queen just waved her off as she gathered her children close.

"Please don't. Why don't you take your lunch now, and they can sit with us."

Jeremiah glanced at Knight, who was smirking at him. It was well-known he didn't have a soft spot for kids the way some of the others did. Priest was busy pulling faces at them, making them laugh.

Jeremiah looked back over at Queen Grace and King James, watching them hold their children like they were precious. He couldn't help but wonder what that would feel like—to be loved that way. He'd only known abandonment and hunger and fear at their age. And as he got older—survival. Distrust. Hatred.

He would kill for his team now. He would die for them. But their bonds weren't forged from affection.

"... should be the one assigned to the family. He has the most practical abilities to protect the family."

Jeremiah blinked, realizing he'd missed part of the conversation. But the way Priest was grinning at him, Storm's eyes were wide with surprise, and Knight was trying to hide a smirk, he realized what they were saying.

"I don't—"

But he couldn't finish the words. The queen regarded him, then nodded. "We want the best, and we've heard that's you. I trust you, Mr. Avril."

He blinked in shock. He didn't hear those words outside of his team often. Or at all.

"My guards can accompany you to the airport to retrieve my son, and I'll have my staff prepare your room for your stay." She rose before Jeremiah could protest, giving her hands a single clap and turning to Thorne. "Please get these gentlemen an ETA on the flight and any resources they need."

Jeremiah rose as the king did and took both their hands a little numbly as they said their goodbyes. He moved closer to Knight as they watched Priest with the kids, and he sighed. "He would be better at this than me."

Knight shook his head and bumped their shoulders together. "You and I both know that's not true. And if the Sirens found out that a sex Demon was living at the castle?"

"You think it's better than a Hellhound?" he challenged. "Storm should stay, then."

He didn't bother suggesting Knight—not only did the Vampire not enjoy working in the field, but it'd be just as scandalous for a *bloodsucker* to be living among the royals.

"He's too likely to defer to his brother." Knight nodded to where Storm and Thorne were chatting on their way out of the receiving room. "You never know. The family might surprise you. And I've seen the crown prince—he's not bad to look at."

Jeremiah tried not to visibly cringe so as not to insult the future king of the Sirens, but he shook his head quickly. "He's a petulant child who's only going to make my job harder."

Knight chuckled lightly, shrugging in concession, then led the way after the guards so they could get working on a viable plan to ensure the royal family survived.

3

REMI

"Gods, we could have taken the car and gotten back faster," Remi muttered, just loud enough to make sure Greg and his other guards heard him, but none of them reacted. In the safety of the private jet, they'd effectively been ignoring him since takeoff.

Luckily, they were about to touch down in Midlona.

Remi held in a sigh as he stared out the window at his future kingdom. The coastline was just barely visible from where they were above the airport, the Bellona Mountains rising like sentries to the north. He couldn't see it, but he could practically feel the suffocating walls surrounding the castle already.

Even after the alcohol had worn off and he'd talked to his mother, who'd been sparse on the details but told him a little more about what had happened during the family's walkabout, he still felt this was all just… a gross overreaction. There had to be some mistake. Crown prince or not, why would someone want to kidnap him except to try to get some money from his family?

A tiny voice in his head pointed out the wrongness of that, especially since they'd tried to take his family too, making a ransom payment impossible, but he pushed his earbuds into his ears harder to drown it out.

He'd hang out at the castle for a few days, maybe a week, and then he'd go back to his life and put the entire thing behind him. He'd dealt with weirder things before—it just came with being royalty. Once, a girl had cornered him at a party and asked to see his tail, getting pissed when he denied her.

Humans, he'd found, were rude but basically harmless. Sirens, on the other hand, could be self-righteous assholes because he wasn't a pureblood. His entire life, he'd heard remarks whenever he was outside the castle walls about what an atrocity it was that he was next in line for the throne. How he wasn't even *really* a Siren, just a weak halfbreed.

He gritted his teeth as the plane finally began its descent, his music unable to cover the unending noise in his head. When he was at university, it was easier to forget all the responsibility and scathing remarks waiting for him in Midlona. But as soon as they crossed the border, it was like all his insecurities knew and came rushing back.

By the time the plane came to a stop, Greg and the others were already up and moving, but he ignored them, not bothering to turn off his music as he unbuckled and gathered his things at a leisurely pace. Used to his antics, Greg waited next to him patiently, hands folded in front of him and eyes never still.

It was sort of funny to him how much more tense Greg and the others were when they were at home. Out among the humans, Remi blended unless someone knew what to look for—his lavender eyes and the way his skin had a barely perceptible iridescence when he was in direct sunlight or water being the biggest giveaways. But in Midlona, surrounded by perfect, pureblood Sirens, he stuck out like a mongoose among swans.

Sticking out meant being noticed, which meant Greg had to work harder to keep him safe.

As he descended the steps, he slipped on a pair of sunglasses, his head pounding at the relentless sunshine Midlona was known for. That and its briny humidity, but the air didn't bother him and his hangover. He was always thirsty in Hillsland, the dryness seeping all the moisture out of him and leaving him feeling parched constantly.

At home, he finally felt like he could breathe again.

There was a large black SUV with tinted windows waiting for them not too far away, the rest of the airport eerily still. He knew once he was in the vehicle and on his way, things would return to normal with people and other planes getting back to their busy lives and schedules. He tried not to visibly cringe thinking about how many people he'd inconvenienced just by arriving.

He was nearly on top of the SUV before he noticed the huge guy leaning against the rear door, arms folded across his miles-wide chest and frown firmly etched into his brow. He was also wearing sunglasses—a dark, basic pair though, nothing like the three-hundred-dollar ones on Remi's face—and his jeans were torn but in a way that looked like it was caused by honest-to-gods wear instead of being trendy. His plain white T-shirt was so tight and worn under his black leather jacket Remi could clearly see the dark hair between his pecs.

Nothing about him should have been appealing. But at the sight of him, Remi felt a vicious tug in the pit of his stomach, nearly making him stumble as he ripped his earbuds out, head spinning.

It wasn't until Greg stepped in front of him, eyes completely black and black sparks dancing around his knuckles, and blue flames appeared in the stranger's hands as he lowered his arms, that Remi realized the stupidly hot guy was a freaking Hellhound. He paused, trying not to show his surprise or apprehension.

"You're the fucking expert?" Greg spat, disgust pouring off him in waves.

Remi turned to him, stunned. He'd never seen Greg react that way—not even when Thad and his other frat brothers made semi-douchey comments or the first time he met Ozias, despite him being a Nephilim. It was his job to protect Remi, and that was it; he didn't have opinions about things or people, but there seemed to be genuine hatred on his face, and the Hellhound's smirk wasn't helping.

"I'm the expert," the guy drawled, not moving a single muscle and extinguishing the hellfire, seeming completely fine with the fact that a Demon looked three seconds away from taking his head off.

Not wanting to get caught in the middle of their pissing match, Remi stepped up next to Greg and asked, "Expert in what, exactly?"

For a moment, neither one seemed like they'd answer him, refusing to look away from each other. Greg's eyes were still pitch-black, but his hands weren't sparking anymore. It was like they were having a staring contest, despite the fact that you couldn't see the Hellhound's eyes at all.

Which… no, just no. Remi was not used to being ignored and immediately didn't like it. "Excuse me, can someone answer me right fucking now?"

Greg started to open his mouth, but the guy beat him to it, pushing off the SUV and saying, "I'm the new nanny. Get the fuck in the car."

Remi bristled and fought the urge to do whatever that deep voice told him to. He was a *prince*. No one spoke to him like that. "How dare you—"

"Please get in the car, Your Highness," Greg said lowly, focus still on the Hellhound. "Your parents are waiting, and

I'm sure everyone inside would like to get back to doing their jobs."

The gentle reminder got him moving, but he still narrowed his eyes on the Hellhound as he moved past him; smoking hot or not, Remi was not putting up with someone like that being in charge of taking care of his brother and sister. The fact that he'd been sent to retrieve Remi from the airport pissed him off as well—he knew his parents still saw him as a child, but he didn't need a damn *nanny* to take care of him!

He slipped into the SUV and fiddled with his earbud case and carry-on, not paying attention as the front passenger door opened and then the other rear door. When a huge, hulking body that radiated immense heat and swamped him in an alluring smoky scent settled next to him, he jerked his head up, staring at the Hellhound in shock, then up to where Greg was in the front, jaw so tense it looked like it would crack at any moment as he stared straight ahead.

"I'd rather Greg sat back here," he said, tone that perfect amount of haughty, do-as-I-say-without-question that he hadn't used since the last time he was in Midlona.

"Too damn bad."

Remi sucked in a breath through his teeth before turning to face the window, refusing to acknowledge the obnoxious man next to him the rest of the way to the castle. Less than five minutes passed before he was twisting back around though.

"What was your name again?"

The Hellhound raised a brow but didn't look up from where he was typing on his phone. His sunglasses were tucked into the front of his shirt, and his overgrown hair was falling over his forehead and into his eyes in a way that *wasn't* adorable. You couldn't be adorable and an enormous hell-beast without an ounce of manners. It was against the rules.

Sighing, Greg turned around in his seat, eyes thankfully back to normal. Remi knew what he was, but the scary, soulless eyes were never fun to witness. "His name's—"

"I can speak for myself, hellspawn," the guy interrupted, still not looking up from his phone.

Greg bristled at the name. "Listen, you arrogant, halfbreed dog—"

Remi flinched at the slur, and the Hellhound finally looked up, frowning at him, as Greg cursed and rubbed at his eyes. A hollow ache began to grow in his chest, and his eyes burned, making him grateful he hadn't bothered to take off his own glasses, even if they weren't as inscrutable as the Hellhound's.

"Your Highness, I apologize. I didn't mean—"

"It's fine," Remi said softly, looking back out his window but no longer seeing the city they were driving through on their way to his parents' castle. "I know you didn't."

No one said anything the rest of the way, or at least Remi didn't hear anything. He couldn't hear anything above the screaming in his head.

Halfbreed. Halfbreed. Halfbreed.

The second the SUV stopped inside the wall that enclosed the castle and its grounds, Remi was out like a shot, unable to sit there and be still for another damn second.

He heard Greg call after him, but he ignored him, not worried about needing protection within his family's walls. Nowhere else was he as safe as he was there—and nowhere else was he as suffocated.

He found the first person he could who'd know where his parents were—one of his mother's handmaidens arranging flowers in one of the eighty million sitting rooms—then took off for the library. So lost in his own thoughts, he was almost there before he noticed the silent shadow behind him. He assumed it was Greg trailing him, but when he turned his head to glance back, he was unexpectedly relieved to see it was the Hellhound instead.

Then he was annoyed.

"I don't actually require a nanny," he snapped. "Go find Sadie and Percy."

He didn't react, simply continuing to follow Remi as he stormed up the stairs. Which was fine. He planned on getting the rude man fired as soon as possible, so best he spend as little time with Remi's siblings as possible.

As he burst into the library, fury driving out the lingering hurt and awkwardness from the car ride, he zeroed in on where his mother was speaking to her personal assistant while flipping through correspondences on a tray in her lap. His father wasn't immediately visible, but he knew he was probably searching the farthest corners of the bookshelves for something he hadn't already read.

"This is ridiculous," Remi snapped, storming toward his mother. "I can't get pulled back home every time some rando decides to take a crack at me. That's literally what Greg and the others are for. They can handle things just fine."

His mother smiled up at her assistant. "Can you give us a moment, Jennette?"

"Of course, Your Majesty." Jennette gave him a soft look on her way past.

Once she closed the door behind her, the queen rose from her seat and approached him, wrapping him in a firm hug. Despite his anger and annoyance, he couldn't help but sink into the embrace, reveling in the strength of her hold and her calming ocean scent.

When she stepped back, he did his best to hold on to his frustration and straightened his spine. Her indulgent smile made his cheeks burn and throw a glance at the looming Hellhound, but he didn't seem to be paying attention to them, eyes scanning the two-story room in a familiar way.

"I know you're upset, dear," his mother began, her lilting voice further soothing his agitation. Even without using her Voice, she had a calming effect on those around her. "However, your father and I will not take any chances when it comes to your safety."

"Which is why I walk around campus with a four-person detail," he said, trying to match her steady calm. "I am safe there."

The Hellhound snorted derisively behind him.

Ire rising once more, he pointed at the annoying man. "And why did you send the *nanny* to meet me at the airport? I'm not a child."

Her opal brows furrowed. "What are—"

"But also, he's a terrible choice for the twins. He's rude and obnoxious. What was wrong with their old nanny? Heather? Feather? Twig? Whatever her name was—she was much nicer and knew how to speak to—"

"Remington," his mother finally interrupted, gaze darting back and forth between him and the Hellhound. "Mr. Avril isn't the nanny. His company does personal protection and security as well as investigates threats. They have been brought on to help us deduce how credible a threat this latest attack is. Mr. Avril will be staying at the castle and providing protection services to the family, in addition to our current guards."

Remi stared at her, a loud buzzing in his ears.

Finally, he asked softly, "He's not the nanny?"

"No, dear."

"He's a new bodyguard?"

Her lips twitched. "Essentially."

Whipping around, he pointed up at the Hellhound's face,

not impressed with the slight tip at the corner of his mouth. "You *jackass*! You will pay for that. I will… I will…" He floundered, unsure what he could do to make the man's life difficult, and finally settled on, "I don't like you. Stay away from me."

"Can't do that… Your Highness."

The pause before his title was noticeable, at least to him, and he knew it was only for his mother's benefit. Bristling, he whirled back to face her. "I don't want him anywhere near me. Greg is the point person on my detail."

"*Greg* nearly lost you at a fucking nightclub," the Hellhound scoffed. Stepping forward, he addressed the queen. "With all due respect, Your Majesty, Remington here is the biggest risk to the family's security. I've read through his protections' reports, and they describe a protectee who is irresponsible, uncooperative, and constantly slipping past their safety net. And"—he raised his voice when Remi tried to defend himself—"I can only assume they're leaving things out due to a sense of loyalty to him. They've been assigned to him since before he left for university, correct?"

His mother's mouth was tight as she nodded. "That's correct."

"That's too long. He doesn't respect their authority anymore, and they've grown complacent. You should be switching out detail assignments every six months."

Remi's mouth dropped open as his mother nodded again and sighed. "You're right. Thorne has been suggesting the same for years, but we've all just gotten so comfortable…"

"Too comfortable," the Hellhound said, voice softening just a little. "I'll speak with Thorne about changing assignments immediately."

"You have got to be kidding me!" Remi exploded, throwing his hands up. "This guy has been here—what? A day? And he's already changing everything. Things worked just fine before."

"If that were true, the group at the hospital wouldn't have gotten so close." The Hellhound turned to him, glowering down at him with glowing blue eyes. "No one should have been able to lay a hand on the boy—"

Remi gasped and met his mother's sad eyes. "They got that close to him and Sadie?"

She glanced at the Hellhound, then turned and moved back to her couch, settling on it once more. "They did. And they got you away from your friends and outside the building before your protection got to you. Mr. Avril is right. About everything."

He flinched at the hard edge her voice had taken, spotting his dad at the end of a nearby bookshelf, sympathetic grimace on his face. He wouldn't interfere though—in Midlona, his mother's word was law, and his dad respected that. He'd never contradict her in front of others, not even if the beast wasn't there and it was just Remi.

"Your recent behavior has me seriously contemplating whether you're mature enough to be attending university so far from home," she continued. His stomach dropped as his face heated at the reprimand. "For the foreseeable future, you will remain here in Midlona, and Mr. Avril will be taking over your protection since you don't seem to listen to or respect any of the others. Mr. Avril has the means to keep you safe, even from yourself."

"Mother—!"

"Your Majesty—"

She held up a hand, and they both stopped. "If we leave the castle grounds, you will, of course, be able to join us."

"*Again,*" the Hellhound said through his teeth, "with all due respect, there will be no leaving the castle grounds. Not until we can ascertain who and why someone is coming after the royal family."

Eyes narrowing, she leveled him with a look that brought most people to their knees, but the Hellhound seemed completely unfazed. Remi couldn't help but be impressed even as he continued to silently fume.

"I cannot hide away in the castle," she said. "The people need to see that we are unafraid, not cowering under our beds."

"I appreciate that, but that's a PR problem, Your Majesty, and I only deal with security. If you want me to do my job effectively, then you need to listen to me. For the next few days at least, your family needs to be in lockdown while my team works to find out what happened."

She didn't look happy, but she finally gave him a slight dip of her chin. "As you wish. We will stay within the grounds for… three days."

"Five."

Eyes narrowing, she said, "Four."

The Hellhound sighed. "Fine. Four days. Starting tomorrow. Your Majesty."

Her lips twitched, and Remi looked between them in confusion. No one told his mother what to do. No one. Yet this hellbeast just negotiated four days of zero movement beyond the walls from a queen known for visiting among her people and allies quite often. Being seen as strong and in control at all times was more important to her than her own safety, he knew that.

But apparently, not more important than her family's.

He started to turn for the door, planning on going to pout in his bedroom for the rest of the day and text Thad about the insanely hot but annoying new bodyguard he just got himself, but her soft words drew him up short.

"And Jeremiah?"

Jeremiah? Who the hell was—

The Hellhound turned back to her. "Your Majesty?"

"I need you to keep my son safe for me. Please."

Remi stared at her, eyes burning with tears at her pleading voice and anguished face. Gone was the stoic queen, replaced by his loving mother, who had only ever wanted him to be happy and protected.

The Hellhound—Jeremiah—nodded brusquely, closed fist covering his heart as he gave a short bow. "I will, ma'am. With my life if necessary. You have my word."

4

SUNSHINE

It didn't even take a full day, and Jeremiah was regretting his promise to the queen.

Not because he couldn't keep her son safe from whatever asshole was trying to come after the royal family. No, because he was pretty sure he was going to kill the kid himself.

After learning the truth of the situation, the crown prince had spent the entire rest of the day in his room with his music turned up so loud it hurt Jeremiah's sensitive ears. A servant had brought him dinner, but the guy couldn't even be bothered to answer the door when she knocked. Jeremiah had ended up taking the tray, then pounding on the door until it finally flung open.

Remington had jerked the food out of his hands without a word, then slammed it shut again.

Jeremiah wasn't sure what infuriated him more: the kid's ungrateful attitude or his seeming inability to take the threats against his family seriously. He didn't know how he'd survived into adulthood without realizing that being the crown prince meant there would be restrictions on his movements and activities. It was like Remi thought he could just live a normal life since he didn't look like he was a Siren. In fact, he and his younger brother both could probably pass as human most of the time.

The young princess, Sadie, was the only child of the king and queen who had noticeable scales along her jaw and down the outside of her forearms, even in the shadows.

But for Remi—and Percy—it was only in direct sunlight that you could see the soft iridescence, marking him as part Siren. That, and when you got up close on him and could see his eyes, their striking lavender color was a dead giveaway.

Not that Jeremiah thought they were striking. He'd barely even noticed them or how pink Remi's lips were. Or how good he smelled—like coconuts and the freshness of a sea breeze.

Regardless, it didn't matter how well Remington thought he could blend into the human world. The prince had to understand that Jeremiah wouldn't put his safety at risk. Period. He didn't care how much the kid pouted in his room about it either. In fact, if he stayed in his room for the next few days, that would make his job even easier. He didn't mind coordinating with his team from the hallway outside.

Of course, he didn't get that lucky.

Once Remi had finally fallen asleep the night before, Jeremiah had let a couple of royal guards come relieve him to make sure the prince didn't do something stupid like sneak out of his bedroom. Even though it had been well past midnight, he'd spent a couple more hours responding to emails and messages he'd missed earlier in the day and then going over some of the threat assessment reports Thorne had provided him and the rest of his team. Jeremiah was focusing on anyone the royal guards had deemed an actual threat, and the others would be reexamining anyone who had been written off to make sure they really weren't a threat.

When he'd shut off the lamp next to his obscenely

comfortable bed, he'd figured he'd be able to sleep in, not anticipating the lazy prince to be an early riser…

Jeremiah was woken up bright and early by sharp, excited screams that had him jolting out of bed, his hellfire heating his hands. He was racing into Remi's room before he was even fully awake, prepared to take on whatever had caused the commotion.

He came to a dead stop when he saw Remi, still lying in bed, covered by his twin siblings, who were jumping up and landing on top of him—first one, then the other—while talking animatedly about all of the things they were going to do now that Remi was home.

Their high-pitched voices were grating on his ears, but their genuine excitement at having their big brother back in the palace made Jeremiah wonder if he'd judged the prince too harshly. He'd seen firsthand how shitty people could be after experiencing a life-threatening incident. Some shut down, some became hysterical, and still others pretended it didn't happen.

He'd assumed the prince was just a spoiled brat who cared more about the fact that his life at university had been interrupted than that his family was being threatened, but maybe that hadn't been fair. Maybe… Maybe Remi had just been trying to protect himself by downplaying the seriousness. It happened, but it usually meant Jeremiah and his team had to work harder to keep the person safe since they were unwilling to change any aspects of their routine.

Luckily, he wouldn't have to worry about that for the time being since he'd convinced the queen to keep the family locked up tight in the castle grounds.

He couldn't really see Remi's face, just the occasional flutter of his hands and a muffled "Okay, okay, whatever you want."

He didn't even sound annoyed, even though he hadn't gotten much more sleep than Jeremiah had and could have arguably been upset at being woken up at the crack of dawn. Something warm unfurled in Jeremiah's chest when Remi wrapped his arms around his brother and sister and started tickling them, sending the twins into hysterical giggles.

Shit. He rubbed between his pecs. Was this heartburn? He didn't think Hellhounds could actually have that.

He didn't make a sound, but something alerted the twins to his presence, and it wasn't until they jolted around and stared at him with wide purple eyes that he realized he was only wearing his boxer briefs. Normally, he slept nude—less chance of losing clothing if he accidently lit up in his sleep—but he was glad he'd kept them on the night before. He definitely hadn't been thinking enough when he'd woken up to stop to put anything on.

Clearing his throat, he crossed his hands over his crotch and stared back at the young royals. "Good morning," he said gruffly, sounding like broken glass over gravel, thanks to the whopping two hours of sleep he'd gotten.

At the sound of his voice, Remi shot upright in his bed, jerking the twins back instinctively before he locked eyes on Jeremiah and relaxed slightly, seeming to remember who the strange man in his bedroom was. The instinctive urge to protect his siblings brought that warming sensation back to Jeremiah's chest, but he did his best to ignore it.

He also did not notice how perfectly flawless the crown prince's bare chest was. Or how his white skin had a light tan that covered every inch Jeremiah could see and looked completely smooth, his narrow chest flushing the longer they stared at each other. Or the fact that his arms and abs weren't rippling with muscles, but there was strength hidden behind all that attitude, his swimmer's body lean but not weak.

He didn't notice any of that because he was a brat and a protectee. He was *more* than off-limits. He wasn't a person to Jeremiah; he was just a job.

He reminded himself of that over and over again as he

slowly backed out of the room, praying he wasn't about to sport wood in front of the four-year-olds still staring at him curiously over their brother's shoulders.

He almost made it to safety.

He was one step from escaping the room so that he could dash down the hallway to his borrowed bedroom when Remi's eyes narrowed. Jeremiah could see the guy remembering that he didn't like him, his whole expression souring before he said in a condescending voice, "The twins and I will be taking our breakfast downstairs by the pool. That is unless you think I'm too stupid not to drown myself in the water."

Usually, Jeremiah was able to keep his cool no matter what a client said or did. That was his job. It was his business and his name on the line at the end of the day. He didn't fuck around when it came to jobs. But between the late night, the unexpected early morning, and the lack of caffeine, he found himself narrowing his eyes right back. He could tell that they were beginning to glow with his ire. "Well, little princeling, I guess we'll see, won't we?"

He could hear Remi's teeth grinding together as he turned and walked back to his bedroom to get dressed. He had a feeling Remi wouldn't be waiting for him.

"At least the food is good there, right? I bet it's really good. They probably have, like, personal chefs from all over come in and make food and all kinds of delicacies and—"

"Priest," Jeremiah interrupted, knowing that the guy could go on and on about eating if he wasn't stopped. Demons and their insatiable appetites, after all. "I haven't eaten anything yet, so I don't know, but I assume they have a private chef or five, yes."

Priest huffed in his ear but didn't remark about the food anymore. Instead, he brought the conversation back around to why Jeremiah had called him—to check in and see if he or any of the others had any leads about who had attacked the royal family. He knew it was doubtful they had anything yet, but after spending all morning watching Remi play with his siblings in the pool and having to exercise breathing techniques to stop himself from getting hard every time the prince stepped out of the water, dripping wet and grinning at the twins, he was praying for a break.

"Storm just got back from the Pearly Gates—"

Jeremiah interrupted again. "Why did you send Storm to the Pearly Gates and not just go yourself? You know how temperamental Azriel can be, especially when it comes to people he doesn't know."

There was a pause on the other end of the line, and Jeremiah knew he was going to be annoyed by whatever was said next. He rubbed at his closed eyes, preparing himself.

Sure enough, Priest mumbled, "Well, I sort of got banned."

Jeremiah sighed, wondering if dunking himself in the pool would relieve the throbbing in his temples. "Do I even want to know why?"

"I swear, I didn't actually do anything wrong. One of the dancers claimed that I was using my powers on her, but I absolutely was not."

Jeremiah frowned. "Azriel actually believed them?"

They had known the fallen angel who owned the strip club for a long time and had cultivated a beneficial relationship for both the agency and the Pearly Gates, passing information back and forth, keeping each other safe. He was surprised that the guy had so readily assumed the worst of Priest, especially considering Priest was there regularly to feed on some of the dancers. *Consensually* feed on them, that is. Azriel knew what was up and had never seemed to care as long as his employees agreed to the arrangement.

"He wasn't there," Priest said, sounding sulky. "It was

that new manager of his that gets all high-and-mighty about the dancers. I tried to explain to him that I wouldn't do that, that just because I'm an Incubus doesn't mean I'm constantly using my thrall on people."

"I know," Jeremiah said quietly. "It's fine. What did Storm find out?"

Priest took a deep breath and settled himself before saying, "He wasn't able to talk to Azriel either. But I sent him with the names of some of the dancers who have talked to us in the past, and he was able to talk to two of them, I think, but neither of them had heard anything yet. It's just a matter of time though. Something this sloppy? People will be talking about it. Bragging. They'll get drunk, they'll go in for a lap dance, and they'll let something slip."

Jeremiah wasn't so sure. To him, it didn't feel sloppy, even though neither kidnapping had been successful. His instincts were telling him the incidents had been more about testing the protection around the family than actually trying to take them. If they'd succeeded, he was sure they wouldn't have thrown the crown prince back, but it smelled more like a... dress rehearsal than a fuckup to him.

He didn't have any proof of that, so didn't say anything to Priest, knowing his guys would keep looking either way. But he had a feeling the next time the group struck, the plan would be a little more sophisticated, and they would have a harder time keeping everyone safe.

Even as he thought it, he turned, finding Remi with his eyes, but he was in the same spot he had been the last time Jeremiah had looked over at him. He was in a lounge chair next to the pool, sunglasses firmly in place and earbuds stuffed in his ears. The twins had been dragged back inside an hour or so ago by a patient but firm nanny explaining it was time to come inside for lunch and then quiet time.

He had thought that Remi would go in too, but the prince had decided to spend the day lounging by the pool. It didn't make sense to Jeremiah since he figured the crown prince would have princely duties and shit to do, but it did make him feel better that he hadn't been wrong about his initial judgment of the young man after all. Jeremiah knew he attended university, but since he was home, that should have meant he had things to do, but apparently not.

He shook off the thought. It wasn't his job to worry if the prince was being lazy or not.

"Get ahold of Azriel," he said to Priest, refocusing on his phone call. "Have him rescind the ban on you so you can go in there tonight or tomorrow night and talk to a few more people."

"Sure thing, Sunshine," Priest said right away. "Is there anything else you want us to do?"

Jeremiah thought about it for a moment and then said, "I know that Storm and Knight are focusing on the correspondences the royal guards had eliminated as potential threats, but I want you to send Storm over to the university."

Priest made a questioning noise. "Where the kid goes?"

"Yeah." He kept his eyes on the crown prince from where he was sitting under the shade of an umbrella. "It's mostly humans, and it's not in a very Supe-friendly country. I want to know who the prince is spending time with and if anybody has taken… an interest in him. Just tell Storm to ask around but to be careful. We aren't going to have a lot of friends there."

"Will do. And if we come across anything, we'll let you know ASAP. I know you're itching to get out of there." Priest said it with a chuckle, but it was the truth; he was the worst with protection detail. He didn't mind running the team, but working one-on-one with the protectee was his least favorite part of the job. He tended to get antsy if he was stuck in one place for too long with nothing interesting to do since most people were smart enough to steer clear of a target being guarded by a Hellhound.

He hung up with Priest but didn't put his phone down, pulling up his emails instead and starting to go through things to see if he needed to respond to anything urgent. He flicked his eyes over toward where Remi was sunbathing every few minutes, noticing he hadn't moved a muscle in over half an hour. He wondered if he'd fallen asleep.

Right as he was about to go over and poke at him, maybe suggest they head in for lunch themselves, he heard footsteps and jerked his head up, becoming alert from one breath to the next.

Heading straight for Remi was his guard from yesterday, the Demon who had hated Jeremiah on sight. He threw a scowl at Jeremiah as he passed, so he assumed he'd been told he'd been reassigned away from the crown prince.

Jeremiah made a note to keep an eye on the man. If he had been overly fond of his protectee, that could prove to be a problem.

The other person who had exited the palace was a young woman he didn't recognize, but she was wearing the same outfit all of the servants wore: black pants with a pale lavender shirt tucked in and polished shoes. She came right over to him, stopping a few feet away, and smiled warily.

He knew he made people nervous, but it didn't suck any less when a stranger looked at him like that. Like they were afraid he'd burst into flames at any second and burn them alive.

"Sir, Her Majesty wanted me to make sure you knew that if you need anything while you're staying here, all you have to do is let us know. We'd be happy to accommodate special dietary needs or anything like that. Or if you need an extra pillow or anything for your room. Please do not hesitate to ask."

Jeremiah stared at her for a moment and then forced a smile that he was sure was almost as scary as his resting face based on the way she blanched and swayed back. "Tell her thank you, but I'm perfectly fine."

She nodded and quickly hurried away from him. He wondered if she had lost a bet or something, having to be the one to come and tell him the queen's message.

He waited until she was back inside and out of sight before turning toward his protectee. He frowned at what he saw. Remi was no longer lounging back in his chair, looking relaxed and sun-kissed. He was standing next to his seat, talking animatedly with Greg, who looked pissed as hell.

Something about the exchange tickled at his instincts, and Jeremiah pushed to his feet, tucking his phone into his pocket and sauntering over.

As soon as Greg saw him coming, he snapped his mouth shut with a glare.

Remi looked over his shoulder, but Jeremiah couldn't read the expression on his face. He had on darker sunglasses than he had the day before, completely covering his eyes, and without being able to see them, he was much harder to read.

"There a problem over here?" Jeremiah asked as he drew closer.

"No, it's nothing," Remi said quickly. Too quickly.

Jeremiah didn't stop until he was between the two, forcing them both to step back, and then he turned and faced Greg. He could feel Remi frowning at the back of his head, but he ignored him for the moment. "You got a problem?"

He could tell the Demon had to force his face to relax, and it set Jeremiah's Hellhound on edge.

"No, no problem," Greg said. "I just wanted to remind Remi to put on sunscreen."

Jeremiah didn't take his eyes off the Demon. There had been a flush in Remi's cheeks when he'd walked up, but was it from embarrassment or the sun? Jeremiah had never heard of a Siren getting a sunburn, no matter how light-skinned or pale they were. They were *Sirens*. They were built to live on the water and in the sun. But maybe because he was only half Siren, Remi could get burned.

Or, maybe, that was a bullshit excuse.

Either way, he knew he needed to nip in the bud whatever was going on with the Demon.

He crossed his arms over his chest, emphasizing how much bigger he was than Greg, and stared him down. "Next time you have a concern about his safety or well-being, you bring it to me. I'm running point on his detail now. Not you." Narrowing his eyes, he added lowly, "Everything that has to do with him is my business, not yours."

Greg's face hardened in an instant, but all he did was nod, turn on his heel, and stalk away.

Jeremiah waited until he was completely out of sight before turning around to face Remi, whose face was mutinous. "Is that true? Do you need to put on sunscreen?'

For a moment, he didn't think he'd answer. Or he'd get some bratty response based on the mulish expression the prince was rocking. But then he seemed to sag into himself, and he just nodded, reaching down to grab a bottle from underneath the chair he'd been lounging in. "Yeah, I'm supposed to reapply it every few hours."

Jeremiah hadn't seen him apply it at all, though he guessed he could have done it in his bedroom before he'd come out in his bright turquoise swim trunks. Inhaling deeply, he thought he could detect a light chemical scent on Remi's skin. Barely. Definitely time to reapply.

He held out a hand, and the prince stared at it with his eyebrows raised.

"Hand it over. I'll do your back. We need to make sure you don't get burned."

Remi just continued to stare at him for a long moment, his Adam's apple bobbing as he swallowed and scent spiking with nerves and… something else. Something that made the saltiness in his scent deepen and tickle at the back of Jeremiah's throat, catching his Hellhound's attention.

He ran his free hand through his hair and wiggled the fingers of his still-outstretched one. It wasn't a big deal. It wasn't like they suddenly liked each other, but he hadn't been lying when he'd told his mother that he'd keep her son safe.

That meant from the sun, too, if need be.

As far as he was concerned, as long as he was in charge of Remi's safety and well-being, not a hair on his head would be hurt. Or a cell on his body burned.

Finally, Remi huffed and slapped the bottle into Jeremiah's hand, his face flushing an even darker pink as he turned and presented his back to him. The tops of his shoulders were a little red too, but he had a feeling that was more sun exposure than embarrassment.

Ignoring how rigidly Remi was standing or how he was grateful no one else from his team was there to see him at the moment, Jeremiah squeezed some of the sunscreen into his palm before tossing the bottle aside.

As soon as Jeremiah put his hands on Remi's upper back, he realized his mistake.

He could tell himself all he wanted that he was annoyed by the prince's behavior, that he didn't see the attractiveness of a protectee no matter what they looked like. That he could remain detached and professional under any circumstances.

But as he slid his palms over the smooth skin of Remi's back, his gut lurched, his Hellhound rippling just beneath the surface. Wanting out. Wanting to rub his scent all over Remi's body.

Marking him as Jeremiah's.

There was only one reason he'd react like that, but his brain fought the instinct. It was impossible. Hellhounds didn't have mates. Not like other Supes. They were an abomination. An unnatural combination of Werewolves and Demons that were never meant to exist.

He watched his hands rub the white lotion into Remi's skin, transfixed.

It didn't matter what his brain was screaming at him, his beast was sure.

He wanted to claim the fucking prince of Midlona as his damn *mate*.

What. The. Fuck.

5

REMI

"—And I swear to every god, if I look over my shoulder to see his ugly face one more time, I'm going to lose it."

Thad laughed darkly. "Throw holy water on him. I heard that shit's deadly to freaks like that. I swear, I can't believe your parents got you a Hellhound bodyguard. It's like they want you to get maimed and left in some alley somewhere. They're literally dogs."

Remi winced, glad for once that Thad couldn't see him. He embraced his humanity because what else was he supposed to do with the fact that his mom's genes had decided to, like, take a nap or something when he was gestating. But he still struggled with how hateful some of his friends were toward Supes. Sure, he found Jeremiah's overbearing presence annoying, but Thad's words grated down his spine, setting him on edge.

"Remiiiii."

He looked up and saw Sadie in his doorway. "Hey, man. I gotta go."

"Lame," Thad whined, but Remi hung up before he could hear the kids and say something that would make Remi want to forget their friendship and knock him out. Thad liked him in spite of the fact that he was half Siren, but he'd always been a little more shitty about the twins.

Fuck, maybe he needed some new friends?

Tossing his phone on the edge of the bed, Remi hopped up and held out his arms just in time to catch his sister. He spun her, slipping into a beam of sunshine filtering through the window, and his heart clenched in his chest at her visible scales. She was like him—half of one thing, half of the other—but she wouldn't have the same struggle he did.

It felt pathetic being jealous of a four-year-old.

"Where's Percy?"

"He's…" she said slowly. "Nuffing."

"He's nothing?" he asked, letting suspicion color his tone.

She started to giggle. "Yeah. He's just nuffing. He's not having cookies."

"Sadie," he said, drawing her name out with a warning. "Is Percy sneaking cookies?"

"Noooo…" She trailed off into a giggle, so he threw her on the bed and dug his fingers into her sides until she kicked him in the balls.

He fell over with a soft cry, and she took the opportunity to race past him as he gasped for air. A second later, there was heat and a looming presence and then a rush of mortification because he was lying on his side, cupping his junk.

"Felled by the little princess?" Jeremiah asked.

Remi flipped him off as he forced himself to breathe. "Let her kick you in the balls and see how well you hold up to it."

Jeremiah's lip twitched—nothing like a smile, but it was different from his scowl. "I'll pass, but thanks."

Remi stood up, straightening his shirt. "What do you want?" He felt a little angrier—a little sharper. Things had been weird since Jeremiah had put his hands all over Remi's exposed body, claiming he needed to protect him from the sun. And Remi's protests had died on the back of his tongue at the first sweep of Jeremiah's hands, which were calloused in some places, soft in others, and so, so warm.

He'd been doing his best to forget. And failing miserably.

He really didn't want to see Jeremiah right then. He was tired of looking at his stupid face. "Seriously, what do you want?" he asked, folding his arms over his chest.

Jeremiah fixed him with a flat look, apart from a single raised eyebrow. "We're leaving."

Remi barked a laugh. "Are you? That's amazing. I guess wishes do come true. You'll forgive me if I don't see you out, but—"

"The car will be waiting for us out front in ten minutes," the Hellhound interrupted.

Rolling his eyes, Remi turned away from him and walked to his mirror, running his fingers through his hair. The slight wave always sat better at home than it did where it was dry and terrible, and he hated that about this place. Yes, he'd eventually rule this gods-forsaken country that hated him for what he was, but a small piece of him had wanted to feel sanctuary somewhere else.

Though, he reminded himself, there was a whole world left to explore. He wasn't out of luck yet. And hell, his parents were probably going to live for longer than he could really contemplate. Maybe he could just wait for the twins to get older and then abdicate.

It wasn't the worst idea he'd had, but could he really do that to them? Leave them to the fate he'd been dreading and avoiding his whole life?

Looking over his shoulder, he breathed a sigh of relief to find Jeremiah gone. His presence was too overwhelming—too looming and dark and yet somehow light and comforting. It was the last fucking thing he wanted to feel when his glorified nanny was hovering over his shoulder.

He understood threats, but he was still convinced his parents were going too damn far. They didn't need to disband his entire security team. And they sure as shit didn't need to blame them for him getting away. Remi just wanted to have a normal life sometimes.

Taking a breath, he squared his shoulders and grabbed his phone before heading for the main hall. He could hear his siblings chattering away excitedly, so he pushed aside his melancholy and frustration for a smile because Sadie and Percy deserved better than his crappy mood.

When he came around the corner and started descending the stairs, Percy made a beeline for him but was stopped by Jeremiah's hand. Remi felt a bubble of rage coursing through him, and he only just managed to bite it back as he reached the landing.

Sweeping Percy into his arms, he nuzzled his nose against his little brother's cheek, making him laugh. "Ignore the big, mean dog," Remi said.

Jeremiah's expression didn't change. He just gestured to the door, and Remi swept past him, heading for the waiting car. He set Percy in, then turned and grabbed Sadie, helping her into her seat. When Jeremiah tried to reach past him to help with their buckles, Remi elbowed him hard enough to make him grunt.

"Calm down, nanny. I've got this."

Jeremiah said nothing, and Remi could feel the weight of his silence.

When the kids were secure, Remi slipped into the seat between them, and they each took one of his hands as Jeremiah climbed in next to the driver. The silence in the car felt like a heavy weight crushing his chest, but all he did was clear his throat and stare out the window, trying his best not to feel like a prisoner trapped in the life he'd been desperate to escape.

It took all of ten minutes to realize they were going to the beach.

The royals had a long stretch of semi-private land along

the cove. Some of the lesser royals and titled Sirens had access to the area, but the guards usually cleared it out when Remi and his family went out for a day. Once upon a time, it had been one of his favorite things to do.

Now, he wished they'd left him home alone so he could wallow while the kids splashed through the shallows.

"Remi?"

He turned to see Percy staring at him with his big, dark purple eyes.

"Yeah, kid?"

"You wanna just… um."

"Um," he said when Percy's attention drifted. He grinned and tugged on his tiny, toddler-fat fingers. "Um um um."

Percy giggled and kicked his feet. "Um. We could build a sandcastle."

"We could," Remi said.

And he would. He didn't love his life. He didn't love the idea of his future or the fact that he'd probably be one of the most universally hated crowned royals thanks to his human blood. He didn't love that he'd be judged for never finding his fated mate because half humans didn't get those. But he loved his siblings more than life itself.

Percy leaned forward as far as he could over his seat straps to catch his sister's eye. "He's gonna build it. A big one."

"Wiff a princess," Sadie said.

"You're a princess," Remi reminded her, tugging on her braid.

She squealed and shoved him away, and he settled back into his seat again. He hadn't packed for the beach, but it didn't matter. There was probably an entire beach house worth of supplies in the trunk of the car, and maybe some sun would do him good.

The best he could get on campus was sunbathing in the commons while his frat brothers played ultimate frisbee. He'd been banned from organized sports for being non-human since the human government didn't know how far his abilities extended.

The sad part was, even if he'd joined the damn swimming team, the only way he'd break any records would be if he shifted to his tail, and there was no way he'd ever want that kind of attention. But he accepted his fate with a quiet reluctance because the last thing he wanted to do was stir the pot.

Closing his eyes, he did his best to think about school but failed ten seconds in when the damn Hellhound's face appeared in the washed-out orange of his eyelids. He was suddenly picturing Jeremiah standing out in the sand with big flippers and arm floaties with his broad, pale bare chest, and all those abs, and…

He opened his eyes and winced at the bright sun before pulling his shades out of his pocket.

God, what the hell was wrong with him?

"Ocean!" Percy cried.

Sadie echoed him, her voice reaching that ear-piercing whistle tone.

Percy tried to ignore the call of the waves, but it didn't matter how human he was. The moment they were close enough to see the water, he felt something humming just under his skin. He felt his Voice tugging at the back of his throat. He rarely sang, his Song not nearly as beautiful or powerful as a full-blooded Siren, but gods, he missed just being comfortable in his own skin. He used to be, hadn't he?

He cleared his throat and tried not to fidget as the driver navigated through the entry gate, then took them down the familiar one-lane road that led toward the sandy dunes. He felt like he was going to shake out of his skin by the time they pulled into a parking spot, and Remi had all but given up on keeping his chill.

The second the car jolted into park, Remi had the door open, and he was quickly scrambling for his siblings' buckles.

As a mostly adult, he had enough control over his faculties to keep the twins' hands in his own as they hurried over the embankment, letting their guards handle the bags, and all three of them had lost their shoes just in time to hit the waves.

He felt a soft, easy ripple from the cool water race up his calves and over his hips. There was a familiar itch behind his knees, his shift clawing at him, but even if he'd wanted to, the moments he could manifest his tail took more effort than he had the energy for that morning.

He'd only done it a few times since he'd gone off to university, but just like his Song, the feeling never left him. It just went quiet sometimes.

The voices behind him got louder, and as he let the kids splash a few feet away, Remi looked over his shoulder to see Jeremiah standing surprisingly near while the rest of the guards set up the tent. Remi normally helped with tasks like that, but it had been so long since he'd been near the water he'd been unable to help himself.

He knew this wasn't exactly helping his cause every time he protested that he wasn't a spoiled royal brat, but really, what the fuck did he care what the hellbeast thought of him? He'd read all about them and knew what Hellhounds were like. Abominations. Untrustworthy and dangerous.

Humans didn't have their own fated mates because they lacked magic.

Hellhounds didn't have them because they were part of a long, cursed line that didn't belong in their world. There was some folklore that contradicted that, but Remi wasn't sure what he believed. Considering Hellhounds had nearly gone extinct, it seemed like maybe it was true.

He met Jeremiah's gaze, and for a second, he thought maybe the bodyguard could hear his thoughts with the way his expression darkened. Then Jeremiah sneered and turned his attention back to the twins. Because he just didn't like Remi.

Even if he'd gotten all handsy with him.

And kind of soft.

No, he told himself. *As a matter of fact, fuck no. You are not going down that road.*

With a breath, he turned and trudged up the sandy incline now that he was sure the kids were being watched, and he grabbed one of the tent poles, shoving it into the hole that Carlos—a Siren who'd protected his family for years—had dug. They shared a little smile, and Remi ducked his head.

"Sorry. I didn't mean to run off on you."

Carlos huffed softly. "It's the same when I haven't been for a while too."

Remi felt a small pulse of appreciation that someone understood what it was like for him.

They worked in silence, and once their stretch of beach was properly shaded, Remi grabbed a pair of swim trunks from a pile of towels and ducked behind the tent flap to change. It wasn't exactly easy, hunched over like some kind of bridge troll, and just before he managed to get the trunks over his ass, he heard a small choking noise.

He spun so fast he lost his footing and hit the tent floor just in time to see Jeremiah's face—bright pink in the cheeks—ducking out of sight.

"Oh, by the grace of all the fucking gods," Remi whispered to himself.

Instead of trying to get up, he flopped back, spread his arms, and willed the sea to just rise and swallow him whole.

Unfortunately, Poseidon didn't seem to give a shit about a random half Siren because nothing happened, and eventually, he got too hot to keep lying there in the closed tent. Turning onto his hands and knees, he crawled out onto the sand.

Jeremiah was talking with the two remaining guards, who turned and left, and Remi felt a small pulse of annoyance. There was no way that fucker had the authority to send anyone away. He swiped sand off his skin as he marched over and squared his shoulders as Jeremiah turned to face him.

Their height difference wasn't profound, but it sure as hell felt that way as Jeremiah stared down his nose. Remi's lips parted on a breath. His skin felt hot all over.

Which made sense. It was definitely the sun beating down on him.

Absolutely no other reason whatsoever to get all pink in the cheeks.

"Where'd they go?"

"The kids are hungry," Jeremiah said, his voice a low rumble, just barely audible over the waves.

In his periphery, Remi could see the twins where they'd set up a sandcastle perimeter a few feet from them. Percy was being Percy and calling out orders, and Sadie was being Sadie and refusing to listen. The gods help their kingdom if those two ever had to share power.

Remi's gaze cut back over to Jeremiah, who hadn't moved an inch. He swallowed thickly, and then his whole body went still as the Hellhound lifted a hand and traced a finger over the bridge of his nose.

"I..."

"You're turning pink."

"Sirens don't burn," Remi said irritably. It was a dumb lie, considering Jeremiah had put sunscreen on him just the other day, but it popped out without thought, the drive to pretend he wasn't different ingrained in him.

"So why are you all red?" Jeremiah's lip twitched up in the corner as Remi took a step back. "I think there's a lot of bullshit surrounding Sirens."

"And I think there's a lot of bullshit about Hellhounds out there," Remi fired back. "They should add nosy as fuck to also being abominations."

Jeremiah's eyes widened, and he flinched. Remi felt immediately like shit. He didn't even mean that, especially because he knew exactly what it felt like to have those kinds of insults flung at him. His own people didn't trust him on either side of his genetics. The humans were afraid, the Sirens thought he was unfit to rule, and everyone else…

Well, hell. He had no idea what Jeremiah thought about him, other than he was a spoiled brat.

"I'm sorry," he said softly.

The expression on Jeremiah's face was gone faster than it had appeared, and he shook his head. "It's fine. We are."

"You're not," Remi said quickly. "That was such a dick thing to say. I'm just…" He let out a soft growl and shoved both hands into his hair.

"I know this situation isn't easy. I know you'd rather be back at school drinking yourself half to death with your little self-important human friends."

Remi's irritation prickled across his skin. "They're not all like, you know, the gross politicians."

Even as he said it, he couldn't quite bring himself to believe it. Sometimes, in the dark, he'd hear echoes of what his fraternity brothers had called his ex, and it hurt almost as badly as if they'd been flinging those insults at him.

But he knew he had to give them a chance to grow. To be better. To meet people like him and understand there was no need to buy into that kind of shit.

He felt like an asshole for defending them though, especially to Jeremiah, who got hate from all sides of every community. But gods, everything Jeremiah said or did seemed to antagonize him, and he couldn't shake the need to keep poking at him every chance he got.

He seriously needed to get drunk. Or… maybe get laid. Properly laid and finally cross that item off his to-do list.

"Look," he started, but before he could say anything else, Jeremiah began to growl. Like an honest-to-gods growl that came from deep inside his chest. Remi started to panic, and even the twins were on their feet, running toward him.

Maybe he'd finally snapped.

Maybe Remi had gone too far, and now he was going to prove everyone right by eating the entire line of royal heirs.

"Don't—" he began to say, ready to beg for the twins' lives, but Jeremiah was in front of him in a single second, half crouched as a light dusting of black fur erupted over his skin. If Remi thought the sun was hot that day, that was nothing compared to the heat rolling off Jeremiah in massive waves.

Hellfire.

Jeremiah's attention was on the hill, and Remi realized why a second later. His panic ratcheted up when he saw two figures rushing through the wispy waves of sea oats. The one in front—a tall, light-haired man with broad shoulders—was holding something between his hands. The man was clearly human, but whatever he had was filled with some kind of power.

Not magic. No. Something else.

"Stay down," Jeremiah growled, his voice a strange, ethereal rumble. "Keep the children back."

"Where the fuck are the guards?" Remi all but shouted.

The two figures began to run just as Jeremiah's entire body erupted into flames. At the same time, whatever the human was holding went flying, and it was in that split second Remi knew whatever it was, was meant to kill his guard.

The worst fear—the worst panic—rushed through him. The idea of Jeremiah dying sent terror like no other rushing through his veins, and he threw himself at the Hellhound, letting the liquid explode against his body.

For a moment, all he could hear was a loud hum, and then time seemed to stop. He was in the middle of burning hellfire, but all he could feel was a gentle warmth. Jeremiah wrapped his arms around him, and their gazes met.

And then suddenly, the flames were extinguished, and they both collapsed to the ground. Remi's ears were ringing, but as they started to clear, he could hear the twins screaming and crying and Jeremiah's ragged breaths. There was a scorched path all the way to the dunes and two bodies lying there, most definitely dead.

Remi's heart was pounding as he climbed onto his hands and knees, and somewhere behind him, he could hear shouting. He felt the presence of the guards—at least one of them half shifted into his Dragon form and towering over him—but he ignored them as he bent over Jeremiah's body.

He was unconscious, and his arms were covered in welts, but his chest was rising and falling. The black fur was gone, and the heat was down to a low simmer. And most importantly, he was very much alive.

Remi could feel the glow of the man's soul still firmly situated in his body.

He let out a small sob as his arms were suddenly filled with shaking children, and he kissed the sides of their heads. "You're okay. We're all okay," he said.

There was a flurry of activity moments later. Carlos took the twins, and Thorne—who Remi hadn't even realized was there, so distracted by the water and his annoying Hellhound bodyguard—helped Remi to his feet.

"Can you walk?"

Remi nodded, rolling his shoulders back and testing his balance. He was fine. He felt drained, the same way he felt whenever he shifted, but he was okay.

"I need to carry him to the car," Thorne said. "Tell me you can walk."

"I can walk," Remi said, his voice slightly shaky. "Is he… Will he be okay?"

"I think so," Thorne answered as he lifted Jeremiah with a single sweep of his arm and plopped him on his shoulder. He was still half shifted, so he was massive with claws and patches of blue scales scattered over his dark skin and glinting in the sun. "But that was holy water."

Remi's body shuddered. Hard. "Are you fucking serious? How did they know? He's been here less than a fucking week!"

"That's what we need to find out. Carlos will call the palace and let them know what happened and then get ahold of Jeremiah's team. They'll meet us back there. We'll get to the bottom of this, Your Highness."

They started forward, and Remi willed his legs not to give out on him as they made their way back to the cars. The twins had stopped crying and were playing with tablets now, settled in one of the cars with Carlos behind the wheel, but when Thorne gestured for him to follow, Remi shook his head.

"I'm going to ride with Jeremiah."

Thorne lifted a brow at him but didn't do more than shrug as he settled Jeremiah in the back seat. Remi climbed in next to him, not touching him but watching his slow, even breathing. He had no idea why the hell he cared so much. No idea why it mattered, but he knew down to his damn soul that if someone tried to separate them before Jeremiah opened his eyes and Remi could know for *certain* he was fine, he would completely fall apart.

6

JEREMIAH

Even raised outside of a Hellhound pack, Jeremiah knew the dangers of holy water bombs. It was one of the few things that could kill him. He could sense it just before the attack, and he'd prepared himself to die in the line of fire but hoping to take out the attackers with him.

It wouldn't have mattered if he had perished, so long as Remi and the twins were safe.

But when the water hit him, it hadn't hurt. He knew he was burned as the water splashed against him, his arms and shoulders screaming in agony. He knew his hellfire should have extinguished seconds after he shot it toward the attackers.

The last thing he saw before everything went black was the subtle lavender of Remi's eyes. He felt the Siren's touch just before everything went numb, and he decided if that was death, there were far worse ways to go.

Except he wasn't dead.

He was very much alive and very much in pain when he finally rose to consciousness. He could smell the acrid stench of antiseptic as he attempted to open his eyes, and his skin felt stretched and seared when he tried to move his arms. The bed beneath him was soft, but the sheets were scratchy against his sensitive, newly healed skin, and he desperately craved his own bed back in his penthouse.

"Well, well, well. Sleeping Beauty finally wakes up from his nap."

Jeremiah managed to flip Priest off as he rolled onto his side, hissing between his teeth. "Why am I not dead?"

"That's a damn good question," Priest said. His words carried his same flippant air, but his tone was anything but. He was shaken.

Jeremiah peeled his eyes open to find his oldest friend leaning close to his bed. The Demon looked paler than usual in his half crouch, his fingers trembling and suit in shambles. "Seriously. It was holy water."

"We know." Priest dragged a hand down his face, then used his considerable strength to shove Jeremiah over. "Move it, Sunshine. I'm getting in."

Jeremiah didn't have time to protest before Priest was under the sheets next to him, turning into a sort of Demon-octopus hybrid. "I'm fine," he grunted.

Priest hummed, but he didn't let go. "Yeah, well, it was touch and go there for a while, asshole. You almost…" He stopped and took a breath.

Jeremiah felt his heart tick up a few beats as he shifted to look at his friend. "The prince?"

"Fine."

"The kids?"

"Also fine," Priest said, smiling just a little. "The king and queen have put the palace on lockdown, but we've collectively agreed that we can't keep this up."

Jeremiah flopped back down and draped his hand over his eyes. Priest was right. "Where?"

"One of Storm's brothers belongs to a Hoard. There's five or six of them, I think. We transported the twins there this morning and set up several wards to accompany the ones the Dragons already set up."

Jeremiah started to nod until he realized one very important person was left out. He sat up halfway, dislodging Priest from his aggressive cuddle. "And the crown prince?"

Priest's lips twitched. "Refused to go."

Jeremiah suddenly had his strength back. He swung his legs over the bed and stood, freezing when Priest wolf whistled at him. He felt the cool rush of air across his naked ass, and he spun.

Priest waggled his eyebrows. "You know what they say about Hellhounds."

"Don't," Jeremiah barked. Literally. His frustration had his shift simmering just under the surface of his skin.

Priest's smile got wider. "Problem?"

"Yes. The fact that one of the targets is still here," he said, trying to control himself. He glanced around until he set eyes on a small pile of clothes folded in perfectly neat squares. That was most definitely the work of Knight. He'd thank him for bringing him more things from his place later. For now, he had a bratty prince to deal with.

Priest chuckled as Jeremiah struggled into his clothes with stiff, burned arms. They were healing—faster than they probably should have, but that was a problem for future Jeremiah to ponder.

"You know he's not going anywhere, right? Like, literally. So you can slow down."

"The longer he's here," Jeremiah said with a grunt as he hopped into his jeans, "the more risk there is of another attack."

Priest sighed. "Look. The outing yesterday was a bad call."

Jeremiah scoffed loudly as he shrugged his shirt on, wincing at the pain as it dragged over his burns. It *had* been a bad call. It had been a call he'd tried to veto, but the king and queen didn't want to take him seriously.

But he couldn't deny he hadn't put up as big of a fight as he should have. He'd been unsettled, but he hadn't considered the fact that someone could lob a holy water bomb at him while—

His breath caught in his chest, and he spun to face Priest. "I burned him."

Priest blinked at him. "What?"

"The prince. Remington," he said, the name feeling odd on his tongue. "He threw himself at me, and my hellfire…"

Priest's brow furrowed in a deep frown. "You might still be a little out of it, man. Your hellfire would have fucked him up."

His heart beat faster, panic settling in. "I know that. That's why I—"

"I just saw him," Priest said slowly. "He's with Knight right now, and he's fine. I swear. It's probably just the holy water attack making things foggy." He tapped his temple.

Jeremiah wanted to argue, but if Remi was fine, then Priest had to be right. He felt better and worse all at the same time. "Maybe I'm not cut out for—"

"You're the only one strong enough," Priest said, throwing his legs over the bed and hopping up. He walked up to Jeremiah and pressed a firm touch over his burns. After a beat, he felt the familiar tingle as his friend began to heal him.

"Don't," he started, but the dark look Priest shot him shut him up.

"It's a couple of burns. It's not going to take me out, and you need to be at full strength."

Demons could heal, but it weakened them. It was something they'd discovered when they were young and on their own, in danger in every city they moved to without legal protection. And some of the crueler species they ran into enjoyed reminding them of that fact.

It had been years since Priest had to heal him though, and he could see more color drain from his friend's face.

It was over after a beat, and Jeremiah felt better than he had in a long while. He flexed his fingers, then cupped his hand around the side of Priest's neck and knocked their foreheads together. "Thank you. But stop being a martyr. I need all of us at peak strength. Make sure you go feed before going home."

This was more than just a small threat. This was an assassination attempt to destroy the current royal line, and Jeremiah was done screwing around.

He eventually found the prince with Knight and a handful of guards in a sitting room. He walked in, remembering to offer a half-hearted bow before he stood in front of the younger man and crossed his arms.

He had a sudden and wild urge to strip Remi down and explore every inch of his skin to make sure he wasn't hurt. Gods, he had to stop turning into a horny little pup whenever the brat was around. He didn't know what the fuck was wrong with his libido, but he definitely needed to get laid when this was all over.

"Can I help you?" Remi asked. His tone was filled with his usual insolence, but there was something in his beautiful eyes that spoke of worry. Almost like he was mirroring Jeremiah's urge to put his hands on him to make sure he was actually okay.

He cleared his throat. "Why aren't you with the twins?"

Remi let out an incredulous laugh as he stood and folded his arms over his chest. "Because I'm not four."

Jeremiah's eyes widened a fraction. "Could have fooled me with the absolute fuckery you've been pulling around here."

Remi took a step back. "You can't talk to me like that!"

"The hell I can't," Jeremiah shot back. "You're not my prince. You're a brat I've been hired to keep alive."

"I'm not the one who okayed a beach trip out in the open while there was an active threat against my family," Remi spat.

That shut him up, his jaw snapping closed with a loud click. The particulars of how the outing happened didn't matter because at the end of the day, Remi and the twins had been his responsibility, and he'd almost failed to keep them safe.

Knight stepped up next to him, attempting to play peacemaker. "Sunshine didn't okay the trip. He got overruled."

Jeremiah stiffened as a grin spread over Remi's mouth. "Did he just call you—"

"I'm going to speak to your parents," Jeremiah interrupted. "I don't know why you have a death wish, but the reason I was hired—"

"Was to protect me. Not pawn me off on a bunch of Dragons," Remi said, shoulders going back and face taking on a haughty edge Jeremiah wasn't a fan of.

Jeremiah wanted to growl and scare the look right off his face. Or… kiss it off. The second option was so appealing he felt his dick twitch in his jeans, and he wanted to slam his head into the wall until it stopped. He needed to get Remi away from him. Whatever the fuck this feeling was, he couldn't concentrate. He couldn't do his damn job properly.

He would have sensed the attackers minutes before if he hadn't been fighting off the urge to run his tongue all over the places Remi was exposed and pink out there by the ocean. Hell, when his beast's instincts had picked them up, it took him a full three seconds to tear his gaze away from Remi's legs where his scales were just barely glinting in the sun.

Turning on his heel, he marched out of the room and down the maze of hallways in an attempt to find the rulers of that godsdamned country. He made it to some ballroom when he sensed a presence behind him, and he absolutely hated the fact that he knew it was Remi.

"Did they teach you that stalking is creepy at school?" Jeremiah asked without turning around. "Or is that just something they tell the peasants."

"There are no peasants in the Siren kingdom," Remi said quietly.

Jeremiah scoffed. "Or you just don't see them. You're too busy being fed with your pretty little silver spoon to look that far down your nose."

Remi was quiet, and Jeremiah felt a sudden pain in his chest. He'd gone too far.

"I know I'm spoiled, but I actually do care about my family," Remi said after a beat. "And I'm pretty sure that the person who wants me and my siblings dead lives here."

Jeremiah whipped around, pinning Remi with a stare. "In this palace?"

"Maybe. Definitely in Midlona."

He stalked closer, and Remi backed up until he hit the wall. "Who?"

At that, Remi let out a bitter laugh. "Take your pick, Hellhound. They're not exactly thrilled to know that at some point, a filthy half human is going to be sitting on the throne."

Jeremiah blinked when he realized that Remi was telling the truth. Or, at least, the truth as he believed it. "That's not—"

"Look, maybe Sirens didn't use a holy water bomb against you, but don't be surprised if you find out that Sirens are in bed with whoever wants to end this line."

Jeremiah shook his head. The kid couldn't possibly know what it was like to be universally hated. A handful of hate mail wasn't even close to the things Jeremiah had seen—what he'd been through. "That doesn't change the fact that you're making my job harder."

Remi laughed in his face. "Am I supposed to make it easier? Roll over and do whatever you tell me like a good dog?"

"Does it make you feel better to say that?" Jeremiah challenged, fed up with the rude comments, even if it wasn't aimed directly at him.

Remi's face erupted into the prettiest red flush, and Jeremiah had to physically stop himself from leaning in to feel the heat with his lips. "I just…"

Jeremiah lowered his head farther. "You just?"

"… think you're an asshole, Sunshine."

He laughed in spite of himself. "You wouldn't be the first person to tell me that."

His nose was flooded with the rich, powerful scent of arousal. If he looked down, he knew he'd see a tent in the younger man's pants matching his own.

Swallowing, he rumbled out, "And you're a spoiled brat who isn't going to get his way. Do you understand me?"

Remi surged forward, bumping their chests together, and Jeremiah felt something hot and intense roll through him. "You can't make me leave. So give it up."

Before Jeremiah could respond, Remi ducked under his arm and ran. His knees felt weak, and he was hard enough to cut diamonds. He lifted his nose to the air and followed his own scent back to his quarters, navigating the maze of hallways with his senses to keep from getting lost, and when he was finally back in his room, he slammed the door. Thank the gods Priest was gone. He couldn't handle any more jokes at his expense.

He was covered in Remi's scent. It was cloying. It stuck to him like cold, stubborn honey, and when he peeled his shirt off, it didn't help. Remi's scent was sweet and rich—like coconuts and salty air—and he wanted to fall to his knees and devour it.

With trembling limbs, he managed to make his way into

the bathroom and start the shower, but the steam only seemed to make the scent worse. He climbed under the spray and eventually lost all control, wrapping his hand around his dick, using the other to brace himself against the tiles as he stroked himself fast and furious.

He was afraid to close his eyes, but he couldn't keep them open for long, and Remi's figure burst into life in the darkness.

"I think you're an asshole, Sunshine."

The words were cruel, but there was heat in his tone. If Jeremiah had kissed him then, Remi would have opened up to him. He would have wrapped his slender arms around Jeremiah and given himself willingly.

Jeremiah would have made him beg for it.

He would have tormented him until his perfect, lush lips were curled around the sounds of begging. And only when he was sobbing and near tears would he give in and pull orgasm after orgasm from him, until he lost all strength.

He'd fuck the brat right out of his body, then curl around him and hold him until that smart mouth was ready to start all over again.

He grunted, thrusting into his fist as he pictured Remi's gorgeous, round ass at the beach. The sight of it had nearly sent him to his knees. It had taken everything in him not to spread his cheeks right there and fuck him with his tongue for all those guards to see.

His dick throbbed. He was so close.

"Remi," he whispered. It felt so right and so fucking wrong, but his body didn't care. The need in his chest didn't care. "Remi," he said again, and then again. His balls twitched. The base of his dick began to swell, though he wasn't close to actually popping a knot.

But it was the closest he'd been in a long, long time.

With another deep moan, he let go on the edge of Remi's name one last time. His arm gave out, and his forehead hit the wall as he spilled down the drain, and he let the water wash away all the evidence of his sin. He was seriously in the shower, lusting after a Siren more than ten years his junior.

And not just that, he was the damn crown prince he was hired to protect.

It was no wonder he was an abomination. This was maybe the worst thing he'd ever done, and he vowed right then that Remi would never, ever find out.

7

REMI

The palace was too quiet without the twins, and he hated it.

He also hated that his stupid body filled with heat and longing every time Jeremiah was within eyesight, like popping wood during their argument after the attack on the beach hadn't been bad enough. Jeremiah had to have known too. Hellhounds had much better senses than Sirens and probably a hundred times better than Remi's half-human ones.

Gods, it was embarrassing.

And yet…

He couldn't stop *poking* at the man.

He knew he should follow Jeremiah's orders and work with him to figure out who was coming after him and his family, but every time they were within ten feet of each other, he couldn't decide if he wanted to strangle the arrogant man or throw himself into his arms.

Which was just… not okay. It left him feeling off-balanced and nervous, and he wasn't okay with that. Without his permission, his mouth would just run away from him, picking at the man to try and get some sort of response out of him. If Remi had to be aroused and miserable all the time, then Jeremiah could at least be pissed off.

For days, everyone walked around the castle like they were afraid another attack could happen around every corner. Remi was followed at all times by *at least* three guards, and if he stepped outside for fresh air—well within the palace walls—Jeremiah was glued to his side, agitation palpable until Remi got so annoyed he just went back inside.

But it had been almost a week. Enough was enough.

"For fuck's sake, can you back off just a little?" he yelled, spinning to face the stony-faced Hellhound.

He'd thought he'd slipped into the gardens without Jeremiah noticing, intent on simply getting away from the tension filling the palace, but less than sixty seconds on the paver-lined path and he'd felt his hulking presence right behind him.

"No."

Gritting his teeth, Remi planted his hands on his hips. "Listen, *Sunshine*, you can't even see the wall from here. I'm perfectly safe."

Jeremiah didn't bother responding, his hard eyes and tight jaw giving nothing away.

"I'm serious. Don't you have anything better to do? Like, say, catch the maniacs coming after us?"

"The team is working on that. Unfortunately, my valuable time is spent making sure my bratty protectee doesn't get himself killed instead of investigating who's behind the attacks." Jeremiah's eyes narrowed on him, taking a half step closer and towering over Remi.

He threw his hands up in the air. "How am I going to get myself killed walking through the *gardens*? You won't be happy until I'm locked in my bedroom twenty-four seven, will you?"

"You could have a lot more freedom if you joined your brother and sister—"

"No," Remi snarled, inching closer. Out of the corner of his eye, he saw the other guards ease back and discreetly disappear around the towering hedges and fruit trees. *Cowards*. "This is my home. My future kingdom. I won't run scared every time there's a little danger."

"A little danger?" Steam began to rise from Jeremiah's stupidly wide shoulders, his irises flickering with blue flames. *"A little danger?"*

Remi rolled his eyes. "Quit being so dramatic."

He was pretty sure he heard one of Jeremiah's molars crack he was clenching his jaws so tightly. "Dramatic? I almost fucking died, little princeling. In case you forgot."

Guilt prickled at his skin and soured his stomach. He hadn't. Gods no. He'd barely slept since their trip to the beach because every time he shut his eyes, he saw Jeremiah barely moving, body covered in burned, welted skin. When he did manage to fall asleep, his mind helpfully provided imaginative ways the day could have gone if Jeremiah hadn't been able to take out the attackers before going down. What they might have done not just to him but Percy and Sadie too.

He shuddered and looked away, taking a deep breath to steady himself before saying more softly, "Hardly. But no one would be stupid enough to try and attack the palace. I'm safe."

"I decide when you're safe. And until whoever is behind these attacks is caught, I wouldn't bet your life on anywhere being completely safe. This place may be formidable, but nowhere is completely impenetrable."

Squeezing his hands into fists, Remi tipped his chin up. "Fine. It's not safe. Whatever. I guess you're stuck trailing after me because I'm not staying cooped up inside all day, every day."

Jeremiah opened his mouth to say something else—probably to call Remi a brat or spoiled or something equally rude but no doubt true—but he spun on his heel and stomped away. He'd just ignore the man and continue with what he'd planned on doing.

He was also going to ignore how his heart rate had sped up, his dick beginning to thicken in his shorts the moment he'd turned and found Jeremiah right behind him and only getting worse the closer they'd gotten.

And when Jeremiah had literally started to smoke with anger?

Gods, that should not be *arousing*. Did he have a death wish or something?

When the enormous fountain in the center of the garden came into view, his body began to relax. Three Siren statues, shifted tails sparkling in the sun, sprayed water from their mouths and outstretched palms in the middle. It was one of Remi's favorite places in the whole kingdom, the water running through the feature pumped in from the coast and perfectly salty.

He stepped up to the stone edge, slipped out of his sandals, and climbed over the short wall. As soon as his bare toes hit the seawater, the remaining tension drained out of his body, and he sighed softly. As traumatic as the trip to the beach had been, he wished he'd been able to spend more time standing in the ocean, letting the waves crash over him and rejuvenate him.

The pool was okay, but the stagnant water didn't feel alive, not like the fountain. It was the closest he could get without returning to the beach, and he knew without asking that was out of the question for the foreseeable future.

The water came all the way up to his knees, getting the hem of his shorts damp. He didn't usually wear clothes when he dipped into the fountain, but he hadn't thought to change into his bathing suit first, wanting to try and get there before his overprotective Hellhound noticed.

Biting his lip, he glanced over his shoulder and saw Jeremiah standing there watching him, arms crossed over his chest, but the other guards were still out of sight. He knew they were still there though, silently keeping him safe from whatever boogeyman Jeremiah thought was lurking in the shadows of the gardens.

Sucking in a deep lungful of briny air, he faced the statues and gripped the hem of his shirt, ripping it over his head in one quick move. He thought he heard a noise behind him, but he refused to turn around, not wanting anyone to see his flushed cheeks. The last thing he wanted was for them to know he was embarrassed, but if they were going to treat him like a prisoner, then he'd take what little pleasures he could get, whether they watched or not.

As he tucked his thumbs into the waistband of his shorts, prepared to shuck them off as well, a hair-raising growl started up right behind him.

He whipped around, an instinctive fear response coalescing in his belly and goose bumps racing down his arms, but Jeremiah wasn't looking at him. His head was turned to the side, teeth bared and hands curled at his sides, where his claws had lengthened. As he lifted his lip in an aggressive snarl, a shiver ran down Remi's spine at the sight of his enormous fangs.

"Leave."

There was a soft rustling as the other guards fled in the face of a Hellhound's wrath.

"Wow. Was that really necessary? What happened to danger lurk—"

Jeremiah turned back to him, and the words died in Remi's throat at the blue glow in his eyes. He looked pissed. Like he was half a second away from tearing Remi's face off kind of pissed.

"What are you playing at?" Jeremiah growled, advancing on the fountain.

Swallowing, Remi licked his lips and shuffled back, closer to the statues. "What do you mean?"

"Do you seriously fucking care so little about your own safety you'd deliberately distract your guards from their duty?"

Shock rippled through him. "*What*?"

"If you want to be a brat, then be a brat. But don't use your naked body to prove some—"

"*What*?" Remi screeched, face flaming. "I wasn't going to get *naked*. Oh my gods."

Jeremiah grunted, looking unconvinced, but some of the fire had left his eyes, his fangs and claws mostly receding. "Whatever you say, little princeling. The fact remains, I won't have you deliberately causing a scene and making it harder for your guards to do their job. I don't know what kind of *relationship* you and Greg had at school, but I won't be so easily manipulated."

Heat crawled down Remi's back at the nasty way Jeremiah said *relationship*, making it very clear what he thought of how close he and his old guard had been. "How dare you! To even suggest Greg was less than a professional—"

Scoffing, Jeremiah crossed his arms over his chest. "Please. The man let you walk all over him, and it doesn't take more than a pair of eyes and working nose to understand why."

Remi didn't like what he was suggesting. The idea of Greg—whom he'd trusted implicitly for years—acting inappropriately or seeing Remi as more than someone under his protection was ridiculous. And gross. They'd grown close over the years, sure, but Remi had never seen him as anything more than maybe an overprotective big brother. He was sure it was the same for Greg too.

Before Remi could untangle his tongue and defend Greg's professionalism again, Jeremiah was continuing, voice dipping down to a deep rumble.

"Furthermore, if you want to go for a swim, you will change in your bedroom and do so in the pool. Stripping your clothes off in front of your protection detail is—"

"Good gods, I wasn't—"

"—is inappropriate and dangerous. None of them need to see you like that."

Remi rolled his eyes and pushed his shorts off, bending to pull them off his legs and then throwing the sopping wet material onto the ground in front of Jeremiah. The Hellhound's nostrils flared, eyes growing hot once more.

Remi held his arms out to his sides. "How is this any different from wearing a bathing suit in front of them? Gods, you're acting like… I don't even know what. A jealous boyfriend."

He didn't know why he said it, but once the words were out there, he couldn't take them back. His cheeks burned, but he held his chin up, refusing to admit how embarrassed the statement made him. Jeremiah obviously didn't see him that way. The growly beast could barely stand to be in his presence.

Jaw tightening, Jeremiah jabbed a finger at him, claw pointed and sharp-looking. "The difference is *watching* you undress. Seeing you peel the clothes off your body. Imagining they get to see more. Do more. Tempting men who are responsible for your safety with thoughts like that is just dumb. Don't do it again, Remington."

For some reason, Remi's heart was racing in his chest, the thudding in his ears nearly drowning out the sound of the running water right behind him. His body felt like it was overheating despite the coolness lapping at his knees.

Did… Did Jeremiah think those things? Was he tempted by the sight of Remi unclothing himself? Was it distracting him?

It seemed impossible.

Ludicrous.

And yet…

Swallowing thickly, Remi sank his teeth into his lip and lowered his head, watching Jeremiah through his lashes. The older man didn't look away, even for a second—hadn't since they'd started the conversation.

"Okay."

His soft word seemed to surprise Jeremiah, his head cocking to the side in a manner that would have been adorable on a less intimidating person. "Okay?"

"Okay. You made your point." Glancing down, he gathered every ounce of courage he could muster, then met Jeremiah's eyes once more. "But since we're already here…"

He slipped his thumbs into the band of his briefs, not letting his nerves stop him from easing the cotton down over his half-full cock and then his legs. He bent and carefully stepped out of them, tossing the material at Jeremiah but unable to bring himself to look back at him again. Instead, he turned away and lowered himself into the cool water, letting it soothe his frazzled edges. He dipped beneath the surface and swam around the statues. Again and again. Barely even coming up for air.

His fourth time past where Jeremiah had remained standing the whole time, and just as his skin was beginning to itch and tighten with the pull of his shift, a strong hand grabbed his arm and jerked him up and out of the water.

A spike of fear ratcheted up his heart once more, but Jeremiah wasn't looking at an advancing attacker.

No, he was staring at Remi.

It took a second for Remi to place the look on his face, having never seen it directed at him before, but then his breath caught in his throat.

Feral need.

Jeremiah *wanted* him.

His lips parted so he could suck in some much-needed air, and Jeremiah's fiery eyes dropped to his mouth, a low growl building in his chest.

"You are playing with hellfire, boy."

Remi shuddered at the dark promise behind those low

words. He wanted to say he wasn't afraid, or maybe something sexy and flirty, but nothing would come. All he could focus on was how hot Jeremiah's hands were where they gripped his upper arms so tightly he might bruise and how closely they were standing to one another.

And the fact that Remi was completely naked.

He definitely couldn't forget that, especially since his body was reacting to Jeremiah's closeness in a way he couldn't control.

Jeremiah inhaled deeply, his eyes fluttering closed for a second, his whole body shuddering, and the tendons in his neck popping to attention. Gods, he was scenting Remi's arousal. He had to be. He was achingly hard, and his nipples were pebbled. But what was distracting him the most was the needy tug of rightness deep in his belly.

The way his blood—still thrumming in his veins from his brief swim and the fact that he was still half-submerged in the water—sang out *yesyesyes pleasepleaseplease*.

He felt like…

Like he'd splinter and crack open if Jeremiah didn't kiss him. Didn't wrap his scorching hot arms around Remi's body and hold him tight against his safe and secure torso. Nothing and no one could get to him while he was locked in Jeremiah's grip. He just knew it.

But he wasn't really thinking about his safety in that moment.

His next breath was shuddery as fuck as he swiped his tongue over his lips.

He felt like he'd never been kissed before, and that definitely wasn't the case. But nothing had ever felt like *this*.

Like the entire world was waiting on their mouths to meet. Like Remi would feel whole for the first time in his life once he could taste Jeremiah's smoky flavor with his tongue.

When Jeremiah moved just a fraction of an inch closer, his heavy-lidded gaze locked on Remi's lips, he couldn't hold back a small sound. The desperation clawing at his insides escaped on a tiny, embarrassing whimper.

"Remi," Jeremiah whispered, voice hoarse and full of some emotion he couldn't place. "We can't..."

When the words died, the sentence going unfinished as Jeremiah's fingers flexed on his upper arms, Remi nodded. "You're right."

But he didn't try and pull away. Anyone could come by at any moment, the other guards could return, his mom could ruin Jeremiah's life and business...

None of that mattered as much to him as his need to know if the inside of Jeremiah's mouth was as scorching hot as he suspected.

Slowly, barely letting himself breathe, Remi raised his hands and inched them forward, not stopping until his wet fingers were pressing into Jeremiah's hard-as-a-rock abs. Grunting, Jeremiah released one of his hands, but before Remi could miss the heat, his long, thick fingers were threading into the hair on the back of Remi's head and tugging, forcing his face up and exposing his throat.

He was so vulnerable to this dangerous predator in front of him.

A shiver raced down his spine as he felt a drop of precome drip from his engorged head.

He wasn't sure if Jeremiah scented that too or what, but he was suddenly looking at gleaming white fangs as the Hellhound snarled softly, then dipped his head down and buried his unshaven face against the side of Remi's neck and sucked in a harsh breath.

"Fuck."

His fingers curled into Jeremiah's downy soft shirt at that rasped expletive, head tipping back to expose more of his throat to him. "Gods, you make me..."

Crazy.

Horny.

Desperate.

Sharp teeth grazed his thin skin, teasing and dangerous all in one. "What?"

Remi shook his head, as much as to try and get his bearings back as to answer. The clear blue sky above them was perfect, not a cloud in the sky to mar the entire expanse as far as he could see.

But he could feel a storm brewing deep in his bones.

"Sunshine…"

The nickname tipped off his tongue without his permission, his own voice so thick with arousal and unspoken pleas he could barely recognize himself.

Jeremiah raised his head, and Remi gasped at the sight of his flaming blue eyes. Gods, he was… breathtaking. They held each other's gazes for one more long, tension-filled moment, and then Jeremiah was dipping closer, the space between them disappearing and filling with their soft, panting breaths.

This was it. It was going to happen. Jeremiah—a *Hellhound*—was going to kiss him, and he just knew his life would never be the s—

A soft sound, barely more than a leaf scuttling over the path behind Jeremiah, had the Hellhound rearing backward, eyes searching the area around them as fire grew in his hands. Instinctively, Remi reacted to his protective stance, crouching mostly behind the wall of the fountain and trying to find the threat.

A pure white rabbit hopped into the circular clearing, paying no attention to the flaming Hellhound and reentering the gardens through another path on the opposite side of the fountain.

They both watched it until it disappeared. Only then did Jeremiah's stance relax, but he didn't turn around. The refreshing water from a few minutes ago now chilled Remi to the bone as he watched Jeremiah's shoulders hunch forward, hands fisting at his sides.

Clearing his throat, Remi stood, the water sloshing around him. "Jer—"

"Get dressed."

Jeremiah stalked forward, only pausing once he was half-hidden by a cherry blossom tree. He still didn't look back though, just waited for Remi to follow his order with his face turned away.

Humiliated and confused, he climbed over the edge of the fountain and pulled on his wet shorts, making a face at how uncomfortable they were, and then tugged his shirt back over his head. As he fed his arms through the sleeves, he glanced around, frowning at the pebbles and leaves and flower petals.

Where the hell was his underwear?

He realized Jeremiah must have tossed them away after Remi had flirtatiously thrown them at him. Cheeks burning, he checked the entrances of the nearby paths and the tops of any hedges he could see but still couldn't find them.

Gods, could the day get any more mortifying? Some poor gardener would probably find them on a tree branch or something in a few days.

Lump lodged firmly in his throat and eyes burning, Remi gave up and accepted he'd probably find them washed and folded on the end of his bed soon and be left to wonder what poor servant had retrieved them.

Holding his head up and tears back with a sheer force of will, he stomped toward the palace, not pausing or glancing at Jeremiah when he passed him.

He wasn't sure if it was better or worse that the broody Hellhound didn't stop him or try and say anything.

8

JEREMIAH

"What do you mean none of you can come take over?" Jeremiah snarled.

Knight sighed like Jeremiah was being particularly obtuse and he had better things to do than follow the orders from his boss. "Everyone is already working on—"

"I know that," he snapped, then took a deep breath, reminding himself he wasn't actually mad at any of his guys. He was furious at *himself.*

And a certain overly tempting prince.

"I'm not a good fit here," he said, working hard to keep his tone even. "I can swap out with you or Priest and take over what you're working on."

When Knight didn't say anything for a long moment, Jeremiah felt his fire stirring in his fingers. Why couldn't they all just *listen* to him for once?

"Are you not fully healed after the attack on the beach?" Knight asked neutrally, but he bristled anyway.

"I'm fine. It's… I don't do protection detail well. We all know this. I should be running point back at HQ, not playing babysitter to a bratty prince."

Especially one too pretty for his own good.

Or Jeremiah's peace of mind.

"You're the boss—"

"Which is why you should do what I say and get your ass over here."

"And the king and queen want the most powerful person on the team protecting their son. That's you and your hellfire, Sunshine. We'll get a break soon, and then you'll be able to come back home, no worse for wear."

Unless his errant hormones got him obliterated by the Siren queen.

Clearing his throat, Jeremiah rubbed at his eyes and paced his bedroom, one ear tuned into Remi's bedroom, but it was still too early to expect the prince to grace anyone with his presence. Without the twins there to beg him to play with them, he went to bed and woke up later and later.

And despite Jeremiah wanting to shove his own foot up his ass for what had happened by that damn fountain, it had at least had the side effect of keeping Remi from trying to sneak out again.

Though the way the prince avoided his eyes and kept even more to himself was making Jeremiah's chest tight and his muscles ache from holding back from comforting him.

He was pissed at himself for letting things get as far as they had last week, and he hated that he'd hurt Remi's feelings, but he couldn't let anything like it happen again. It just couldn't happen.

Remi's safety was more important than his dick.

And his Hellhound could just fucking chill already and stop clawing to get out.

"Still no clear suspect on who tipped them off about our trip to the beach?" he asked, and he could practically hear Knight's ass unclench at the change of subject.

"No. We've checked all known numbers and any devices within the palace grounds capable of sending so much as a smoke signal. Nothing."

Jeremiah planted his hand on his hip and stared at the rug his bed sat on, not seeing the colors or pattern. They were missing something. They had to be. That trip hadn't been planned, so it wasn't like someone could have accidentally let it slip in the days leading up to it. It had been spontaneous, and only those guards who had gone with them had known where they were going.

One of them had to have had leaked the information somehow.

"You're sure the place isn't bugged?"

"Swept the whole palace twice," Knight reminded him, the Vampire sounding less and less patient, but Jeremiah didn't give a shit.

"Do it again." He pinched the bridge of his nose, trying to stave off a headache he'd had building for a week, ever since he'd seen a dripping wet Remi practically begging to be kissed. "Then get the queen's permission to search the guards' and servants' private quarters and homes. If someone has an unregistered phone, I want to know. Hell, if anyone has a fucking typewriter, take it."

"Will do. Anything else?"

Come and relieve me, you dick. "No. Keep me updated."

"Yessir."

Jeremiah shoved his phone away a second before someone knocked at the door of his borrowed bedroom. Frowning, he strode over and tugged it open, surprised to find the queen's personal assistant on the other side. The sun was barely up, the day just beginning, yet she looked like she'd been at it for hours.

"Her Majesty would like to see you."

Jeremiah had a bad feeling his shit day was about to get a hell of a lot worse.

"This is a terrible idea," he said for the third time, but he kept the complaint under his breath, knowing the queen wasn't going to listen any more than she had back at the palace.

A fucking walkabout. What was she thinking?

"My people need to see me and know we aren't afraid. If we act like everything is fine, they'll remain calm."

Jeremiah lifted his lip in a silent snarl. He hated having his damn hands tied by a client, and the queen was one of the worst he'd ever had to deal with, used to being able to do whatever the hell she wanted and having everyone bow down to her wishes. There was such a fine line between protesting and being insolent, and he was getting tired as shit of having to walk that tightrope.

Diplomatic, he was not.

When he'd insisted Remi at least stay at home, she'd completely ignored him.

He knew she loved her son, but in her mind, he was safe as long as Jeremiah was next to him. He'd told her—more than once over the last couple of weeks—that while he was willing to sacrifice his life for his protectee, he couldn't guarantee that nothing would ever happen. Jeremiah could be the very best bodyguard in the world—and he knew he and his men were top-tier—but there was only so much he could do, especially when Remi and his mother refused to fucking *listen*.

He scanned the crowded street around their small group, instincts crawling with agitation. They were too exposed. The palace guards were doing their best to set up perimeters along the route the queen had said she'd be taking, but people were swarming to get a glimpse at her and her family too fast for them to keep up with.

A young woman, scales along her jaw an alluring mauve, hurried forward suddenly, eyes locked on Remi.

He was moving before Remi could do more than widen his eyes in surprise at her, planting himself between the woman and the prince. Letting his fangs lengthen, he growled lowly.

"Stop."

She gasped and jerked backward, staring up at him like he was about to rip her throat out.

Which... she wasn't *wrong*.

But then Remi was shoving an elbow in his side and stepping around him with a fierce scowl. "What are you doing?" he hissed. "Chill the fuck out before my mom fires your ass for terrifying innocent people."

Jeremiah didn't take his eyes off the young woman, noting she had something clutched in her right hand. It was too small for him to see, so probably not a weapon, but he planted a hand on Remi's chest to hold him back anyway.

"Show me what's in your hand," he said, ignoring the people around them staring and whispering.

Her mahogany skin flushed as she looked away in embarrassment, but she held out her hand, palm up. It was a small, decorative box, looking harmless, but Jeremiah jerked his head toward where Jennette and a few other support staff people were bringing up the rear of the group.

"Give it to one of them."

Nodding quickly, she scurried off and shoved the token into the chest of one of the young men who Jeremiah couldn't remember the name of, then disappeared back into the crowd. Jeremiah ran his gaze over the massive group of gawkers filling the street and creeping up onto the sidewalk where the queen and her entourage were, having stopped so she could buy a bouquet of flowers from a shop.

Slender fingers gripped at his elbow, bringing his attention back to a furious Remi. "What the hell was that?"

"Me doing my job. You don't accept anything from anyone you don't know, Your Highness."

Remi rolled his eyes, turning his back enough that most of the onlookers couldn't see his face. "Do you honestly think that girl was some sort of assassin? You're getting paranoid, Sunshine."

Narrowing his eyes, Jeremiah leaned down so they were practically nose-to-nose. "I don't make assumptions about people based on their appearances, little princeling. Anyone can be a threat. That's not paranoia, that's *experience*."

Remi sucked in a deep breath, his slender chest expanding with the force of it and drawing Jeremiah's eyes down his body without his permission. Letting it out slowly, Remi said, "This isn't working. I'm going to talk to my mother, and we'll figure out another person to run my protection detail."

Despite the fact that Jeremiah had been trying to do that exact same thing earlier that morning, hearing Remi say the words had his hellfire roaring to life under his skin. Like fucking *hell* someone else would protect him.

"Your mother was very clear that she wanted me and only me for the job of keeping you safe."

"Things change," Remi said through gritted teeth.

Jeremiah noticed the Siren in question watching them out of the corner of her eye, even while she smiled and thanked another person for their kind words and gift that Jennette accepted. He had no doubt she'd rip them both a new one for making a scene if they didn't finish their conversation later.

Stepping back, Jeremiah scanned the street around them. "Maybe. But I think my chances are pretty damn good, brat."

The small gasp he got for the insult made him want to grin, but he slipped his impassive face back into place and pretended he didn't notice.

"Time to go back to smiling, little princeling. People are beginning to notice."

With his peripheral vision, he saw Remi straighten up, shoulders tensing, then whip around to face the crowd once more, lifting a hand in a wave.

Jeremiah would never really understand how it happened

—one moment, their group was on the move again, and the next, he'd somehow lost sight of Remi.

His heart rate picked up, but his training kicked in as well, keeping him calm as he meticulously searched the area around them, ignoring the noise of the swelling crowd. People were shouting and crying, begging the queen to stop and talk to them for a moment, but it all became white noise in his ears as he relied on his other senses.

He pushed through people, heading back the way they'd come. Somehow, Remi must have stopped without anyone noticing. It was the only thing that made sense, but Jeremiah didn't know how he hadn't seen it. He always kept the boy in his sightline, even as he checked the crowd.

Except when they'd crossed the street and several people had gotten between them.

He broke through a knot of people and ignored the annoyed shouts at his rough treatment.

There.

In the shadowy alcove of a shop's doorway, Remi was crouched down, talking to a crying boy around the twins' age. "Remington!"

Remi's head whipped around, finding Jeremiah on the opposite side of the street and heading toward them. He waved a hand like he wanted Jeremiah to stop, but he ignored it, growling in anger when a huge family stepped between them, and he lost sight of Remi once more.

In the seconds it took him to finally get through them, Remi had stood and picked up the boy, wrapping his arms around him and heading in Jeremiah's direction. They were only a dozen feet away from each other when his instincts prickled, his Hellhound snarling and clawing for release.

He rushed forward as he looked up and down the street, trying to find what was setting him off, and his blood ran cold when he pinpointed the man in a hoodie behind Remi. He couldn't make out his shadowed face but saw the gun in his hand just fine.

"Get down!"

Even as fast as he was, he knew he wouldn't be able to get between Remi and the shooter before it was too late, but he still tried, pouring every ounce of speed into his legs as he sprinted the final distance. Remi—for once in his damn life—dropped to the ground, curling his body around the small boy, who screamed in confusion and terror.

Jeremiah heard the first pop when he was still a couple of feet away, and the crowd lost its collective mind, shrieking and starting to run in every possible direction. His beast burst from his skin as he leapt, shredding his clothes and roaring in fury. He landed on the other side of Remi, planting his body between him and the threat.

He howled in protest as the man turned and fled, but he couldn't leave Remi, not when he still didn't know if he was hurt or not. Royal guards were starting to swarm around them, encircling them and demanding to know what the fuck was going on.

It wasn't until Jeremiah shifted back to order some of the guards to go after the man that he felt the twinge in his thigh. Confused, he glanced down his naked body and saw the oozing bullet hole.

"Jeremiah!" Remi screamed.

He whipped around, claws and fangs at the ready and his beast half a second from taking over again, but Remi wasn't in danger anymore. He was being held in place by several guards, staring at Jeremiah's leg in horror. All of the blood had drained from his face, making him look like he was the one who'd been shot and was bleeding all over the street. A surge of something that felt eerily like affection pumped through his veins at the sight of Remi's shaking hand holding the back of the small boy's head, forcing him to keep his face tucked in Remi's neck. One of the guards kept trying to take the kid, but Remi finally just bared his teeth and told him to back off.

"Remi." His voice was soft, but somehow, he heard him over the cacophony of the street, eyes locking on him with an intenseness that stirred Jeremiah's Hellhound. "Let him go."

A split second later, Remi was squishing the poor boy between them, trying to hug Jeremiah and fuss over his wound at the same time. "Oh my gods. Are you okay? Of course you're not okay. Holy shit. I can't believe someone shot you. We need to get you to a doctor—"

"Remi." He cupped the prince's face, forcing his wild eyes to focus on his once more. The little boy peeked up at him, tears clumping his lashes and streaking down his face, but Jeremiah ignored him for the moment. "Take a breath, brat. I'm fine."

"But you were—"

"It's already healing." And it was. He could feel the wound closing, the blood barely more than a trickle. He'd have to get checked over later to see if the bullet needed to come out, but he wasn't close to death's door or anything. "We need to get back to the palace, okay? Do you know this kid?"

"Hm?" Remi glanced down at the boy, frows furrowed, then shook his head. "This is Trey. He lost his mom and dad in the crowd and couldn't find them, so I told him I'd help."

Warmth flushed through him, but Jeremiah ignored it, the need to get Remi to safety overruling everything else. A commotion nearby drew his attention, and he narrowed his eyes, already moving to put himself between the boys and whatever it was before he realized the young couple was crying and reaching toward them with a desperation only a terrified parent could have.

He moved aside and took the kid from Remi's arms. "I think we found them. Stay here."

He waited until Remi nodded and another guard came

over to stand next to him before he strode over and handed the little boy to his father, the man looking like his knees were about to give out for a moment as he wrapped his arms around his son and sobbed.

"Thank you," his mom said wetly, placing a trembling hand on the boy's head like Remi had. "The crowd got so big… I don't know how I lost him."

"He's alright. The prince kept him safe."

She glanced at him with wide eyes, then looked past him at where Remi was still watching, face tense with worry and hands wringing in front of him. "He did?"

Jeremiah nodded before turning and heading back toward Remi, ready to get him in an SUV and on the way to the palace. A pair of sweats appeared in front of him, stopping him in his tracks. He followed the hand holding them up the arm to the unreadable face of Greg. Jeremiah hadn't wanted him to come on the walkabout, but Thorne had overruled him, saying they needed the Demon's experience.

Without saying a word, Jeremiah accepted the pants and pulled them on, then continued on his way, collecting Remi from the other guard and hustling him toward the car waiting for them around the corner. He knew the queen was already probably back to the palace and knew he'd get ripped into as soon as they got back, like he hadn't been the one to say it was too dangerous.

But that didn't matter, and he knew that. Clients didn't always listen; they had lives to live and didn't always want to accept the restrictions Jeremiah and his team suggested be put in place. It was his job to keep them safe, even when they went against his counsel.

And he'd nearly fucking lost Remi.

After he climbed in behind the prince and ordered the driver to get them back to the palace as fast as possible, he let Remi scoot closer and hover a hand over where he'd been shot. His light eyes still looked terrified as he stared up at Jeremiah, bottom lip trembling.

"Are you sure you're okay?"

"I'm sure. Probably won't even scar."

Remi sucked in a shaky breath and nodded, gaze skating down his bare torso. "I can't believe someone would try and kill you out in the open like that. That was—"

"Remington." He paused, sure he'd misheard. "I wasn't… That man wasn't after me."

Pale purple eyes shot back up to his own, damp lips parting. "But… you were the one hurt…"

"Brat," he murmured, unable to stop himself from cupping Remi's chin and rubbing his thumb against that pouty lip. "We got fucking lucky. He was aiming for you."

"Me?"

"You. They aren't trying to take you anymore, it seems. Now, they're trying to kill you."

9

REMI

It had only been a few days, but it felt like weeks since his Hellhound had been shot. And it had been almost exactly that long since he'd started thinking of the obnoxious Hellhound as his. He'd managed not to slip up when he interacted with Jeremiah, but it wasn't easy. The longer he was in the castle, watching Remi's every move, the more… possessive Remi was starting to feel.

It was almost like he could sense where Jeremiah was at any given time, which was definitely not normal. At least, he was pretty sure it wasn't normal. He sure as hell hadn't felt like that when he was dating Oz. Hell, thinking back to Oz, it felt like some schoolboy crush when he compared it to the heat Jeremiah caused every time he was anywhere near Remi.

But it was a little more than that too. Jeremiah had healed exactly like he promised, but Remi had been refusing to leave the castle. He'd canceled all of his appointments, and while his parents weren't exactly putting up a fight about it, he felt like shit. Walkabouts were important, as were his charity meetings and the three visits to schools that had been added to his calendar while he was home.

The problem wasn't that he was afraid for himself—

though he didn't want to be maimed or killed by whatever fringe terrorist group had decided to target him and his family. It was more the fact that every time someone tried to hurt him, they ended up hurting Jeremiah, and he wouldn't be able to live with himself if anything else happened to his Hellhound.

The only thing he could do in the moment was try to avoid Jeremiah at all costs. He made his way down to the pool in the early afternoon, and he could feel him prowling nearby, but he appreciated the space between them. Jeremiah seemed just as shaken by their odd connection as he was, and Remi was going to use that to his advantage to get some breathing room.

"Missing school terribly, aren't you?" came a welcome voice to his right.

Remi, who was lounging on his back with his feet in the water, turned his head to see his father walking toward him. Behind the castle walls, James was not a king. He was just a dad in his high-waisted jeans and polo shirt tucked in way too tightly. He was so human—so fragile and powerless—but Remi had never been afraid when his dad was nearby.

He felt that comfort now as James kicked off his shoes, rolled up his cuffs, and took a seat. He hissed when he dipped his toes into the cool water, and Remi wondered what it was like to not feel connected to the water down to his very atoms.

"I like learning," Remi said, pushing his shades a little higher up on his nose.

James snorted. "You definitely get that from me. Your mom once told me she was allergic to reading."

Remi rolled his eyes. "Unless they're Gargoyle romances."

James let out a hefty laugh, shaking his head. "Never tell her you know that."

"Uh, yeah," Remi said. "I value my life."

James's smile softened, and he reached over, laying a hand

over Remi's wrist. "Seriously though. Your mother and I are both worried about you. This week hasn't been easy."

Remi couldn't help a bitter chuckle. "The last *few* weeks have been a goddamn nightmare. Jeremiah's gotten hurt twice, the twins are off with strangers, and I feel completely helpless to do anything except cower. They *shot* him, Dad, because of me. Because of who we are."

"You never cower," James told him, squeezing his grip a little tighter. "And you didn't that day. I was there."

Remi let out a trembling breath. He supposed that was true. He didn't cower. He just also didn't do anything, and mostly because he didn't know how. His Siren powers were weak at best, diluted from his human side, and even then, he didn't know any battle Songs. He hadn't grown up in a time of conflict, so the most he was ever taught was how his ancestors fought for their lands with Voice, claws, and spears.

And what was he?

A bratty, spoiled princeling, as Jeremiah insisted over and over.

There was a rustle in the brush, and Remi's head whipped to the side, though he could feel an odd, pulsing tug somewhere deep in his sternum telling him it was the Hellhound. He flushed, glancing back at his father, who was giving him an odd look.

"How are you getting on with your guard?"

"Fine," he said, trying and failing to mask his irritation. "He's a dick, but I haven't died, so I guess he's succeeding at his job."

The look on his father's face was one of pure and utter disbelief. "Is that all you think of him?"

"What else is there?" Remi asked, sitting up. He felt irritation crawling under his skin like tiny fire ants, and he couldn't shake it off. "I just want this to be over so he can go home and I never have to see him again. Things will be better… back to normal."

James hummed softly. "I see."

Remi folded his arms, feeling like a petulant child. It was no wonder Jeremiah called him a brat, but he couldn't seem to help the way he was feeling. Like some adolescent hitting his first hormone surge, and godsdamn it all, but he was supposed to be past that now.

"Remi..."

"I need to go inside," Remi said with a huff, pulling his legs out of the water. He caught a glimpse of his scales, which would have made him happy since it was so much harder for him to shift than full Sirens, but all he felt was a strange, longing pulse in his chest that he didn't know how to relieve.

He appreciated that his father didn't try to stop him when he left, but he felt very alone as he navigated the corridors back to his room and even worse when the door shut, cutting him off from the small thread that was linking him to his bodyguard.

Another two days passed before Remi snapped. He was not only going stir-crazy, but every time Remi so much as moved, Jeremiah tensed like Remi was about to be blown into pieces.

It was late at night—somewhere past midnight—when Remi snuck out of his room. He followed the odd feeling in his chest, the pulsing getting stronger as he got closer to the Hellhound, and it was no surprise when he found him in the guards' training arena.

It was completely empty that late at night, though Remi could see guards posted on the walls a few yards from the courtyard, but he ignored them in favor of approaching the Hellhound, who was taking out all of his aggression on one of the heavy bags.

There were claw marks on the side, and Remi was pretty sure it was done for.

"Why aren't you getting your beauty sleep, princeling?"

Remi bristled at the name but didn't let himself react to it. "Why are you beating down this bag like it owes you money?"

Jeremiah snorted a laugh, then reared back like the sound surprised him. He didn't look over, which was fine with Remi because he got the perfect view of the Hellhound's ass as he sauntered toward the table and snapped up his water bottle.

Remi could see the line of Jeremiah's throat and the way it bobbed as he swallowed down mouthful after mouthful of water.

"Is there something you need?" Jeremiah asked after swiping the back of his hand over his wet, pink lips.

Remi swallowed heavily, shook his head, then changed course and nodded. "Yeah. Yes."

Jeremiah raised a brow, staring at him pointedly.

In that moment, Remi almost panicked and ran. He felt small and young and pathetic. If that odd connection between them hadn't tethered Remi to the spot, he actually might have. Instead, he took a breath, then said, "Teach me to fight."

Jeremiah choked on his second drink of water. "Sorry?"

Remi squared his shoulders. "I said, teach me to fight."

Jeremiah slowly set the bottle down, then folded his arms over his massive chest and turned to face Remi. "Teach you to fight," he echoed.

"Am I speaking a new language?" Remi demanded.

Jeremiah shook his head, but he wasn't saying no. He looked incredulous and maybe even a little annoyed. "What makes you think I have time to waste on that?"

Remi's eyes widened. "Waste—dude, fuck you. It's not a waste of time to teach me how to defend myself."

"Yes," Jeremiah said slowly, like he was talking to a toddler, "it is. I'm in the middle of running an investigation while also trying to protect your pretty face from getting smeared all over the pavement by some group of maniacs who have it out for your family."

Remi's cheeks flushed. Pretty? His face was pretty? Objectively, he knew that, but… He stopped and cleared his throat. "Wouldn't it make your life a lot easier if I could defend myself?"

Jeremiah laughed, and it wasn't very kind. "It would make my life a lot easier if my team could track down who the fucking leak in the castle is. Then we could take this person down, and you could get back to your life."

"And you can forget all about me," Remi said. He didn't mean to, but the words tumbled out of his mouth, and he regretted it almost immediately. He turned, mortified that he'd shown his hand like that, but before he could run, searing hot fingers brushed the back of his neck.

His entire body went stiff, but he moved when Jeremiah urged him to turn, and he looked up when that same fiery touch pressed against the underside of his chin.

"That's not what I meant," Jeremiah said, softer than he'd ever spoken to Remi.

His heart felt like it was trying to beat straight out of his chest. "It's fine, you know. I know I'm pathetic. You're not wrong about me being a brat. But I'm tired of feeling useless, because I'm not. I get that being half human makes me weaker, but…"

"Being any sort of human doesn't make you weaker," Jeremiah said, his voice deep and rich. "I don't know who the fuck told you that, but I'm willing to bet it wasn't your parents."

Remi laughed bitterly. "No. Just everyone else who spent the last twenty-five years protesting my parents' marriage, then the birth of me, and then the birth of the twins. Tell me you didn't see the signs when we were on the walkabout."

Jeremiah blinked, looking a little shocked. "The signs?"

Remi scoffed. "Halfbreed is the most common one. They

can't really get in trouble for telling it like it is. But the shit they say is worse." He threw up his arms in frustration. "And I don't even care if they say it to me, but the twins are going to start understanding what that garbage means, and—"

His words cut off when Jeremiah pressed his palm to the side of Remi's neck. "I understand."

Remi scoffed. "Yeah, right. A fucking Hellhound—one of the most powerful species on the planet—understands."

Jeremiah gave him a look he couldn't quite read, but there was something in his gaze that almost seemed to crawl under Remi's skin, like an emotion he was being forced to feel. It was grief and loneliness and anger all rolled into one. And it was gone as quickly as it had come.

"You really want to learn how to fight?"

Remi pulled back. "Yeah. I do. I'm not trying to be some problem child here. The other day, with the shooting? That scared the shit out of me. I want to be able to defend myself, but I'm not the only one who's vulnerable."

Jeremiah stared at him a long moment, and then his arms dropped to his sides, and he took several steps back. "Fine. But you can't quit if it gets hard or painful. I don't do anything half-assed."

Remi knew he meant that in training alone, but his mind immediately went elsewhere. It went to a deep, dark place of Jeremiah taking him to the very limits of pleasure, and gods…

No, he couldn't let himself think about that now. Swallowing his pride like this was embarrassing enough. He took a breath, then held his fists up in a fighting stance. "Okay, let's do this."

Jeremiah laughed, and before Remi could even blink, he was on his ass.

"Drop your weight," Jeremiah growled.

The tone of his voice, how deep it was, pulsed through Remi, and he might have reacted differently if his heart wasn't racing from exertion and a little bit of fear. There was something wild and primal about a Hellhound pinning his arms behind his back, holding him with a force no one had ever been brave enough to use on the crown prince.

Remi grunted and attempted to drop his weight, but when it didn't work, he kicked backward, aiming for the Hellhound's balls. Jeremiah just laughed and shoved Remi's chest against the wall, hard enough to steal his breath.

"Had enough, princeling?"

"Fuck you," Remi spat. "Fuck you. I'm not weak."

"Never said you were," Jeremiah rumbled against the back of his ear. "You're untrained, and you don't know how to use your assets to your benefit. Which means anyone who gets their hands on you will use them against you. You have power. Show me."

Rage flooded through him, the feeling odd and foreign but strangely good. Remi felt suddenly like he was floating outside of his body, and he managed to bring his hands together, his left fingers tugging at his signet ring. He'd been knocked around all goddamn night and made a fool of, and while it made sense because everything Jeremiah said was true, it pissed him off.

He was tired of being pathetic.

He was tired of being vulnerable.

"Let go." With his ring gone, the suppression spell was broken, and his Voice purred out of him. He felt Jeremiah's grip slacken—not enough for Remi to break his guard's grip, but enough for him to drop his weight so he could slip out of the hold. He laid a sucker punch to Jeremiah's right kidney, dropping him to his knees, and then he had the Hellhound flat on his back with his bare foot to the larger man's heaving chest.

Jeremiah's eyes were glowing. He stared at Remi, their gazes locked, and Remi smirked down at him.

"Ha. I wo—"

Before he could finish his words, Jeremiah took him by the ankle, and the next thing Remi knew, he was on the ground with Jeremiah's weight pinning him.

"Your second mistake—you got cocky and assumed you'd disarmed me."

"You should have told me Hellhounds were immune to Siren Voice," Remi snarled.

Jeremiah grinned down at him. "We're not. You just lacked focus."

Remi didn't think that was true. He'd never felt so in tune with his Siren side before. It should have dropped Jeremiah entirely—should have put him under a thrall that would have been impossible to break. At least, that's what would have happened if Remi wasn't half human.

It was the only explanation.

Frustration and shame coursed through him, and he closed his eyes, feeling Jeremiah's weight and the heat of his hellfire that burned beneath his skin. It should have terrified him, but it was comforting in ways he didn't want to admit.

"I have no right to rule," Remi eventually said. His words were hoarse, choked with his self-loathing, and he only opened his eyes when he felt Jeremiah's grip tighten.

"Why do you think that? Because you can't take down a trained guard? You do know your parents hired me because I'm the best in this business, don't you?"

Remi shoved Jeremiah, and he knew it wasn't his own strength that moved him. Jeremiah rolled away, and Remi stood, brushing invisible dust from his pants. "It's not about you. Not everything's about you."

Jeremiah laughed. "You don't have to sell me on that, princeling. It's never been about me. But it's my business when you ask me to train you and it turns into a self-pity party."

"That's not what I'm saying," Remi shouted, throwing his hands up before dragging fingers through his mussed hair. "I'm... Everyone is right about me. How the hell am I supposed to rule this entire kingdom when I'm so..."

"What?" Jeremiah pressed. He stalked closer, and Remi found himself taking steps back until he hit the wall. "Clever? Calculating? Charming?"

Remi rolled his eyes, in no mood to be mocked by a man he shouldn't want so goddamn much. It only made the pain of it all worse. "Human."

Jeremiah stopped. "Is that such a bad thing?"

"Humans aren't meant for this," Remi said, his voice barely above a whisper.

"Do you think that about your father?"

Guilt hit Remi even harder, and he winced. "That's different. He's different. He's strong and humble and brave all at the same time. I'm exactly what you said I am."

"And what is that?"

"A spoiled, weak brat," Remi fired back, lifting his chin.

Something flared in Jeremiah's eyes, and then his hand slammed against the wall beside Remi's head. Before he could react, Jeremiah had him by the jaw, his grip iron-tight and unforgiving. Their lips were barely a breath apart. "I have never," he said, a rumbling growl coming from his chest, "called you weak."

Remi opened his mouth, but before he could fight back, warm lips were on his own. Jeremiah fit against him perfectly, like they were born as separate halves of a whole. Remi's entire body lit up when the Hellhound dragged a rough, warm tongue over his lips, and Jeremiah swallowed down Remi's soul-deep groan as sparks shot across his skin.

His eyes were closed, but as Jeremiah deepened the kiss, Remi swore he was glowing with the light of his hellfire. His hips moved, seeking friction, but before they found it, Jeremiah ripped himself away, and it was like ice being poured over Remi's entire body.

"I—"

"We can't," Jeremiah gasped. He looked like he was in agony, several feet away, one hand in his hair, the other clenched at his side. Remi caught a faint whiff of something sharp and metallic, and he saw blood dripping from Jeremiah's fingers. His claws were out. "This is... I can't. I can't do this."

Remi stood there, immobile and confused, as Jeremiah spun on his heel and left. He didn't move for what felt like a short eternity, and it was only when another guard showed up, silently slipping into the room and waiting patiently, that he realized Jeremiah wasn't coming back.

He hadn't done anything. Jeremiah had kissed him, but he couldn't stop the painful feeling deep in his chest that somehow, that single moment had ruined everything.

10

JEREMIAH

His hands shook as he gripped his glass, the alcohol burning his throat. There were few spirits that actually worked on him, and those that did were mostly made by Dragons. Lucky for him, he had a member on his team with a family that had been in the distillery business for generations.

"Better?" Knight asked with a small smile.

He was sitting across the room, dressed to the nines in his suit despite the fact it was the middle of the night, his ankle crossed over his knee. A highball glass dangled from the tips of his fingers, the liquid inside dark red and glinting from the low light in the corner of Jeremiah's room. He used to find the scent of blood disconcerting, but he'd grown used to it over the years since Knight predominately fed from a glass to avoid contact with people.

Jeremiah grunted and took another long swallow from his glass.

"Come on, Sunshine. That would burn the scales off a Siren. Sip it, you heathen."

Jeremiah winced in spite of himself as he took another drink. The alcohol worked just enough to take the edge off his nerves, but he'd never be able to consume enough to forget what he'd done. He'd broken every moral code they had—and a few of his own.

Remi was a client, and he was young, and he was *vulnerable*. Whatever the hell he was feeling, it wasn't normal. It wasn't natural. And it was clear it wasn't something either of them could control. Remi's want had poured off him like clouds of pheromones, and Jeremiah's hound was clawing at his chest to be let loose, to claim.

And he'd let go for just a second.

There was no taking it back.

"You need to take over for me," Jeremiah said roughly.

Knight sighed. "We've been through this. The queen and king—"

"They're going to throw me out on my ass if—*when* they find out what I did," Jeremiah said, shoving his fingers into his hair and tugging. He started to sit, but halfway into his crouch, he shot back up again and started pacing. "We've barely made any headway with this investigation, we've made almost no progress in tracking down the leak, and now I've molested—"

"Whoa, wait. What the fuck?" Knight asked. He was on his feet, his fangs dropping and eyes flooding with a red glow. "You did what?"

Jeremiah wanted to sink into the floor. "I kissed him."

"Against his will?" Knight growled.

Jeremiah slapped a hand over his face and dragged it down. "No, but—"

"Oh, by the everlasting fucking gods," Knight said and collapsed back down. "Can you please not use the word 'molested' when you're talking about making out with a man who clearly wants to climb you like a tree? Swim you like an ocean?" Knight added with a frown. "Whatever the equivalent is for Sirens."

Jeremiah gave him a withering look, and Knight just

tipped his glass at him in a cheers, then gulped it all down, his eyes glowing once more as the blood hit his system.

"Why are you not understanding the gravity of this situation?" Jeremiah growled. "It doesn't matter that he wanted it. I'm in a position of power over him—"

"I hate to break it to you, but he's a crown prince, and you're technically on *his* payroll. He's the one with the power," Knight said. "And you're treating him like a child because you feel guilty that you finally gave in to something you wanted."

"You think so?" Jeremiah snarled sarcastically.

Knight spread his hands, unmoved and unintimidated by Jeremiah's voice. "I call it like I see it, and I do that because I love you. And because you're acting like a moron."

Jeremiah wanted to put his fist through the wall and debated whether or not he'd settle for putting his fist through Knight's chest. The fucker would heal. "I can't keep this up. Every time I'm around him, I want to…"

"Tear his clothes off?"

Jeremiah swallowed heavily and couldn't bring himself to lie. "And I don't think he's going to stay away from me anymore, which is making going to make it that much harder."

"It or you?" Knight said with a wink, refilling his glass from the thermos he'd brought with him when Jeremiah had called freaking out.

"Will you please, for the love of all the gods, take this seriously?" Jeremiah begged.

Knight sighed and set his glass down, then rested his forearms on his thighs, looking up at Jeremiah. "I'm not saying it's ideal to fall for a client, and I'm not saying you should continue to act on it. But I'm also not *not* saying that."

"I'm going to light you on fire and bury you in concrete."

Knight spread his hands as he sat back and picked up his glass once more. "I've survived worse. In fact, we've both survived worse. And that's the very reason you're panicking about this."

Jeremiah froze, and his brows dipped. "What?"

Knight let out a small sigh and pinched the bridge of his nose. "It's too bad I'm too pretty to go into psychology." He leaned forward again, capturing Jeremiah's gaze with the barest hint of thrall that Jeremiah didn't bother to fight. "You forget that we're cut from the same cloth. That the world hates my kind almost as much as they hate yours. I've heard similar insults ever since I was turned—that I'm little more than a diseased human. That I'm a freak. That I don't belong." His jaw was tight but his eyes strangely blank as he rattled off the things they'd both had spewed at them. "So I know what you're thinking when you look at that well-dressed, proper little prince."

"That he's going to get himself killed?" Jeremiah asked roughly.

"That you'll sully him if you put your hands on him. That you don't want to ruin him because you're a Hellhound."

Jeremiah closed his eyes and hated with every fiber of his being how well Knight understood him. "I have no business with him. And whatever this feeling is," he said, rubbing his chest, "it won't matter. He's the crown prince. Even if I wasn't a Hellhound, you know he's probably betrothed so some... princess or duchess or whatever."

"From my research, I can tell you he's not," Knight said. "The queen and king married for love, and they seem pretty determined that their children all do the same."

That was the last thing Jeremiah wanted to hear. He didn't need false hope, even if it was nothing more than a glimmer. "You're missing the point."

Knight sighed, pushing to his feet. "No. You're missing the point, and I'm not going to enable your bullshit anymore. I love you, Sunshine. You're my brother in more ways than I've learned how to count. But you're also a dumbass, and I'm not going to sit here and watch you keep getting in your own way."

Before Jeremiah could stop him, Knight was gone with a speed even he couldn't follow. A surge of anger hit him, and he flung his empty glass at the wall, feeling only a moment of satisfaction as it shattered. He stared at all the broken pieces like a kaleidoscope on the ground, glass glinting in the dim light, and then he turned on his heel, determined to find the queen and king and put an end to the madness.

The castle was like a goddamn maze, and he found himself in some conference room with chairs set up in front of two thrones like they were in stasis, waiting for the rulers of the country. He was exhausted and ready to give up looking for any member of the royal family. Why had he thought doing this immediately was a good idea?

It was late, and the queen and king were both feeling low, having sent the twins off for safekeeping, so there was every chance they'd turned in early.

Jeremiah had never loved anyone as much as those two loved their offspring. And he most certainly hadn't been that loved himself, so he couldn't quite comprehend how it would feel, but it had to be close to how he got every time one of the members of his team got injured on the job. The heart-racing, gut-twisting fear he felt any time one of them went down was almost too much to bear.

He wasn't sure he'd survive this life loving someone even more than that…

And that, above all, was what terrified him about Remi. He didn't think the prince was weak. Far from it. He'd proven in the last week that he was brave, if maybe a little reckless, but the way he wanted to protect his family was behind all the ridiculous decisions he made. And Jeremiah could understand that.

He'd thrown himself into danger before to protect the others. He'd do the same for any member of this house without regret.

But those were moments, not forever, and he had to figure out how to shake the feeling he was having because it wasn't sustainable. His only real option was to confess what happened and let the royals fire him so he could move on. He could work behind the scenes where he belonged and not have to see Remi's face every single day.

He wouldn't have to feel the damned longing that hadn't left his chest since he looked into Remi's eyes and realized there was more to him than a vapid, self-absorbed brat.

Even if he was still a bit of a brat.

"You look lost."

Jeremiah jumped and hated himself for dropping his guard. It was half a dozen times now, and every single one of those moments had been either watching Remi or thinking about him. It was a problem. He spun to find King James standing in the doorway of the conference room, a gently amused look on his face.

"Did I frighten you?"

Jeremiah rolled his eyes, but he didn't hesitate to admit the truth. "A little."

"Never thought I'd hear the day a Hellhound admitted that to a human."

Jeremiah pursed his lips, then gestured to the seat beside him. "I'm not like most Hellhounds."

"I've never met any others, but I have a feeling you're right," James said as he walked in and lowered himself beside Jeremiah. He looked very unkingly in his pajama pants and matching shirt, and the thought almost made Jeremiah smile. He'd never really considered royal families could ever be average, but then again, he didn't spend a lot of time considering royals.

Up to this point, his only motivation in life was to stay alive and get paid.

"Are you lost?" James asked after a beat.

"No, Your Majes—"

"Just James, I think," the king said with a tiny sigh. "If you don't mind. Things are a little upside-down right now, and I need to feel a bit like myself."

Jeremiah nodded, staring down at his hands. "I'm sorry it's taking so long, James."

"So am I. I'll never regret sending my children away, but not seeing them every day is hell. My time with them is limited as it is, with how busy I am. I… I love my wife, and I'd do anything for her, but there are days when I miss who I was."

"Human?"

"Average. Unremarkable," James said. "The spare to an heir who married young and has given me so many nieces and nephews I never stood a chance of inheriting the throne. No one paid any attention to what I did. But now…"

Jeremiah snorted. "That's where he gets it."

"Who?"

Jeremiah flushed. He hadn't meant to blurt that out, but it was too late now. "Your son seems to think he's entirely too human to be worthy of the throne."

James glanced away, pain flooding his face. "They would have hated him here, even if we weren't royal, but it's so much worse because we are. His entire life, he's been told by strangers that he's unworthy. That he doesn't belong. That's he's not Siren enough, not human enough. And I think my own inferiority has been a bit too obvious."

Jeremiah stared at him for a long time. He could see so much of James in his son and so much of his mother as well. He was the perfect blend of the two—a brand-new creature that belonged only to himself. There was a sort of tragic beauty in it that he doubted Remi would ever see.

"He doesn't think of you that way, if that helps," Jeremiah said quietly. "If anything, he wants to be more like you. I think this has just taken a toll on him in ways he wasn't expecting."

"I've noticed." James froze suddenly, and before Jeremiah could panic that something was wrong, another figure filled the door.

The queen walked in wearing a matching pajama set to her husband's, her feet bare and tapping on the cool stone floor. Her hair was tied back in a long braid, and she was wearing a small smile as she carried three mugs filled with steaming liquid on a tray.

"A little birdie told me that we had a midnight wanderer."

Jeremiah jumped to his feet and started to bow, but she scoffed, and he stopped halfway. "Ma'am."

"Gods, please don't. I know James has already been on you about it tonight."

Jeremiah glanced down at the king, who was smirking. "I can show myself back to my room."

"Or you can sit and drink some cocoa," Grace said, holding out two mugs.

James took his, and after a beat, Jeremiah did the same because the last thing he wanted to do was refuse the Siren queen. She smiled, satisfied, and took a seat in the row in front of them, twisting her body so she could stare over the back of the short chair.

"Is it a personal crisis or just work keeping you up?" she asked.

Jeremiah rubbed his temple with two fingers as he brought the mug to his lips, and at the first sip, his entire body went warm. "What…"

"Old family recipe," Grace said with a wink. "Don't ask

me what's in it. I'm sworn to secrecy until my death, and that's going to be a long time from now."

Jeremiah's eyes cut over to James, and he couldn't help but wonder if being fated to her meant his life was extended. It seemed a rude question, so he kept it to himself.

"Well?" Grace demanded after a long beat.

Jeremiah blinked, then remembered she'd asked him a question. "Both."

"I suspected as much. James was a lot like you when he moved in here. Wandering, trying to find his place. Trying to figure out why I'd chosen him."

"Oh, you're making it out to be so much more complicated than it was," James grumbled into his drink, failing to hide a small grin. "The simple fact was, a queen of an entire species saw me—a throwaway son from a tiny human kingdom—and decided I was for her."

"The simple fact *was* that I saw the man fated to be mine," Grace said, her voice low and silky. "And it helped that he had an amazing, huge—"

"Grace!" James said, lurching forward to slap a hand over her mouth.

Her laughter was like bells ringing through the empty room, and even a man as heartless as Jeremiah couldn't help his own grin or the way their love made him warm in ways his hellfire never could.

"Library of books," she said, wagging a finger at him. "What did you think I was going to say?"

James flushed a brilliant red. "Thank you for that, my love. As if I'm not awkward enough as it is."

"I think you're wonderful," she said softly. She leaned forward to set her mug down, then rested her arm on the back of the chair and laid her chin on her hand. She seemed so normal, and he couldn't help but envy the love Remi must have grown up with. "The truth is, this isn't an easy life. Not for ones brought in and not for the ones born to it. But we take strength in each other. I only wish my son would understand that."

"I think he does," Jeremiah said, wishing he could keep it in, but he couldn't help it. So much of him ached for Remi, and it was terrifying. "I think he's afraid, but he's going to do amazing things. He'll be a fantastic king."

"If he wants to be," Grace said with a small, knowing smile Jeremiah couldn't hope to understand. "But I hope you give yourself credit."

Jeremiah jolted. "For what?"

"Bringing out a side of him he's been hiding for a long time. I know you two might seem like oil and water, but I've been around for a long time, and I know better." When Grace reached for him, Jeremiah couldn't bring himself to pull away. Her hand was almost painfully cold against his perpetually hot skin, but he didn't hate her touch. "I don't know what has you wandering the halls after midnight, but I hope you know how grateful we are that you're here."

Even if I kissed your son? Even if I put him in danger because I was so caught up in him?

But as much as he'd resolved to tell them the truth so they'd force him out, he couldn't bring himself to say it aloud. He'd never had parents before, and the way they were with him—near him like they wanted to be, like they didn't care that he was an abomination—it was too addictive, and he wasn't ready to let go.

"I should leave you two and get to bed," he finally managed, extracting himself from her fingers and standing.

The pair exchanged a look, and then James climbed to his feet. "Let me walk you back."

Jeremiah wanted to say that wasn't necessary, but he was still craving the company, so he didn't put up a fight when the king matched his pace and they started down the corridor. Silence settled between them, comforting and easy in a strange way, and Jeremiah almost regretted it when James took a breath.

"There are days I still don't feel like I belong. The weight of hatred is sometimes too much to bear, and I don't know that Remi will want to live with that for the rest of his life. I think he's afraid if he decides to turn down the throne, we'll be disappointed in him."

"Have you told him you won't be?"

James scoffed. "More times than I can count, but you know how kids are with their parents."

"I don't," Jeremiah admitted. "I never knew mine. I was abandoned as a child. Hellhounds around here don't usually keep their children."

James's eyes darkened with sadness. "I regret that your parents didn't get to know how you turned out."

Jeremiah could only think of a dozen self-deprecating things, so he said nothing at all.

"I just wanted you to know that whatever Remi chooses, we will always support him. And for however long you stick around, we're glad to have you." James clasped his shoulder and squeezed with more strength than Jeremiah was expecting.

Before he could say anything, James turned and disappeared around the corner, leaving Jeremiah more confused than when he'd left his room, determined to burn this job to the ground.

What the hell had been in that cocoa?

11

REMI

Remi stopped outside the gym and listened to the steady beat of fists hitting leather.

For the first time since the attack on the beach, he had gone an entire day without seeing Jeremiah. Even when he'd been outside swimming in the pool, there had been no sign of the Hellhound, just a half dozen palace guards.

The fact that Jeremiah was obviously avoiding him had soured his mood. Having a man kiss him and then run away had been bad enough, but then to not see him at all when it was his damn job to keep Remi safe?

Ridiculous.

He'd seen the handsome Vampire from Jeremiah's team stop by about an hour after their… interaction the night before, and he'd thought for sure the man was going to be swapping in for Jeremiah as the head of his detail.

But he'd found out the following morning that the Vampire had left almost as soon as he had arrived. He kept expecting to see Jeremiah at some point or to at least feel him just outside of his line of sight, hiding in a hallway or in the bushes when he was outside. But that strange pulsing sensation to let him know when the Hellhound was near hadn't triggered at all, not until just a moment ago as he'd neared the gym. He had spent most of the day trying to decide what he would say once he did see Jeremiah again. As much as he'd told himself that he wasn't upset about the aborted kiss, he knew that was a lie. Watching Jeremiah literally flee the room after kissing him had left his chest feeling flayed open, vulnerable. His whole body ached in a way he wasn't familiar with.

It wasn't like he'd never been rejected before. At school, most people didn't know who he was. If he went out to a club or to a party, he was just another guy. Hell, Oz—his one semi-serious boyfriend—had dumped him spectacularly when Remi had suggested they have sex.

He'd learned how to take a no and roll with it, but for some reason, he couldn't seem to shake off the devastation that had settled over him the night before, and that pissed him off.

How dare Jeremiah touch his face so gently, tell him he didn't think he was weak, and then kiss him, only to flee like the entire thing had been a horrifying mistake.

Remi had half a mind to get the man fired, but as the day had progressed, he'd realized he couldn't do that no matter how upset he was. The idea of not seeing Jeremiah's scowling face lurking around the palace he loved and feared in equal measure wasn't something he could handle.

He knew it would happen eventually. He wasn't delusional.

Jeremiah and his team were too good not to figure out who was after Remi and his family. And once they did and neutralized the threat, there wouldn't be a need for Jeremiah to be there anymore. He and his team would go back to wherever it was they'd come from, Sadie and Percy would get to come home, and Remi… Well, he supposed he would go back to school and try to figure out how the hell he was supposed to be king one day.

But *knowing* that at some point in the future Jeremiah would leave wasn't the same as forcing him to go. He couldn't do it.

Just the idea made his heart race, his lungs struggling to draw full breaths.

Jeremiah might have run off after their last training session, but Remi was serious about wanting to learn to protect himself. To protect his brother and sister, if need be. He wanted to stop simply being a liability. He wanted to feel strong and powerful.

If Jeremiah no longer wanted to teach him, he'd find somebody else, but a not-small part of him wanted it to be his grumpy Hellhound. As hard as it had been the day before and as much as his muscles ached from the strain, he wanted to spend the extra time near him, having Jeremiah's hot hands on his skin as he corrected his form or they sparred.

Was he a despicable person for wanting that with a man who had turned tail and run at the idea of kissing him? Maybe. But Remi was just enough of the selfish prince people saw him as to decide he was going to go after what he wanted anyway. It was so damn rare for him to actually *get* what he wanted he was going to hold on with both hands until Jeremiah told him to stop.

Straightening his shoulders, he took one more deep breath and then strode into the gym like his nerves weren't on high alert and his skin prickling.

The second he entered the room, Jeremiah froze, his head twisting around, and bright, glowing blue eyes landed right on him. He wondered if Jeremiah felt it too, if he had sensed Remi come into the gym rather than hear or smell him.

But he was too afraid to ask.

Partially because he didn't know what it meant, but mostly because he was afraid of the answer, afraid that Jeremiah would say no. He would rather go on thinking they had some undefinable connection than know for sure that it was completely one-sided.

"What is it, Remi?" Jeremiah growled at him, turning to face him head-on and swiping at his sweaty brow with his forearm.

Remi tried not to stare at what he was wearing. The thin gray sweatpants molded to every muscle in his thick thighs, and the big gaping holes down his sides where the sleeves had been torn off his old T-shirt. It felt scandalous to see so much of the bare skin of his torso, despite the fact that Jeremiah saw a lot more of Remi when he swam in the pool.

In fact, he'd seen *all* of Remi when he went for his dip in the fountain.

But up until that point, he'd never seen anything other than Jeremiah's forearms.

He could see hints of his ridged abdomen when he moved, but what caught and held his attention when Jeremiah raised his arm was the large black-and-gray tattoo all down his side.

Remi had never seen a fully shifted Hellhound before the day of the shooting, but he recognized Jeremiah's hound, shivering as he remembered the huge animal panting and growling as he'd stood between Remi and danger. The rolling heat from the flames dancing down his black-furred back had been intense.

Why would Jeremiah ink his shifted form into his skin? Was it a Hellhound thing, or had Jeremiah chosen to do it, to mark himself for some reason with the beast inside him so many feared?

The snarling face was terrifying, but it was also… beautiful. The details were amazingly captured—from the long, sharp claws to the wet-looking fangs bared in anger. The wisps of smoke rising from the beast's back and ears looked delicate, belying the truth behind its fiery danger.

Gods, all Remi wanted to do was run his tongue over the ink.

Swallowing, he dragged his eyes away, forcing himself to look Jeremiah in the face. He ignored the frown that had somehow deepened in the moment it had taken Remi to answer and spit out the words he'd been practicing for an hour.

"You're still going to teach me self-defense."

Jeremiah's eyes narrowed, and he took a step forward, his hands fisted at his sides. "It isn't a good idea—"

Remi didn't give him a chance to finish. Lifting his chin, he said clearly, "You're going to teach me, or I'll find somebody who will."

"All of my men are too busy to—"

"Greg said he would." Remi let the lie hang in the air between them, watching Jeremiah's flushed cheeks darken with anger and his eyes start to glow with blue flames once more.

A thrilling shiver of awareness raced down his spine. Jeremiah truly seemed *jealous* of his relationship with his old bodyguard.

Jeremiah was jealous. Over him.

As much as he was sure Greg *would* teach him, he wanted it to be Jeremiah. Needed his grumpy little puppy to be the one to show him how to defend himself.

For… reasons.

"I know what you're doing," Jeremiah said lowly, advancing on him.

Heart speeding up, Remi held his ground and pasted on an innocent smile. "I don't know what you're talking about."

Steam was rising from Jeremiah's heaving shoulders as he stepped in close, looming over him and blocking out the rest of the world. Their gazes locked and held, and Remi had to stop himself from putting a hand over his belly when it swooped at the dark desire he saw shining back at him so brightly.

"Fine," Jeremiah bit out, fangs just a little longer than was polite. "Get in position."

"This was a terrible idea," Remi said after he hit the ground—*again*—with a grunt. He wasn't looking, but he could feel Jeremiah rolling his eyes at him. If he'd thought the Hellhound was tough on him the day before, he'd been proven wrong within the first twenty minutes.

"Quit being a whiner."

"I'm not a whiner."

"Get back on your feet, Remi."

"No," Remi said, drawing out the word in what was most definitely a whine. He threw his arms over his eyes and panted, letting the mat beneath him cool off his overheated body.

He wasn't meant to be working so hard or sweating so much. He was a *prince*.

What the hell had he been thinking?

"This was your idea," Jeremiah reminded him.

For the first time in an hour, Remi was almost positive there was amusement in his voice. Lifting his forearms off his face, he glared up at the Hellhound. Yep, definitely a smirk.

"Well, I changed my mind," Remi sniped and then let his arms fall back over his head. He was sure his face was already red from the exertion, but just in case, he wanted to hide any evidence of a blush as he admitted his mistake. "This is dumb. I don't know why I thought I could do this. There's no way I could take out some lunatic who's trying to kill me."

A bare foot nudged one of his calves. "What we're doing isn't about you taking down anyone," Jeremiah said slowly.

"Your only job is to get away and get to somebody whose job it is to take down the bad guys."

Remi puffed out his cheeks and then let out a noisy breath. "Well, it doesn't matter because it's pointless either way. Out of the water, I just don't have any sort of grace."

Jeremiah grunted and dropped to one knee next to him. "Look at me, Remington."

He didn't, at least not right away. He had a feeling all he'd see was pity on the Hellhound's face. That was the last thing he wanted, especially because that damn connection he felt to the man had only grown stronger the longer they'd been in the gym together.

It was like a string was tied between their chests, and the more time they spent in close proximity, breathing the same air, touching each other's skin, the tighter the string became, reeling them closer together. It was the strangest sensation.

Remi wasn't even a hundred percent sure he liked it, but there was no denying the visceral pull he had toward his stupid bodyguard.

"Remi," Jeremiah said again.

He let his arms fall out to the sides but kept staring at the ceiling. "I just thought I could…" He trailed off, not quite sure how to explain what it was he was feeling.

He knew he would never be a badass like Jeremiah or the rest of his team, and that wasn't what he'd wanted. Those guys had probably been training most of their lives to do the things that they could. All Remi wanted was to feel like he wasn't completely helpless.

But that was beginning to feel more and more unrealistic.

If the assholes who were after him and his family got their hands on him again, he doubted he'd be able to get away. The first time at the club was a complete fluke, and that realization was humbling… and terrifying.

It was obvious to him now that Jeremiah had been right. Whoever was behind the attempt hadn't been as organized as they were now and had simply taken the opportunity to go after him at the same time they'd targeted the rest of his family.

But dumb luck wouldn't keep him alive for much longer. He just knew it. He could feel it in his bones. Something was coming. Some*one* was coming. And if he didn't figure out how to keep himself safe, it wouldn't matter whether he was worried he'd never be ready to take over the throne or not.

"Talk to me, little princeling," Jeremiah said, settling on his ass and crossing his legs as he rested his arms on his knees.

Remi tried not to look at how his bare torso was glistening under the fluorescent lighting of the gym. He wasn't exactly sure what number it had been when he hit the ground, but it had one hundred percent been Jeremiah's fault because he'd whipped his shirt off and then went right back to sparring like it was no big deal. Remi's hands hadn't been able to keep up, too distracted by the ridiculous amount of muscles on Jeremiah's torso and the way his hair had gotten messed up.

Pulling himself up into a sitting position, Remi cleared his throat. "It's fine. Like you said, I'm just whining. Maybe we should call it a night, though, and continue tomorrow."

As he started to climb to his feet, he was surprised when Jeremiah grabbed his wrist, holding him in place on the mat. "No, you need to tell me what's going on. One minute, you're all gung ho, and now it's like you want to give up. Did you really think it would be easy?"

Remi shrugged. "A little bit. I mean, I know I'm half human, but the other half of me is supposed to have amazing reflexes and superhuman strength. But it's like all of me is human when it comes to stuff like this."

That time, he got the privilege of seeing Jeremiah rolling his eyes at him. "Listen, kid, if all it took was some fancy DNA for people to know how to protect themselves, to fight, how to survive when a threat is looming over them, I'd be out of business. Just having an edge over humans doesn't mean most of us know how to use it. You just need to create the muscle memory. Learn how to break a hold, throw a punch, a kick, whatever is necessary to get you away from whatever the threat is."

Remi nodded along, considering Jeremiah's words. He supposed it made sense. Why else would Jeremiah be able to make a living protecting mostly non-humans otherwise?

"Yeah, okay," Remi said slowly. He looked down at where Jeremiah was still holding on to his wrist, the heat from his fingers seeping into his skin.

It was like Jeremiah didn't realize he'd still been doing it. As soon as Remi drew his attention to it, he jerked his hand back like he'd gotten a jolt of electricity and jumped to his feet.

Remi stood more slowly, keeping an eye on the jumpy Hellhound, but Jeremiah kept his back to him, shoulders hunched forward.

Biting back his sigh of disappointment, Remi rubbed at the dull ache between his pecs at the rude dismissal.

He focused on keeping his breathing even as he padded across the mats toward the exit, keeping his spine ramrod straight.

"Hold up a second."

Remi took a deep breath, steadying himself, and then turned around. He'd nearly made it to the door, so he was forced to watch Jeremiah's brutishly elegant body jog toward him. His bare feet slapped on the mats, ringing out in the giant, empty space. He wasn't sure exactly how everyone knew to stay away while they were working, but he had a feeling it had to do with the man coming toward him.

Whether because he'd told them to steer clear or because they were too scared of Jeremiah to interrupt was hard to say.

Jeremiah slowed as he drew near. "Before you go, I need you to be straight with me. Is all of this—" He gestured at the room around them. "—because you don't feel safe under my protection? Because if that's what's really going on, I can get another one of my guys in here tomorrow."

Remi was shaking his head before Jeremiah even finished his ridiculous question. "No. Gods, no!" He studied Jeremiah's closed-off expression as he took a few steps closer. "It is the opposite of that. No one has ever made me feel as safe as you do. You have saved my life twice." Remi held up two fingers right in front of Jeremiah's face, smiling at the instant scowl that earned him. "You almost died the first time, and you were shot the second time. How could you even think, for half a second, that I would want anyone else? That'd I'd want someone less amazing than a badass superhuman Hellhound who has managed to keep me alive—even when my dumb ass wasn't listening and wasn't taking the threat seriously? I don't understand how you could ever think—"

Remi's tirade was cut short by Jeremiah's lips pressing against his, stealing his words and his breath and his damn *thoughts*.

He stood frozen for a moment, unsure what was happening, his brain needing to reboot to catch up. Just as the pressure started to lessen, like possibly Jeremiah was about to pull away, Remi reached up, clasped both sides of his face, and held on for dear life. He returned the kiss with as much passion and gusto as he could, sighing with relief when Jeremiah wrapped his arms around his waist and held on to him.

He held on like he was worried *Remi* would be the one to run away this time.

Yeah, like that would ever happen.

As the kiss went on and on and on, the only clear thought tumbling through Remi's head was that Jeremiah didn't seem like he was about to flee either.

Thank the gods.

He was overwhelmed with the feeling of Jeremiah's soft lips moving carefully against his own and how hot his hands felt through his shirt when they lightly smoothed up and down his back before settling on his hips.

He had never felt as small and delicate as he did in that moment, pressed up against Jeremiah's bigger and stronger body. Every nerve ending in his body sang with joy that it was finally happening. The tugging sensation in his chest eased, relaxing into a pool of warmth that spread throughout him, filling all the lonely nooks and crannies of his body.

It was magical, and all of those sensations were why it took him so long to notice that Jeremiah was holding back. He was participating in the kiss, sure, but he was letting Remi lead, keeping his touch light and his mouth shut. Frustrated, Remi tried to kiss him harder, tried to provoke a response out of him. He felt Jeremiah's long fingers twitch against his low back, but that was it.

Peeling his mouth away, he panted against the rough scruff of Jeremiah's jaw. "Please," he begged, delving his hands into Jeremiah's hair, grasping at him desperately. "Please, Sunshine."

He wasn't sure if it was the begging or the nickname, but the next thing Remi knew, his back was hitting the wall next to the door, and Jeremiah's warm, sweaty body was pressed tight against his front.

Jeremiah latched onto the sensitive skin on the side of his throat just beneath the corner of his jaw. He used his teeth, biting just hard enough to make Remi moan, before licking over the spot and saying darkly, "I was working so hard to be good, but gods, you are simply too much temptation."

Moving his head to the side to offer up more of his skin for consumption, Remi arched to press his hardening arousal firmly against him and reveled at the thick erection he felt in return. "Does this feel bad to you?"

Jeremiah growled. "You feel like perfection."

"Then stop thinking so godsdamned much and just touch me. Just be here in this moment," Remi pleaded, digging his fingers into the back of Jeremiah's head. "Just be here with me."

Jeremiah didn't verbally respond, but his lips landed on Remi's, tongue swiping until Remi granted him entrance and then dipping into his mouth. Jeremiah was very clearly in control, taking every little piece of Remi and then demanding more.

It was all-consuming. Remi had never been kissed like that before in his life. Oz had always treated him gently, like he was worried Remi would break if he wasn't careful.

Jeremiah slid a hand down his back, following the curve of his ass and gripping him tightly. Right in the middle. The only thing stopping Jeremiah's fingers from pressing against his entrance was Remi's clothes.

He squeezed harder, groaning into Remi's mouth, and Remi shuddered, clutching at Jeremiah as his knees went weak.

This. This was what he'd been missing. The rough and sweet. The desperation that made them both too needy to be careful.

Holding back had become second nature to Remi, even from his ex, who he'd tried to convince himself he could fall in love with. But with Jeremiah?

He couldn't have held back if he wanted to.

His body sank into his scorching heat, and he gladly gave everything he had, knowing without a shadow of a doubt that Jeremiah would give him what he needed.

If the man wanted, he could have him on the floor of the gym in that moment, and all Remi would say was, "Yes, please."

Remi moaned as Jeremiah licked inside his mouth, tasting every inch of him and giving Remi the same. He was a little light-headed at how good Jeremiah felt and how much stronger his alluring scent was this close, how he could relish it on his tongue.

Smoke.

Danger.

Home.

But he needed more.

He peeled his mouth away, but Jeremiah simply dropped his face down, licking and sucking at the thin skin of his throat. His hips jerked forward, and the friction was so good, shooting lightning through him and ratcheting up his desire, he couldn't help but moan, "Please… Touch me, *please.*"

Jeremiah chuckled and nipped at his Adam's apple. "I am touching you, princeling."

He tried to move against Jeremiah's body again, half out of his mind with the need driving him, but strong hands stopped him. Tears sprang up in the corners of his eyes. "No, please, I need… Gods! I need you. Need to come."

A low growl rumbled out of Jeremiah, and he felt it where he was pressed against his chest. "You need me?"

Was he serious? Of course he did.

Remi nodded, digging his fingers into Jeremiah's strong back. "I need you."

"I've got you, little prince."

He gave Remi's ass another squeeze, and then his hand disappeared, causing Remi to whimper. The sound choked off into a groan, though, when that same hand reappeared between them, palming Remi's erection through his pants.

"So perfect," Jeremiah rumbled, tracing the outline of his shaft and making Remi shiver. "Let me see, little princeling."

Panting, Remi peeled his fingers off Jeremiah's rock-hard back and fumbled at the tie on his sweats. Heat was radiating off the Hellhound, warming Remi all over and tempting him to curl up against Jeremiah and take a nap like he would on a sun-warmed beach.

Well, he'd be more tempted if he wasn't so horny at the moment.

Maybe he'd take a nice little snooze on the Hellhound later.

Much, much later.

As soon as his dick was free, Jeremiah's hand was there once more, cupping the underside of his shaft and holding him in place. "A pretty cock for my pretty prince."

Remi's cheeks flushed, and he sank his teeth into his bottom lip, driving his hips forward to move his dick in the light grip.

Jeremiah's other hand landed on the side of his neck, his thumb pressing into his throat. "Hold still, little princeling."

"Oh gods…" His eyes just about rolled into the back of his head, and he let himself collapse back against the wall.

"That's it." Jeremiah tightened his hold on his dick, giving him a rough squeeze that sent fire down his spine. "Good boy."

Remi made an embarrassingly high-pitched, needy noise, and Jeremiah's flaming eyes locked on his, a knowing look on his face. "Jeremiah… please…"

"Shh, let me take care of you," he rumbled, holding Remi's gaze and stroking at a steady, mind-bending pace. Every few tugs, he'd rub his callused thumb across his weeping head, causing Remi to jolt and moan.

Pitifully fast, Remi was on the edge of release, half-formed pleas falling from his lips as he clutched at Jeremiah's massive biceps. Pleasure was clouding his head, and his eyes were squeezed shut as he tried to hold off, tried to make it last. He was terrified this would be his only chance with Jeremiah, and he hadn't even managed to get his hands on anything below his waist. Every time he even loosened his grip on his arms, Jeremiah would rub against that spot just beneath the head of his cock and fry his brain all over again.

Soft lips brushed against his own, and then Jeremiah's voice was in his ear, rougher and deeper than usual, the hand on the side of his neck sliding over to cover his throat. "Be a good little prince and come for me."

Gasping, Remi sank his nails into Jeremiah's burning skin and exploded, every muscle in his body contracting while his ecstasy detonated across his nerve endings. His vision whited out as half-bitten-off sounds fell from his lips, his dick shooting longer and more than he ever had before.

Through it all, Jeremiah kept stroking him, kept telling him how pretty he was and how good he was doing, and kept that firm hold on his neck, his searing palm covering the entire length of his throat.

It was… *everything*.

Little jolts of pleasure kept going off in his body even as his muscles loosened, and he sagged against the cool, unforgiving wall behind him. Jeremiah's overwhelming heat pressed all down his front, his huge size blocking out the gym and keeping him safe and steady as he struggled to catch his breath.

His arms were hanging at his sides, no strength left in him. He sucked in a shaky breath at the firm, possessive fingers tucking him back into his pants and then sliding around to his low back. Jeremiah's chest was moving faster than normal, small tremors cascading down his limbs where they were pressed together.

It took Remi's blissed-out brain an embarrassingly long time to realize why.

He tipped his head back to try and see Jeremiah's face, but he was tucked too close, his stubbly jaw rubbing against Remi's temple with his movements. Slowly, the words taking more focus than usual, he said, "Once I can move my arms again, I'll return the favor."

Jeremiah huffed out a breath, ruffling Remi's hair. "I can wait. Let's get you upstairs before you pass out standing up."

He tried to protest—by the gods, he could and *would* muster the strength to touch Jeremiah's cock!—but his mouth was having problems forming his argument, his eyes sliding shut even as Jeremiah tugged him away from the wall and wrapped an arm around his back, supporting and guiding him.

"'m not even that tired," he slurred, almost falling on the steps leading up to their rooms.

Sighing, Jeremiah didn't bother replying, simply scooping him into his arms and carrying him the rest of the way. Remi thought about fighting it, but his Hellhound was just so warm. He leaned into the heat and moaned, nuzzling into Jeremiah's shoulder.

The last thing he remembered before finally surrendering to the sleep pulling him under was soft, warm lips pressing against his forehead. "What am I going to do with you, little princeling?"

Remi had a few X-rated ideas.

He'd be sure to share them just as soon as he woke up.

12

SUNSHINE

"Jeez, man, what'd you do to that kid last night?"

Jeremiah jerked his head up from the report he'd been reading—and doing his best not to feel Remi's phantom fingers clutching at him or hearing his breathy voice in his head begging for release—his fingers heating in fury before he noticed the friendly smile on the Gargoyle's face. He forced himself to relax and stop acting guilty or weird before someone figured out how his session with Remi had ended.

Besides, the guy asking was a palace guard and one of the few who'd actually treated Jeremiah with respect from day one, and he didn't look suspicious or angry on the royals' behalf. Still, Jeremiah kept his face blank as he responded.

"I don't know what you're talking about."

The man's eyebrows popped up. "During your self-defense lesson last night. My buddy is on morning shift and said the prince is limping pretty bad even after his swim. You remember he's the one we're protecting, right?"

A few of the other palace guards chuckled at the Gargoyle's teasing, but they shut their mouths as soon as Jeremiah sent a glare around the room. They'd been using the space every morning for meetings since he'd arrived, and anyone not on active protection duty was required to be there. He didn't share everything his team was doing or the few small leads they'd found, but he made each of them report anything and everything they discovered.

"He's fine," Jeremiah finally said, flicking a hand toward an open seat. The last thing he wanted to do was talk about Remi and what had happened between them the night before in a room full of people he didn't trust and who were trained to detect deceptions. When the Gargoyle crossed his arms and stubbornly held his ground though, Jeremiah sighed. "I'll check on him after the meeting. I'm sure he's just sore because he's not used to it."

"And from being a weak little halfbreed," someone muttered from the back of the room.

Jeremiah's hackles rose, his temperature spiking. "Stand up. Whoever fucking said that—stand up right now."

There was a long moment of tense silence, and then a big guy with long blond hair braided down his back rose to his feet, sneer curling his lip as he eyed Jeremiah. Werewolf. They always thought they were so much better than him.

Not that he gave two shits about what this guy thought about him in that moment.

He turned to the Gargoyle. "How long has he worked for the palace?"

"Two years, sir." The Gargoyle—he should really start to learn their names—looked equally unimpressed, scowling at the wolf. Jeremiah was sure the honorific was on purpose too, to send a message to the rest of the room.

"Two years and you still think it's okay to disrespect the crown prince of Midlona in a room full of witnesses." Jeremiah kept his voice level, even though his hound was dying to rip this asshole to shreds. He knew being part human was something Remi struggled with accepting about himself, and to hear some dipshit who was responsible for his well-being call him the very slur people had been hurling at both of them their whole lives? Fuck no, he wasn't going to stand for that. He turned to the Gargoyle. "Take this asshole to Thorne's office while I let him know he's being fired."

The wolf howled in outrage, storming forward, but several other guards held him back, telling him to chill out.

"Let him go," Jeremiah growled, letting his Hellhound come forward and simmer just beneath the surface, lighting up his eyes and lengthening his fangs. Hellfire danced between his fingers, and the first row of people scrambled away from him.

Chest heaving, the wolf eyed his hands with obvious fear, then shook his head. "Fuck you and this job."

He turned and stomped out of the room.

Jeremiah took a deep breath, settling his bloodthirsty beast and promising him a fight in the ring later with one of his guys. He stopped the Gargoyle before he could leave too. "What's your name?"

His craggy face looked even more unimpressed somehow, but Jeremiah didn't really care. Shaking his head, he sighed and said, "Evan."

Jeremiah nodded and pulled out his phone, shooting a message to the palace's head of security.

Evan is bringing someone to your office. I just fired him. Make sure you put a tracker on the piece of shit. I want to know exactly what he does, where he goes, and who he talks to.

The Dragon's response came through immediately from somewhere else in the palace where he was on the queen's detail.

Thorne: *Understood. I'll handle it.*

Satisfied, he put the device away and took in the rest of the group. They were silently waiting and more than a smidge wary after his little power display.

Good.

"Anyone else have something they want to say about me,

the royals, or their assignments?" he asked, making sure to meet the eyes of each person in the room and taking note of anyone who looked pissed.

No one spoke up.

"Alright, then, let's get this shit going."

It was a couple of hours before he could track down his little princeling, and he couldn't help but grin as he watched Remi limp out of a room, one of the palace's PR people right behind him and still chattering about some event she wanted him to attend next month.

In Hillsland.

Mood souring, Jeremiah waited down the hall until Remi promised her he'd consider going to the fundraiser, and she hurried away, typing on her phone. Once she was out of sight, he closed the distance between them. Remi jumped when Jeremiah wrapped a hand around his elbow.

"Oh, it's you." Remi slapped a hand to his chest over his racing heart, the sound teasing at Jeremiah's predator instincts. Smiling up at him, Remi bit his lower lip. "Where have you been all morning?"

"I was busy." He tried not to be affected by the flash of hurt on Remi's face at his sharp tone. "Is there something you need to tell me?"

"Something I need to tell you?" Remi frowned, taking a half step back. "What are you talking about?"

The sound of footsteps approaching stopped him from pressing for more information right there. He glanced around and then decided they were close enough to the stairs that led up to their rooms that they should just go there for privacy.

"Come on."

He waited for Remi—who rolled his eyes but followed, his

gait stiff and far less amusing than it had been a few minutes ago—then led the way up to his borrowed bedroom.

As soon as the door was closed behind him, he turned on the prince. "Are you seriously fucking making plans to go back to school?"

Remi's lavender eyes widened in surprise before narrowing. "Excuse me? Do you think I truly have a say in *anything* that happens in my life? Have you not been paying attention?"

Jeremiah jerked back at the raw pain and anger in his prince's voice, the hurt radiating off him and seeping into Jeremiah's nose and heart. "Why was that woman asking you about some fundraiser, then?"

Making an annoyed noise, Remi limped away from him, hands moving in the air as he explained. "Because my mother has decided that if there hasn't been another attack or progress made on finding the culprits by the end of the month, then things can go back to normal basically. She's going to bring the twins home and fly me back to school, but with a larger protection detail to be on the safe side. She said she was going to talk to you about it, but obviously she hasn't if you're this upset about—"

Jeremiah grabbed one of his waving hands as he moved past him, giving it a tug until Remi tumbled against him. His protective instincts finally began to settle once they were pressed against one another. He knew all the way down into his useless, damaged soul that the only place Remi would ever truly be safe was with him.

"She hasn't said anything to me about that, no," he said softly, clasping the back of Remi's neck with his free hand to hold him even more firmly. Heat raced through him at the way Remi shivered and made a tiny sound of pleasure. "I'll let her know I don't think it's a good idea. That only gives us a couple of weeks to—"

"It won't matter," Remi said softly, eyes falling to half-mast. He leaned forward and buried his face against Jeremiah's chest, inhaling deeply. "Once she decides something, you can't change her mind. And…"

"What?"

"She said your contract is up at the end of the month and you'll be leaving anyway."

Jeremiah snarled, shifting his hand up into Remi's hair, gripping firmly, and jerking his head back so he could meet his eyes. "I don't give a fuck about the contract. If she insists on sending you back to Hillsland before we find who's behind this, then I'm coming with you."

Remi's perfect pink lips parted. "You will?"

"Little princeling…" Gods, he wanted to say so much. To tell him he'd never let him go. That his Hellhound had decided for the both of them long before Jeremiah had even admitted to himself that he was attracted to Remi. That he would claim him as his mate in every way imaginable and tie them together for eternity.

But he couldn't say any of that.

Because Remi was a *prince*.

And Jeremiah… he was simply a patchwork monster. A beast created by two things that should never have crossed. He had no family. No title.

Nothing to offer a man like Remi.

"Sunshine?" Remi whispered, his hands slowly creeping up his abs and a tiny, hopeful smile on his lips.

Glancing away, Jeremiah cleared his throat and said gruffly, "I will. It's my job to keep you safe, and I take that seriously."

Remi stiffened against him, then tried to break free, but Jeremiah couldn't convince his hands to release their hold. Putting emotional distance between them was what he'd wanted, but he had no control over his body as his arm wrapped around Remi to hold him more securely.

"Let me go."

"Remi—"

"I mean it!"

He leaned down into Remi's face and growled. "No."

Completely unafraid, Remi lifted his chin. "Yes. You made yourself abundantly clear. You're a professional, and I'm just a job to you. Got it."

"I didn't say that," Jeremiah gritted out, knowing he was a hypocrite even as the words spilled out of him as he refused to let him go. "But what happened last night… it can't happen again. We can't… We just can't, Remington. It was just something that happened, and we should move past it."

Remi sucked in a breath like Jeremiah had slapped him, but then his face turned frigid. "Good to know. I didn't realize hand jobs came with self-defense lessons, or I'd have asked Greg to teach me years ago."

Even knowing Remi was baiting him, Jeremiah couldn't control the jealousy ripping through him. Fire licked at the edges of his control, begging to be released, to destroy anyone who even dared to look at his mate. "If that black-eyed motherfucker even thinks about—"

"Why do you even care?" Remi pushed against his chest, but Jeremiah held firm. "I'm just a job to you, remember? I can suck off my whole protection detail if I want, and you can't say—"

"Stop!"

Remi froze at his shout, but his lavender eyes were still lit up beautifully with his anger.

Sighing, Jeremiah pressed his forehead against his temple and inhaled his sweet, salty scent, letting it calm him. "Just stop," he said softly, nuzzling against the side of Remi's face. Everything inside him felt all twisted and out of sorts, but he still couldn't make himself back off. "Why are you punishing me?"

"Me?" Remi choked out, hands fisting in Jeremiah's shirt. "You're the one who keeps flipping hot and cold—acting like you actually care and then pulling away just as fast. It's giving me fucking whiplash, Jeremiah."

"I know. I just… You're a prince. The next in line to the throne. You can't get caught up in someone like me because I happened to be here when you needed someone to make you feel safe."

One of Remi's slender hands slid up and curled around the side of his neck, his touch gentling him and his fiery beast even more. No one had ever had so much control over him before. He'd never *let* anyone have so much control. It was terrifying.

And thrilling.

"Is that what you think? That I'm attracted to you just because you're here?"

"It happens," Jeremiah tried to explain, to make his case, even as he ran his nose down the side of Remi's face until he could burrow into the crook of his neck. Hunched over the slender prince who held his heart in his delicate hands without even knowing it was the most vulnerable Jeremiah had felt since he was a scared and lonely child. "People fall for their bodyguards all the time, but it's not real. It's just the circumstances and adrenaline."

"That's not what this is," Remi said quietly, holding him so gently Jeremiah's eyes were burning for some fucking reason. "You don't just make me feel safe. I can't… Gods, I can't breathe when you're not near me. My whole body aches for you. The only time I feel whole is when I'm in your arms."

The words reverberated through him, setting off a vibration of awareness. His declaration was an echo of the throbbing need Jeremiah had been doing his best to ignore for weeks.

"It doesn't change who you are—"

"Forget who I am," Remi said fiercely, but his touch stayed soft and soothing. "When I'm with you, I'm not the future king. I'm not too human or not enough Siren. I'm just… me. Remi. Just—"

"Mine."

Remi shuddered in his arms. "Just yours," he exhaled.

The twister of emotions in his chest fell away at his easy agreement. The logical part of Jeremiah's brain knew it didn't fix the reality of their situation. No matter how accepting the king and queen may have seemed, there was no way the people of Midlona would accept a *Hellhound* as their future king's chosen mate.

But in that moment, he didn't care.

He didn't have any fight left in him.

Letting out a long breath, he ran his hands up and down Remi's lithe back a few times before letting them rest at the swell on the top of his ass. "While you're just mine, I should do a better job of taking care of you."

"No one has ever taken care of me as well as you."

While his hound rumbled with pleasure, he hoped that wasn't actually true because until recently, he'd done a piss-poor job. He'd let his assumptions about this boy color his perception for too long, but he promised himself he'd do better.

For as long as he was allowed.

Humming, he smoothed one hand down to fully cup one plump cheek, grinning against Remi's smooth neck when he sucked in a breath. "If I was doing such a good job, then why are you limping, little princeling?"

Remi groaned and sagged against him. So dramatic. "Because I'm so sore. You were abhorrent to me last night."

"I remember being pretty nice to you too," he said with a chuckle as he raised his head, getting lost for a long moment in those pretty eyes.

Remi's lips twisted like he was going to smile, but then he forced them into a pout. "Were you? I don't remember. The pain is fogging my memories."

"We can't have that," Jeremiah murmured, pressing a soft kiss to those plush lips. When he lifted his head, Remi rose onto his toes, chasing his mouth. Fuck, he was perfection. "How about I make things better?"

"How?" Remi's eyes lit up with excitement. "With a kiss where it hurts?"

He snorted. "A massage, you deviant."

There was that pout again. "I think kisses would help more."

Jeremiah shook his head and gave Remi's ass a rough pat. "Such a brat. Get on the bed, princeling."

Bottom lip still sticking out, Remi stomped over to the bed, then hesitated before climbing up. He peeked at Jeremiah over his shoulder. "Should I take my clothes off first?"

Desire punched through him, stealing his breath and thoughts. Clearing his throat, he had to reach down and rearrange himself in his jeans—the little brat watching with a smirk on his face. "Yes, Remington. Take off your clothes for me."

The humor drained from his face, replaced with excitement and pure lust as he tugged his linen shirt over his head and let it fall on the floor. He kicked off his sandals, then tucked his thumbs into the waistband of his shorts and held Jeremiah's eyes as he peeled them down his hips.

Jeremiah couldn't look away from the masterpiece that was Remi's body. Every other time he'd seen him—even the night before—he hadn't had the chance to truly *look*. He had very little hair on his body and only a small patch at the base of his long, slender cock. His legs, arms, and torso weren't bulky but showed the amount of time he spent in the water, the strength in him hidden just out of sight.

"You're so fucking beautiful," he croaked out, nearly overcome by the idea that this gorgeous *prince* would choose him. Even if it was only for now and not forever, the fact humbled him.

Cheeks flushing, Remi smiled and ducked his head. "Thank you."

He got lost, tracing the lines of Remi's body with his eyes and making a plan of where he'd lick first and how many love bites he'd leave hidden under his clothes, but he almost swallowed his damn tongue when Remi turned and clambered onto his unmade bed.

It wasn't like he hadn't seen Remi's ass before. Between stripping at the fountain, changing at the beach, and the tiny bathing suits he liked to swim in, Jeremiah had already been aware of how perfect it was.

And yet… Now that he could take his time to look, his fucking mouth began to water.

Remi had barely laid himself out on his stomach, and Jeremiah was on the bed, kneeling between his parted legs. "Where's it hurt most?"

Groaning, Remi spread his thighs wider, making space for him. "Gods, everywhere, but especially my legs and… glutes."

Jeremiah grinned, setting his palms on the smooth skin on the back of Remi's knees. "Your glutes are sore?"

"So sore. They probably need the most attention," Remi said, sounding haughty as shit, but Jeremiah could see the flush on the back of his neck.

"Yes, my prince."

Pressing firmly with the heel of his hands, he pushed up the back of Remi's legs, not stopping until he met the shelf of Remi's perfect ass. Remi moaned and squirmed against the mattress, so Jeremiah did it again.

"Gods, that feels so good. Your hands are so warm it's melting away the tension in the muscles," Remi muttered.

"Good," he said softly, focusing on first one thigh and then the other, working out as much stiffness as he could.

When he hit a particularly sensitive spot, Remi arched and

swore loudly. "Why are you so good at this? Forget protecting people, this is your true calling."

He hadn't thought to dig up some lotion or anything, but even without visible scales, Remi's skin seemed resistant to friction, allowing him to rub along the muscles over and over without worry he was causing him pain. When he shifted out of the way and told Remi to put his legs together, he complied without hesitation, docile under Jeremiah's caretaking.

Skipping over his glutes for the moment, he dug the heel of his hands into the base of Remi's spine and pressed upward along either side.

"*Fuck*." Remi melted into the bed. "Seriously. This is getting added to your official duties."

"Yes, my prince."

He wasn't surprised to find tension in Remi's shoulders. A few weeks ago, it would have shocked him, but he knew better now. Knew how much strain he was under and the worries he carried with him constantly. With as much care as he was able, Jeremiah did what he could to take some of that away and relieve some of the burden.

As he made his way back down Remi's body, he eyed the side of his peaceful face. "Did you fall asleep?"

The edge of his mouth that Jeremiah could see tilted up. "Not yet, but I am feeling pretty relaxed."

"Relaxed is good," he murmured, shuffling down to straddle Remi's thighs, then leaning forward to plaster himself to his prince's back. "But asleep isn't really my kink."

Remi sucked in a breath, his lips parting as Jeremiah settled his straining erection against his untouched ass and thrust. "Oh no? I suppose that's good to know."

Jeremiah grinned. Remi was going for nonchalant, but he'd fallen short, the husky quality in his tone giving him away. "Definitely not. I prefer my partners to be... active participants."

Remi's fingers clutched at his pillow, jaw tightening.

"Don't… Please don't talk about other people you've fucked while you're in bed with me."

Jeremiah's heart clenched. "Remi—"

His prince buried his face into the pillow, muffling his voice. "I get you have more experience than me, but I *hate* the idea of you being with anyone else."

"Shh." Jeremiah smoothed his hands up Remi's arms to his wrists, then gripped lightly as he nuzzled into the back of his head, doing his best to soothe and scent him. "You're right. I'd hate to hear about other people you've been with too. It makes me… angry just to think about."

Remi huffed and turned his head, and Jeremiah took advantage, rubbing their cheeks together. His instincts were driving him to cover as much of Remi as possible with his scent, to claim him in every way possible. Remi made a soft sound and nuzzled back, thrilling Jeremiah and his beast.

"I haven't…"

When he didn't finish, Jeremiah nipped at his ear. "You haven't what?"

Breathing shakily, Remi whispered, "Been with anyone else. Not… completely."

Jeremiah froze for a second, his brain stuttering to a halt, and then he squeezed Remi's wrists and growled. "What?"

He didn't mean to sound angry—he was just in shock. There was no way he'd just heard what he thought he had. When Remi flinched at his sharp tone, he felt like complete shit.

"I'm sorry if you feel like I misled you," Remi said brokenly, tugging at Jeremiah's hold and grunting in frustration when he didn't let go.

"That's not… I'm not upset." Jeremiah focused on steadying his breathing and relaxing against Remi's back. "I'm just surprised. You're so fucking beautiful. You must be beating them off you with a stick at school."

Remi scoffed, and it wasn't a nice sound. "Hardly. And

my one semi-serious boyfriend… Well, let's just say it was less serious for Ozias than it was for me. When I suggested we, you know, take things to the next level, he dumped me instead."

The pain in Remi's voice was like a knife to the gut. He wasn't sure what was worse: the idea of Remi still hurting over a breakup with another man or the fact that he'd been hurt at all.

"He's an idiot," Jeremiah snarled, meaning it with every fiber of his being.

"He's not." Remi sighed. "He just wasn't interested enough in me. Said we weren't meant for each other and apologized for leading me on."

"I could kill him and make it so no one ever found his body."

He was… half-joking.

Remi laughed and craned his neck around. Jeremiah met him halfway, unable to resist stealing a quick, hard kiss. "That's sweet, I think."

He wasn't sure if he should inform his sweet little prince that he'd do just about anything for him. Take a bullet. Kill a rival. Destroy an empire.

There was no limit to his and his hound's devotion.

Knowing it would be better to keep that to himself since there could be no real future for the two of them, he instead peppered kisses down Remi's neck and across his shoulders, giving them both this moment, at least. One day soon, he'd have to watch Remi walk away from him, but for now, he was Jeremiah's little princeling.

It would have to be enough.

Before long, Remi was squirming beneath him, letting out soft, sexy moans.

"You're still hard," Remi whispered, wiggling his ass and rubbing against Jeremiah's cock.

He huffed a laugh. "I'm pressed against your naked body. Of course I'm hard."

"Are you going to do something about it?" His husky voice, combined with the way he peered over his shoulder and bit his lip, had precome leaking from Jeremiah's aching cock.

Humming, he gently bit right where Remi's neck met his shoulder, being careful not to break the skin. But fuck did he want to. To sink his teeth and dick inside Remi at the same time and make it crystal fucking clear to everyone in a mile-wide radius that the crown prince of Midlona was *his*.

Remi whimpering and canting his head to the side didn't make pulling away from that deliciously tempting spot of skin any easier.

He gave Remi's delicate wrists one more squeeze, then shifted Remi's arms so he could clasp his hands together. "Keep your hands right here."

Remi's back shuddered as he inhaled deeply and nodded.

"Good boy."

Gods, the way his prince moaned at those two words.

Sitting up, he gave himself a second to just take in the golden perfection before him. Remi was so perfectly put together, lean but strong. He followed the dip of his spine all the way down his back and smiled at the two small dimples just above the swell of his ass. He was smooth everywhere, made for cutting through the water.

His perfect Siren prince.

In the quiet of his borrowed bedroom, he lowered the zipper on his jeans, grinning at the goose bumps that appeared on the back of Remi's thighs at the sound. He grabbed the back of his shirt and jerked it over his head, tossing it aside, and then shoved his jeans and boxers down to mid-thigh.

His ruddy, plum-shaped head pointed right at his target as soon as his cock was free.

When his hands landed just beneath Remi's cheeks, his prince jolted and then slid his legs farther apart. Making room for him. Inviting him in.

Jeremiah grinned and slid his hands upward, digging the heels into the sore muscles he'd neglected before.

"Oh gods," Remi moaned, arching his back.

"Good?"

"So good."

His beast rumbled with pleasure at the low, dirty sounds he coaxed out of Remi as he worked him over thighs to low back. Once Remi was rocking gently against the mattress with each rub of his hands, Jeremiah gripped both of his cheeks and spread them, exposing his tightly furled hole. Remi sucked in a sharp breath, peeking over his shoulder.

Grinning and holding his eyes, Jeremiah leaned down and ran his tongue from the back of his nuts all the way up to those two little dimples, pressing a kiss to each one.

Remi shuddered. "Oh *gods*."

Jeremiah did it again.

And again.

After the third swipe, Remi arched up against his face, silently demanding more, and he decided to stop teasing him. He shuffled forward and eased himself down, laying his bigger body over Remi's once more, covering him completely and wedging his cock between his cheeks.

And then he thrust.

His saliva, combined with the natural silkiness of Remi's skin, was just enough to smooth away any friction, creating the perfect warm tunnel for him to drive his cock through. Remi moaned beneath him and moved against the bed, scrambling to grab onto the sheets as Jeremiah's strong thrusts slid him forward.

"You feel so good, little princeling," he groaned, threading his fingers through Remi's and holding tight.

"You're not going to—oh shit, more, please." Remi pushed

up against him, whimpering when the head of Jeremiah's cock caught on his hole before slipping past once more.

"Not going to what?" Jeremiah licked up the back of Remi's neck, his fangs itching to break his prince's perfectly unblemished skin. "Fuck you?"

"You—I need—fuck, please!" Remi twisted beneath him, but he held on, holding him in place.

"Not today, not when I need you this badly," he groaned, shuttling his hips faster and chasing the pleasure that was building beneath his skin. "I can't be careful with you right now, and that's what you need for your first time. It's what you deserve."

"I don't need anything but you," Remi whispered and then groaned, his eyes squeezing shut and body going tense beneath him.

The scent of his come hit Jeremiah's nose, and he couldn't hold back any longer. He rutted against Remi's ass like a possessed animal and pressed his open, panting mouth to the side of his neck. The sound that left him as his release crested was barely human, but he couldn't stop, couldn't pull away.

His hips stuttered forward a few more times, Remi's soft skin milking every last drop from him. His body was soft and relaxed beneath him, but Jeremiah's instincts weren't done. Shuffling back, he stared for a long moment at the gut-wrenchingly sexy sight of his come splattered on Remi's low back and smeared between his plump cheeks.

Gods above…

Before he could stop himself, he laid a hand over the largest pool and dragged his seed up Remi's spine, coating him in his essence as much as possible.

Remi huffed a tired chuckle. "What are you doing?"

He gritted his teeth, unable to explain the instinct but knowing he had to do it. He needed everyone to know who Remi belonged to. He needed to mark him.

When he didn't answer, Remi raised his head and looked

back at him, eyes half-lidded. He watched as Jeremiah covered one of his fingers and then separated Remi's cheeks and pressed at his hole.

Remi moaned but relaxed back down onto the bed, spreading his thighs farther and arching his back.

"Sorry," Jeremiah murmured even as he pushed harder, forcing himself inside Remi's body so he could leave a piece of him behind.

"Don't be," Remi said, then moaned and pushed back, driving him deeper. "Whatever you need to do, you can. I don't… I don't think there's a single thing I wouldn't let you do."

Jeremiah growled, pumping his finger in and out a few times and then slowly pulling free. He crawled up Remi's body and plastered himself to his back again and nipped at his earlobe. "You shouldn't say that to me. The things I want to do to you, little princeling…"

"Do your worst, Sunshine."

13

REMI

The sun was a balm against his skin, the early afternoon softness of the season soothing to Remi in ways he knew humans couldn't feel. It was easy to forget some days that he wasn't fully human, but moments where he was shifted, his tail stretched along the sun bench in the pool and his Song bubbling against the back of his throat, he felt like…

Himself.

Or as close to himself as he'd ever been.

Escaping to the pool had been necessary that morning since gossip was spreading like wildfire through the servants and guards. Remi had spent his entire life pretending like he couldn't hear them whispering about him—pretending like he wasn't tucking all their words behind his heart, letting their judgment and prejudices shape him into who he was.

But now, the talk had morphed. No one had any idea what he and Jeremiah had actually done together, but they all knew his Hellhound's focus had grown even more intense over the last few days. He'd heard the word "thrall" on the lips of so many people that morning he wanted to pull his own face off.

"—he might be a Hellhound, but stooping to pant after the

halfbreed prince? It has to be the Siren thrall. I bet he's using his Voice on him."

Remi had almost thrown up his breakfast into a potted plant decorating the long hallway that led to the throne room. That was the moment he'd snapped. The moment he'd lost his ability to pretend like he didn't care what everyone was saying about him.

He was wild about Jeremiah in ways he couldn't explain. Every time Jeremiah touched him, Remi felt the connection grow stronger, and he couldn't explain it. He wasn't foolish enough to believe that there was anything fated about the two of them. That wasn't possible. Remi's human half was far too strong, and Jeremiah wasn't even the same species as him.

But he couldn't deny that every waking moment he wasn't thinking of the twins and the dangers they were all in, he was thinking of his gorgeous guard and his rough mouth and strong hands and the way he made Remi feel like there was no one else in the world. It was addictive and terrifying, and he never wanted it to stop.

But listening to the whispers about them did nothing more than remind him it was just one more thing that made him a freak.

For the moment, no one knew the truth, but if they did, all hell would break loose.

There would be a coup, no doubt. They'd force Remi to abdicate. They barely tolerated him as it was, but with a Hell-hound at his side? No one would follow a king like that.

"Not that I fucking want the damn throne," Remi muttered to himself as he lay back and covered his face with his tablet.

His escape to the pool had been under the guise of trying to get some actual work done so he didn't go back to campus weeks behind everyone else, but every time he attempted to do his reading, he'd start... remembering. He'd remember Jeremiah's hellfire-hot fingers tracing lines over his body. And the way he felt with Jeremiah's weight pressing him into the mattress as he rubbed off between his cheeks.

He flushed bright and hot as he remembered just how badly he'd wanted Jeremiah inside of him. His tail twitched, splashing a little bit of water onto the concrete deck.

Gods, he was screwed.

Bzzt, bzzt, bzzt.

Remi sat up with a short gasp before realizing the odd noise was his phone. He pawed around for it, then stared at the screen and fought back a sigh before answering. "Now's not a good time."

"Aww, bro. It's never a good time for me anymore," Thad whined.

Remi had almost forgotten what his best friend sounded like, and strangely, he'd almost forgotten why he was even friends with the guy. "Sorry. It's been a total shit-show here."

Thad snorted. "Yeah? Getting that royal dick all wet while you're on vacation? God, I wish I was royal. I'd be drowning in so much servant pussy I couldn't see straight. How many guards did you blow this week?"

Nothing about Thad's question was a surprise. In fact, it was a lot tamer than the shit he usually said, but something about it pissed him off. He felt suddenly possessive and angry, and he had to swallow it all back before he said something he regretted. He couldn't just blow up his life because things were weird right now.

"Yeah, this is definitely not a vacation, man. I'm not even allowed to leave the grounds."

"Eh. You'll get over it. When are they letting you come back?"

Remi sighed. "I don't know. Soon, probably. I mean, nothing's happened since that last attack, and I think my parents are starting to calm down. Jer—uh—my guard is on edge, but that's his job, so I don't know."

"Boring," Thad drawled. "You need to come back. There's

been a frat-house party war going on all week, and you are missing some prime opportunities to get dicked the fuck down."

Remi said nothing to that. He never said anything to that. He knew he didn't fit in with the rest of his fraternity brothers, and it felt even harder to pretend now that he knew what Jeremiah's lips tasted like. "I'll let you know if they start to give in."

"Sweet. Oh, by the way, you'll never guess who we ran into last night."

"Who?" Remi asked, closing his eyes and turning his face up toward the sun. He watched his veins in the orange glow. "And am I going to actually care?"

"You fucking better. It was Ozias."

Remi waited for his heart to do that painful, aching thud-thud against his chest, but it didn't come. There was just a sort of echo of old pain leftover from Oz's rejection. "Tell me you didn't harass him."

"Dude, not to his face," Thad said. "The fuck do you take us for? Nah, we were a lot more clever than that."

Remi swallowed down bitter bile that had risen against the back of his throat. "What did you do?"

"Dave may or may not have made an anonymous phone call that some Supe freak was soliciting underage human girls at the bar."

"What the fuck?" Remi demanded.

"Don't get your panties in a twist. This is revenge for what he did to you," Thad defended.

It would have been awful either way, but something about Thad's glee didn't sit right. And if he was being honest with himself, it never had. Not really. Thad's prejudices ran deep, thanks to his father, but Remi had convinced himself that being friends with him was changing that.

"Just leave him alone. I'm over him," Remi said, lying

back down. He put his hand over his eyes and squeezed them tight enough he saw sparks.

"Whatever you say," Thad said, sounding bored and distracted. "See you when you get back?"

The call ended before Remi could respond, so he let his phone fall to the grass, and he shifted lower into the water, swishing his tail back and forth. Opening his eyes a little, he watched the sun play off his scales. His arm stretched forward, his fingers elongated, his skin iridescent.

This was maybe the longest he'd been able to hold his shift in… hell. Ever? The only time it had ever felt this easy was when his mother was with him. He took a breath, then glanced around him and couldn't see a single creature lurking.

He wasn't sure that was entirely true, but he felt safe enough to open his mouth and let a few notes escape. This was the only place he was allowed to sing. The only place the guards were ordered to keep away so they could have the freedom to be themselves.

Though this had never been Remi's self before.

But something had shifted. His power felt strong—like a ball of Jeremiah's hellfire sitting in his chest. His Song felt like it was going to burst free from his chest if he didn't let it out. He slipped all the way into the water, diving under before pulling oxygen through his gills, parting his lips, and letting it out.

A single note trilled through the salty currents, bouncing off the concrete walls all wrong because his Song belonged in the ocean waves. But the relief was almost palpable, and the urge calmed to a low simmer just under his skin.

He gave a push with his tail, shooting to the other side of the pool and back, twisting and turning to the rhythm of the notes spilling from his throat. The words were in their ancient language—one he understood on instinct alone. They were reminiscent of the Song his mother used to put him to sleep with, only… it wasn't exactly the same.

He felt love, but there was something else behind it. Something big, and powerful, and all-consuming.

He wanted to stop, but he didn't know if he could.

Curling his tail, he shot up to the surface, the Song dancing through the air, and for a moment, he thought he'd never be able to stop.

And then he saw him.

Jeremiah was less than twenty feet from the edge of the pool, his eyes almost glowing as he watched Remi. His hands were in fists at his sides, and he was taking steps toward the water like he had no choice. Like he was under Remi's spell.

The Song died in his throat, and panic took its place as Remi raced to the edge of the water, prepared to stop Jeremiah before he dove in. He pushed his tail against the bottom of the pool and rose as Jeremiah fell to his knees, impossibly warm hands cradling his face.

"You…" Jeremiah whispered.

Remi's heart began to beat faster. He knew he should stop this. He couldn't let Jeremiah touch him while he was under a thrall. He would have no ability to consent. No ability to decide for himself if this was what he wanted.

But by the gods, his touch sent sparks through Remi's entire body.

"So beautiful," Jeremiah murmured. His fingers traced a touch over the faint outline of Remi's scales that decorated his torso. He pressed a flat palm to his sternum, then dragged it down until it reached the place where his skin became tail. It was sensitive, and he couldn't help a heavy groan as Jeremiah pulled him closer.

The hand still touching his face pressed harder, his thumb grazing a line over Remi's jaw.

"Kiss me," Remi whispered.

Jeremiah's eyes went even more dazed as he nodded and leaned in.

Seconds before their lips brushed, Remi snapped back to reality. With a strength he hadn't even realized he possessed, he sent Jeremiah flying backward with a single shove, and he dove under the water. He took huge gulps of it through his gills, the chill calming the heat racing through his veins, and he looked up to see that his Hellhound was back, peering over the edge.

"I can't," he murmured to himself, no sound coming from his throat. "I'm sorry. I can't."

He was too human, except for all the moments he wasn't, and his Siren side was dangerous. It had stripped Jeremiah of reason and will, and Remi would rather die than ever, ever put him at risk again.

He looked through the rippling surface and saw Jeremiah was no longer wearing his shirt and was removing his pants. Panic gripped him, and Remi shot to the surface, holding up his hand.

"Don't!"

Jeremiah looked at him with a familiar expression of fond annoyance, and he dropped down to his ass, putting both feet in the water. "I know how to swim, princeling."

"You're under my thrall," Remi said. Fuck, even under a spell, and the man was still so goddamn stubborn. "*Stop*," Remi ordered, calling on his Voice.

Jeremiah pushed through the order, and seconds later, he was in the water. It was too deep for him to stand, so he swam forward with powerful strokes, and Remi backed up until he hit the edge of the sun bench. Jeremiah was on him in seconds, using his grip on Remi's waist to keep his head above the water.

"Breathe," Jeremiah ordered.

Remi realized he'd been holding his breath, and he let one out through his lungs. "You have to get away from me."

Jeremiah just raised a brow. "Why's that?"

"My Song. I… it's…" He licked his lips and fought the urge to put his arms around Jeremiah and wrap him close. "I didn't mean to."

Jeremiah closed his eyes, then suddenly, he laughed. "You didn't do anything."

"I saw your face."

His expression going soft, Jeremiah tipped his head lower to meet Remi's gaze. "Your Song is beautiful, Remi. And so are you. I didn't know if I'd get the chance to see you shifted."

Remi's breath trembled in his chest. "I know how the Song works, Jer—"

"So do I," Jeremiah said. "But it doesn't work on me, apparently. I'm… a freak of nature. I'm a hellbeast," he said like it was a curse, and Remi wanted to claw the face off anyone who had ever made Jeremiah feel like that was a bad thing. Jeremiah tipped Remi's chin up with a finger. "Look at me. I'm in this water because I want you—but it's not because of your Song. The other night wasn't because of your Song."

Remi flushed a deep, rippling indigo, and Jeremiah groaned, leaning in and dragging a rough tongue over his collarbone. "Please," Remi whispered.

Jeremiah chuckled hotly and pulled Remi so their bodies were flush. "Whatever you want, my prince."

Remi shuddered, then wrapped his tail around Jeremiah's legs, supporting him so he didn't have to hold on so tightly. "Touch me."

"Where?"

Remi's fingers shook as he reached for Jeremiah's wrist. He'd never been able to shift long enough for this, but he knew what he wanted. This wasn't the first time he'd felt a need when he was in the water. Gripping his Hellhound's wrist, he dragged his hand low—lower—until two fingers pressed against a barely there slit.

Jeremiah's eyes widened, and his breath stuttered. "Is this—"

"Yes," Remi said, closing his eyes on the edge of a groan as Jeremiah traced the opening. Jeremiah's nails carefully moved over Remi's scales, and Remi felt himself thicken—felt his cock trying to extrude. "Inside. Put… put them inside me."

Jeremiah sucked in air, and he turned his hips so Remi could feel him, searing hot and throbbing against his hip. There was a moment when Remi thought maybe it was too much—maybe Jeremiah was wrong and the thrall was just wearing off… and then suddenly, two fingers pushed inside him.

Remi gasped, his hips thrusting forward, his cock heavy and so fucking wet as Jeremiah's fingers made a wide V around it and began to stroke in and out. He'd never felt like this before. Never. Nothing had ever been this good.

"I—fuck. Unf," he gasped, writhing under Jeremiah's weight as the Hellhound pressed him back against the sun bench. Remi slid over it, taking Jeremiah with him, and he groaned when two powerful thighs straddled his tail. "In me. P-please," he stuttered, begging. "I need it. I need you."

Jeremiah stared down at him with glowing eyes that held a hint of fire in the irises—the glowing blue flames that only Hellhounds could produce. Fuck, he was so beautiful.

"Are you sure you want this?" *Are you sure you want me,* Remi heard—words the Hellhound wasn't actually saying.

He grabbed Jeremiah's hips. "Please don't make me beg."

Jeremiah's eyes darkened, and he traced around Remi's lips. "What if I like how you sound when you beg?"

Remi's eyes slammed shut, and his cock thrust forward just enough to push the tip out. Jeremiah groaned, and when Remi peeked, he saw he was staring down at him. "It's…"

"Gorgeous," Jeremiah said before Remi could say anything self-deprecating. "You're so fucking beautiful I can't control myself. Let me fuck you, princeling. Let me give you what you want."

There was a growl behind his words that made him sound almost feral, and Remi's entire body was singing with every sweep of Jeremiah's hands.

"Please," he gasped again. "I need it. I need to feel you. Last time, I wanted—but you didn't," he babbled.

Jeremiah touched the side of his cheek, thumb pressed to his chin, and Remi slowly opened his eyes. "I wanted it to be perfect."

"It is," Remi told him. "I don't know what this feeling is, but I know I need you. Please, please."

Without any more warning, Jeremiah shifted his angle, and a second later, he was inside. His thick cock filled Remi's slit, sliding alongside Remi's aching, soaking-wet cock. The water around them seemed to pulse in time with Jeremiah's thrusts as he got both hands around the backside of Remi's tail and held him, hips pumping with a rhythm Remi had no hope of keeping up with.

His eyes rolled back in his head as pleasure erupted under his skin in ways he'd never, ever known. He felt like he was flying and falling all at the same time, and he clung to his Hellhound like he might disappear if he let go.

"You like that?" Jeremiah grunted.

Remi opened his eyes, his lip between his teeth to keep from screaming as Jeremiah adjusted his angle and hit something inside him that sent him wild with lust.

"Oh, you do, don't you, little princeling? You fucking love it. You fucking love the way I fill you."

"Yeah, yes, fuck," Remi gasped, unable to form a coherent sentence. It felt like his soul was trying to escape his body and burrow into Jeremiah, and he wanted to let it. He had no idea what it meant, but he found himself tilting his head, bearing his neck like he wanted to be bitten.

Jeremiah growled louder, the sound rumbling from his

chest and racing over the top of Remi's skin. The water around them felt wild, like their lust was in command of it, and he lifted his tail, wrapping it around Jeremiah as best he could as he thrust mindlessly and helplessly. He was so fucking full, his cock throbbing in his slit, Jeremiah's cock sliding against it goddamn maddening.

It was too much and not enough, and he needed… something.

"Gods," Jeremiah whispered. He lowered his head into the crook of Remi's neck, and then he felt it. Fangs. Sharp and dangerous, grazing his tendons.

"Yes. Do it," he begged. He didn't know what he was asking for; he just knew that it had to happen.

Between one breath and the next, Jeremiah's hips stuttered forward, and then he sank his fangs into Remi's neck. The pain was exquisite, blinding as his vision whited out, and the feeling of pleasure was so overwhelming he wasn't sure he'd ever come down. A rough tongue started licking over the mark, and then Jeremiah let out a furious groan, and Remi felt something inside him expanding. More and more, he was opened on it, and he was so clouded with ecstasy it took him far too long to realize it was a knot.

It was Jeremiah's knot.

"Did you—?"

Jeremiah let out a long moan against Remi's shoulder, and when Remi tried to move, Jeremiah bit him again, keeping him still. "Just," he said, his voice muffled against Remi's warm skin, "just wait."

Remi stilled, though tendrils of pleasure were still fizzing through his limbs. His cock was pulsing with the aftershocks of release, and every time Jeremiah's knot throbbed and spilled inside him, he felt like he was coming all over again.

"It's so much," he gasped.

"I don't… fuck," Jeremiah said, and he buried his face in

Remi's neck, rubbing his stubbled jaw back and forth. "This has never happened to me before."

"It's a knot," Remi said, "right? Or is it… I'm sorry. I don't want to say the wrong thing."

Jeremiah pulled back, his eyes a blazing hellfire blue. He cradled Remi's face with one hand, using the other to keep himself half propped up. "You couldn't say the wrong thing."

Remi laughed and rolled his eyes. "Trust me, if anyone could, it would be me. That seems to be my unofficial motto in life. The one who always fucks it up."

He hated this compulsion to be so fucking honest with Jeremiah. He wanted to be suave and cool and sexy. Instead, he was just some mostly virginal nerd who was losing it over a knot.

Jeremiah leaned in and kissed him. It was a soft, slow press of hot lips and demanding tongue, and Remi groaned, shifting his tail again. Jeremiah grunted and thrust forward, making Remi gasp into his mouth.

"If you don't stop, it's never going to go down," Jeremiah growled.

Remi nodded, then suddenly burst into laughter, clinging hard to Jeremiah, who tried to pull back in offense. "I'm sorry. Gods, baby, I'm so sorry. I'm just… I've never been able to shift for more than a minute or two, and the one time I managed it, you knot me."

Jeremiah stilled and looked down at him. His face was mostly unreadable, but Remi got an odd pulse of emotion that didn't feel like his own. Something like worry and confusion and… hope? "You never shift?"

Remi shrugged and tried not to gasp as his tail moved again. "Not really, no. Usually I can manage it for a really short time in the water, but you must have noticed by now I'm mostly human."

"You're not mostly human," Jeremiah said, then let out a

hissing breath when his knot started to reduce. Not enough to pull out, but enough that Remi didn't feel like he was being tormented anymore. "That's not a thing, you know?"

Remi shrugged, and as Jeremiah finally began to slip out, he felt the familiar spark along his spine that came with the shift. His tail spasmed and flapped, then began to shrink before it split into two, and his legs formed. He glanced down at his cock, which was floating in the water, and it was human again—tucked inside foreskin and definitely still a little slick.

Jeremiah was watching him when Remi lifted his gaze, and his lips softened into something not quite like a smile but close. "We should get cleaned up. I didn't come down here for that reason."

Remi pushed himself to sit and wiggled his hips from side to side as he reacclimated to having legs again. "Did you need me for something?"

"No, I just… I hadn't seen you in hours and needed to put eyes on you."

Remi chuckled and pushed himself up on the ledge, standing when he no longer felt his knees wobble. "You know I'm safe here, right? If nowhere else, I am here."

He started toward his clothes but paused when he heard a splash, and then a warm hand caught his wrist and pulled him against a taut, hairy chest that burned like fire. "I know. I just… I needed to see you."

Remi breathed out, shaky and needy all over again, and he lifted his fingers to the spot where Jeremiah had bitten him. His skin was tender but smooth, and he knew that somehow, it was significant; he just didn't know how exactly. "I needed to see you too."

Jeremiah laid a kiss to that sensitive spot, then backed away. "I've got to get back, but I'll see you later, yeah?"

Remi nodded and watched Jeremiah walk away without another word and without bothering to stop to grab his clothes, leaving Remi wondering if he was going to wake soon to find out it was all a dream.

Gods, he hoped not.

14

JEREMIAH

Jeremiah wanted to pretend like he was surprised when he came down to dinner a week later to find his team sitting at the table next to the queen and king, mostly because he wanted to believe that whatever was happening between him and Remi was going to last longer.

But he wasn't.

He held back a resigned sigh and took a seat to Remi's left, smiling his best at the royal couple.

"So. Obviously, you have news," Remi said, his tone sour.

Jeremiah would have chalked it up to him being a brat—which he was—but he knew that wasn't it. What happened in the pool a week ago had changed something between them, and he knew they both were feeling on edge, wanting the threat to be found but not wanting their time together to end. It was why he'd been finding the urge all week to whisk Remi off to some private island where no one could bother them.

He wanted to fuck Remi again—in every form the prince had. He wanted to dip his tongue into his slit and draw his cock out, sucking it until he couldn't see straight. He wanted to spread his cheeks and lick his hole until Remi was crying and begging to come. He wanted to stare into his eyes as he drove into his body, not stopping until Remi passed out from exhaustion.

He wanted to worship him in every single way possible and then hold him as they slept so Remi would never feel unsafe, unloved, or unwanted ever again.

And that terrified him beyond all reason. He hadn't signed up for that. He'd agreed to a well-paying job with people he wouldn't mind owing his team.

Danger and even death came with the territory, but falling for a crown prince?

Jeremiah glanced over at his team and wished they'd actually want to do something practical—like eviscerate him for being so fucking foolish. But they all seemed to be enjoying this, and that made him want to throw himself into the sun.

Gods, maybe he was a little dramatic?

"—time to move on," the queen said, and Jeremiah's attention snapped back to her. By the gods, he could not afford this distraction.

"Are you saying you don't want us to continue working this case?" Knight asked, darting a glance at Jeremiah. "The initial contract expires in a few days, but we're willing to renew it and stay on this until we figure out who's behind it."

King James gave Jeremiah a knowing look that made his cheeks burn like he was a damn pup and then shook his head. "Not at all. We were hoping Jeremiah would be willing to accompany Remi to campus. We don't trust that whoever's trying to harm our family is gone, but they're not going to make a move until they feel like he's vulnerable. As much as we'd love to keep him safe and protected here forever, we know that just isn't feasible. But putting a nearly indestructible Hellhound right next to him…"

Knight chuckled under his breath. "If you ever get tired of being king, we could use more strategic minds on our team."

James laughed. "I think my wife might kill me if I took a job like that, but I appreciate it."

Grace leaned forward and winked. "Ask me again next time he keeps me up all night with his snoring."

Priest burst into laughter. "Amazing. I think I love you both. Can I pledge myself to your country?"

"If it were only up to me," Grace said, eyes sliding to Remi and Jeremiah and smile turning sad, "my answer would be yes."

But public perception and their fickle support could be a bitch. Jeremiah was far too aware of the way the world and its politics worked, thanks to his job, and it left a heavy stone sitting in his gut. He was falling in love—he could admit that to himself, at the very least. But there was no hope for him. For them.

Not with the crown standing in the way.

He swallowed heavily and said, "I want at least one of you here with the children when I leave."

Priest's hand shot in the air, a sly grin on his face. "I'd be happy to. So long as you don't mind a Demon in the house."

Grace smiled at him. "We'd be glad to have you. I hope you like cocoa. We've already forced it on Jeremiah."

Priest lit up like a torch. "I love cocoa. Even more than his grumpy ass."

"Then consider it your official invite," she said. "Now, I'll have one of our guards bringing back the twins, and—"

"I want to get them," Remi cut in, speaking up for the first time. The room fell silent, and he crossed his arms, giving everyone a defiant stare. "I want to see them before I go. I… Anything could happen. And I trust this team, but I want to do this. Jeremiah can come with me."

"They will be safe with us," Jeremiah said, and Remi shot him a grateful look before turning his attention back to his parents.

"Please?" He straightened his shoulders. "But I'm not really asking."

Grace sighed. "I don't like the idea of all my children in one place with the threat against you. And if the press catches wind of anything..."

Jeremiah swallowed roughly at her implication, but Remi just bristled next to him.

"Fuck the press. All they do is attempt to make everyone in this family miserable, and they never waste an opportunity to remind me I have no business taking the throne," Remi spat.

His mother gave him an unimpressed look, but when James opened his mouth, she held up her hand. "There might be consequences, but at worst, there will be some unflattering op-ed pieces."

Jeremiah shifted uncomfortably, dropping his eyes to the table. He knew she wasn't talking about pieces being written about Remi going to get the twins himself. She was warning the two of them of what could happen if they weren't discreet.

And he knew op-ed pieces wouldn't be the worst of it.

If word that the man next in line to the throne was sleeping with a Hellhound got out?

Things could get way worse for Remi than a few cruelly worded news stories.

Remi seemed unconcerned though, snorting and rolling his eyes. "They did that when someone got some creepy pap shot of me dancing on a bar last year."

"You were in your underwear," James said flatly.

"At an invite-only, private party," Remi said. "They acted like I destroyed the reputations of all Sirens, like they don't get fucking dirty when—"

"Enough," Grace said firmly, though she was obviously trying to hide a smile. "It doesn't matter. You understand the risk, and I'm giving you permission."

I'm giving you permission.

To… be together? No, she couldn't have meant that.

Remi shot Jeremiah a satisfied smile. "When do we leave?"

Clearing his throat, he refocused on the immediate concerns facing them. "Tomorrow. We'll have some of the palace guards and Storm accompany us as well."

"There's a private room on the jet," Remi said quietly, slipping a hand onto Jeremiah's forearm, and his face flushed all over again. If he'd wanted to confirm to everyone within hearing distance that they were fucking, that was the way to do it.

Luckily, because Knight covered Priest's mouth with one of his hands and everyone else in the room had manners, no one called them out on it.

"You are a brat," Jeremiah hissed, pressing Remi against the wall. He licked over the spot he'd bitten days ago, confused why the impulse had been so godsdamn overwhelming and why he wanted to do it again. Thankfully, Remi had healed almost immediately after he'd laved his tongue over the bite, the wound disappearing.

He'd wanted to ask about it since Remi was always so quick to call himself mostly human, but he'd still been reeling from how it felt to fuck Remi. Though it hadn't felt like fucking. He wouldn't be so saccharine as to call it making love, but there had been a moment he swore he could feel his soul reach out and touch Remi's.

Even now, he was getting hard just thinking about it, and having Remi looking at him with a small smirk on his lush lips was pushing him near the edge. They hadn't had much time alone together since the pool, barely more than a few stolen kisses, and Jeremiah couldn't help but look forward to being in Hillsland with only a small detail with them instead of an entire palace.

"You like me that way," Remi said.

Jeremiah leaned in and laid a biting kiss to his lips. "Yes. Gods give me strength, but I do."

Remi smiled against his mouth, and Jeremiah felt dangerously happy in spite of knowing they had no real hope for a future. Whatever the feeling was in his chest, he prayed it would fade when he and Remi were forced to separate. But he'd been denied so much his entire life, godsdamn him to the pits of hell, but he wanted to be selfish for this little bit.

"What's wrong?" Remi asked.

Jeremiah shook his head. "What makes you think there's something wrong?"

"I don't know," Remi said, then lifted his hand between them and pressed his palm to Jeremiah's racing heart. "Just a feeling."

He sighed, then knocked their foreheads together. "I need to do rounds and speak to my team. Then I want to check in with your parents about Priest staying here."

Remi pulled back. "Is his name seriously Priest? A Demon?"

Jeremiah laughed softly and shrugged. "No. That's not his actual name. But he never uses it, and neither do the others. They've all pretty much adopted their code names."

"But you protest going by Sunshine?" Remi asked with a laugh.

Jeremiah nipped his jaw. "That's different. That was a joke that stuck and became my code name."

"I think it's cute," Remi argued, and he dragged his hands down Jeremiah's back, cupping his ass. "You light up like the sun when I do this."

Jeremiah let out a deep growl from the pit of his stomach, watching as it made Remi erupt into a blush. He fought the urge to give in to his hound and lick the heat from his cheeks.

Gods, Remi made him feel so connected to his animal side. It had taken a lot of his control not to shift when he saw Remi's tail. And when he slipped inside him…

Remi moaned and thrust his hard cock against Jeremiah's hip. He was so turned on, but some of the feeling in his chest didn't seem to be his own, and he had no idea what to make of that.

"Behave, brat," he ordered.

Remi grinned, clearly trying to look innocent. "Make me."

Jeremiah gripped him by the jaw and met his gaze, his eyes burning. "Don't think I won't, little prince. I'll be back soon."

"You're going out with that?" Remi asked, brushing his hand over the front of Jeremiah's pants.

Jeremiah bared his teeth. "And I'll make you sorry for that when I get back too."

It took all of his control to let go and walk away, and he kept to a dark corner of the corridor until he willed his erection to go down enough to casually and carefully tuck it away.

He was wound up and still hot when he rounded a corner and found Knight waiting for him, and he wanted to knock the shit-eating grin off his face.

"Happiness looks good on you, Sunshine."

"If you like the way your fangs look in your mouth, you'll drop it," Jeremiah warned.

"I don't know why you're all tied up in knots," Knight told him, elbowing him gently. The touch was fleeting but still more than he did to anyone outside the Alpha Team. "He likes you just as much."

Jeremiah hated how that made him feel all warm in the chest. "It's impossible. You realize that, right?"

"The king and queen support—"

"I know," Jeremiah interrupted. The ache of knowing he'd need to let go of something that everyone who *should* matter supported was far too real. "But that doesn't change anything. Remi is already fighting for his position because of his human half. Imagine what his people—not to mention those assholes in the press—will do if he announced he wanted to bond with a damn Hellhound."

Knight bowed his head and said nothing because there was nothing to say. As a Vampire, he understood. He wasn't as universally hated the same way Hellhounds were, but his species was a close second. Of course, Knight had never shown interest in anyone, and Jeremiah couldn't imagine him falling for someone like Remi, but he knew if it happened, Knight would probably walk away, thanks to all the shit in his head from his past.

And Jeremiah should do that too.

And he would. After the job was done and Remi could go back to his normal life. Until he was sure he was safe, he wasn't letting Remi out of his sight.

"I don't want to see you lose hope," Knight said as they approached the royals' receiving room, and he stopped Jeremiah with a firm hand on his elbow. "We've suffered enough, haven't we? If we have the chance to finally be happy…"

"Not at his expense. Not with everything it'll cost him," Jeremiah said, a small growl coming from his chest. His hound was fighting tooth and nail against it, but he wouldn't let it win. He couldn't. He took a breath, then stepped forward and knocked, waiting to be let in.

Jeremiah woke to an alien sensation—warmth against his back and something tight around his waist. He felt a single moment of panic, ripped back to his past as a vulnerable child afraid of what might happen to him when he slept. Then he remembered.

He felt something in his chest, almost like the beat of a

second heart, and warm breath ghosting along the side of his neck. He stretched out his arm, extending his claws for a second before pulling his beast back and laying his palm over Remi's. The Siren was clinging to him like he was afraid to let go, and Jeremiah had no words to describe how that made him feel.

He saved people for a living, yes, but people rarely considered him safe. He was a Hellhound—a pariah. He was the scourge of the earth in the eyes of most beings, but Remi looked at him like he was worth something.

Shifting onto his side, Remi groaned and loosened his grip a little before blinking his eyes open. They were a little foggy and red from sleep, but as their focus sharpened, his lips curled into a smile.

Jeremiah was unused to anyone looking at him like that either.

"Morning," Remi said, his voice rough and thick with sleep. As worried as Jeremiah had been about him staying the night in his room, he was grateful beyond words to have any extra time together he could get.

Jeremiah leaned forward, helpless to do anything except kiss him. His mind wandered back to the night before—to when he finally made it back to the room after confirming with the royals that they were comfortable with Priest and with him accompanying Remi to pick up the twins before heading to Hillsland. Remi had been waiting for him, flat on his back in Jeremiah's bed, completely naked, his hand around his cock.

It had taken all of Jeremiah's control not to half shift, pin him with teeth, and fuck him until neither of them could speak. Instead, he'd slowly undressed, enjoying the tortured way Remi had moaned, the way he squirmed at being forced into patience.

He was a prince used to getting his way, a brat used to instant gratification, and Jeremiah could only dream of having years of tormenting him. There was nothing better than begging words falling from Remi's lips like an unrestrained waterfall.

The sex hadn't been as intense as it had been in the water, but Jeremiah had lost himself at the end, and he'd bitten Remi again. He hadn't popped a knot—he had no idea what that even meant, and it wasn't something he could think about just yet—but his tongue lapped up the sweet Siren blood until nothing but fresh, pink skin remained.

He'd fallen asleep curled up behind Remi with his limp cock between his lover's thighs, feeling sated in ways he hadn't thought possible.

"Please tell me we have a little time," Remi said.

Jeremiah was willing to say yes to anything, even if it was a lie, but he rolled over to check his phone before sighing. "Ten minutes at the most. Do you want to—"

He didn't get the rest of the words out. Remi pinned him by the shoulders, kissing the rest of the sentence off his tongue before sliding down, dragging blunt teeth and warm lips over his torso, his belly, and eventually breathing hotly over his dick.

With a heavy groan, Jeremiah thrust upward, feeling almost overwhelmed with the way Remi laughed, then parted his lips and took him down in a single swallow. Remi had been a little shy at first, mostly driven by instinct, but he'd quickly gotten over that and now took Jeremiah's cock like he was starving for it.

He pushed fingers into Remi's hair, his claws coming out to drag over his scalp, and Remi moaned loudly, the vibrations shooting right to Jeremiah's balls. He relaxed his jaw as Jeremiah gripped him under the chin to guide him, and when their gazes met, Remi's eyes were glassy.

Fuck, he was completely gone.

"Good boy," Jeremiah rumbled.

Remi moaned again and let Jeremiah hold him tight to

fuck his face. He wasn't going to take long. Not with the way Remi was looking at him. Not with the way he was drooling and humping the bed between Jeremiah's spread legs.

He felt the familiar tingle at the base of his cock, and he gripped it, willing to keep his knot down as his orgasm crept up on him. He had only enough time to grunt out a warning before he shot his load, and Remi took it all down in heavy swallows.

He felt that same feral part of his animal clawing to the surface, and he couldn't stop himself from pulling out and smearing what was left over Remi's lips before flipping him over and kissing the taste out of his mouth. He only just managed to pull his claws back before gripping Remi's dick, and he stroked him hard and fast, watching color rise along his neck, outlining scales that were rising to the surface.

Remi bucked his hips, his mouth open, making needy, desperate sounds, and Jeremiah leaned in, laying a wet, hot kiss over the spot he couldn't stop biting. His fangs ached to sink in again, almost like they were trying to close the gap of something invisible and intangible, but he stopped himself this time.

He didn't want Remi to show up to a Dragon Hoard with fresh bite marks, looking like he'd been defiled by some hellbeast.

Though it might have been too late for that as his back arched and he came hard with a silent cry, spilling all over Jeremiah's knuckles.

He stroked Remi through it, until he was twitching and pulling away, and then he kissed him softly as he let go, licking his hand clean. He felt Remi's eyes on him and looked over with a small smirk as he pulled his middle finger out of his mouth with a loud pop.

"That's one way to wake up," Remi said, his voice still hoarse.

Jeremiah snorted. "You started it, little princeling."

"And you sure as fuck finished it," Remi shot back. He darted forward for another kiss, then jumped out of bed with an energy only someone in their early twenties could have. Jeremiah watched him stretch, his gorgeous, lean body twisting and turning, and then he stopped and winked. "Shower?"

Jeremiah swung his legs over the bed and stalked forward, taking Remi by the throat. He had no idea what the fuck was coming over him, but he suddenly couldn't bring himself to care. He was bringing Remi into a Dragon Hoard full of horny, polyamorous, gorgeous men.

Like fuck he was washing off his scent.

"Don't you dare."

"Shit," Remi whispered, eyes fluttering shut as he leaned into Jeremiah's possessive hold.

"You're mine. And they're going to know it."

Remi licked his lips, then nodded, and only then did Jeremiah let go, entirely satisfied.

15

REMI

Being allowed to have Jeremiah the way he wanted him felt a little like he'd been standing in front of opaque glass with only his silhouette, then having that wall shattered. Not only was he allowed to reach out and touch Jeremiah in any way he wanted, but Jeremiah was acting like a possessive beast.

Not in a terrifying way though. Remi had never in his life felt safer. No, Jeremiah refusing to let him shower so he smelled owned in front of all the Dragons made him feel wanted. Needed. It filled in all the empty gaps in his life he'd spent wondering if anyone would want a halfbreed freak like him.

Jeremiah was also the picture of professionalism too, which was driving Remi wild. He refused to rise to Remi's provocations when they were in the car. Remi had crept his hand toward his Hellhound's crotch, and Jeremiah hadn't done more than offer him a warning growl before threading their fingers together and gripping him just shy of painful.

Remi was half-hard all the way to the airport, and the Dragon member of the Alpha Team could definitely tell if the smirk on his face was anything to go by. Remi knew he should probably mind, but Jeremiah didn't shy away from touching him in small, subtle ways, and Remi didn't feel like anyone's dirty secret.

On the plane, the three of them sat in seats facing each other with the palace guards huddled together on the other end, Jeremiah's hand on his thigh while the Dragon—Storm—sat across from them, and he and Jeremiah went over the information they had. Nothing had changed, and no new information had come to light, and Remi could tell both Alpha Team members were frustrated.

"Maybe they just wanted to freak us out," Remi offered into the tense silence that had fallen over the jet.

Jeremiah gave him a pinched look. "No one uses that kind of power or force if they just want to scare you. I should have died at the beach."

Remi shuddered, remembering how horrible it had been to see him so hurt. The idea of losing him… He took a breath. "So why do you think they've gone quiet?"

"I want to say it's because they're trying to lull us into a false sense of security, but I don't think that's it," Jeremiah said.

Storm rumbled his assent. "Anyone with the knowledge and power they possess knows us better than that. We don't drop our guard."

Remi sighed and looked out the window at the mountaintops. They were passing over the border into Averna—the Kingdom of the Gargoyles. The Dragons lived in mated groups called Hoards, in the forests, ocean, and mountains there, trusting almost no one but the alliance they had with the Gargoyles.

All of that had been drilled into Remi's head from his childhood—necessary education if he was going to sit on the throne and be an effective ruler. The thought of that was like another weight pressing on his chest, and he looked at Jeremiah, who was staring at him with a concerned frown.

"What's wrong?"

Remi rubbed his sternum, feeling a spark of… not quite fear but something like it. Jeremiah seemed to sense his emotions, and it was happening to him too. He desperately wanted to speak to someone about it, but he was too afraid.

He wanted to hope that it meant something—that fate would give him someone like Jeremiah—but he would be laughed out of the conversation if he asked. Humans *rarely* found mates, and only with a particularly strong Supe, like his dad did with his mom. Remi might have been shifting easier now, but he was still so damn human.

"We're landing in fifteen," Storm said, startling Remi out of his thoughts. There was a frown on his face, and Remi recognized it a little too well. It was the look of a man who didn't want to be noticed by the people he was about to see.

"Are you okay?"

Storm looked at him, surprised. "Why do you ask?"

"Because you're making the same face I make whenever I have to give an interview."

Snorting, Storm rolled his eyes. "The Hoard that took in your brother and sister belong to one of my brothers. They're very powerful and very kind, but…"

Remi waited, but Storm just swallowed thickly and shot Jeremiah a pleading glance.

Jeremiah sighed and lifted Remi's hand, kissing his knuckles. "Storm was politely asked to leave their Thunder."

A Thunder was like a clan, Remi knew, made up of Hoards of bonded Dragons, who always had three or more mates. He also knew it was rare for a Dragon of Storm's age to not have a single mate yet or not have found another Thunder to join. Even the palace guards who were Dragons belonged to a Thunder and had long stretches of time off to spend with their mates and families.

"Is it rude for me to ask why?"

Storm shook his head. "No. It's just... difficult for me to speak about."

Jeremiah drew Remi's attention back to him. "He's... different. He has no desire to be with a Hoard. Wanting only one mate isn't something tolerated by most Thunders. He came out to them when he was a teenager, and he was disowned by his parents. But then he found us and our merry little band of outcasts."

"You're not—" Remi started, but Jeremiah touched his cheek gently, stopping him.

"We are, and we're not ashamed of it. Storm's made peace with some of his brothers—this one and Thorne in particular. But it's not easy for him to go home."

"You could have stayed," Remi said.

Storm smiled politely. "No. I'm acting as an envoy. Dragons are fiercely secretive—to the point of xenophobia sometimes. My brother's not as much as some of the others, but it's safer this way."

With that, Storm rose and walked to the back of the plane to give instructions to the palace guards, and Remi turned in his seat to better face his Hellhound.

"He's still hurt."

"Something I think you understand a bit too well," Jeremiah said.

Remi swallowed heavily, and Jeremiah tugged him over for a quick kiss. "I wish none of you had to feel that way."

"I wish the same for you," Jeremiah said. "But I meant it when I said we're not ashamed. We've created our own family."

Remi desperately wanted to ask to be part of it, but he couldn't call forth the words. So instead, he clung to Jeremiah's hand until they landed and were forced to walk apart.

"Remi!"

He hadn't realized just how badly he needed to see the twins until he was on his knees, his arms around them tightly. They seemed not only fine but thriving and happy, and something settled in his chest as he stood back up and let them each take a hand, their mouths running a mile a minute.

"And we got to fly!"

"And there was this deer, and he just... boom! Took it."

"We ate it! We ate it for dinner!"

"And we... we gots to go in the hot springs, which wasn't too hot!"

"And we shifted, Remi! We shifted in the hot springs even though it wasn't Siren water!"

Remi smiled down at them. "That's amazing. I'm so happy you had a good time."

Percy nodded, then wrinkled his nose. "You smell weird."

Remi shot a withering look over his shoulder at Jeremiah, whose cheeks were pink, but he was pretending he hadn't heard Percy. "Uh. It's just from the long plane ride and being around the palace guards and Jeremiah..."

"No. The others don't smell like that," Sadie told him pointedly.

A tall Dragon wearing thick-rimmed glasses and an honest-to-gods sweater vest appeared and held his arms out as Percy and Sadie leapt into him. "Sometimes they do." He winked at Remi, then managed to stick out his hand from under Sadie. "I'm Caspian. It's really nice to meet you. Thanks for letting the kids hang out. We haven't had hatchlings in a long while. And it's been hard since..." He cleared his throat. "We sort of lost someone."

Remi's chest burned with sympathy. "I'm so sorry."

Caspian shook his head, then let the twins down so they could run over to Jeremiah and talk his ear off for a bit.

"Humans," Caspian said once they were out of earshot.

"But we didn't say anything in front of the twins about him or what happened. We didn't want them to think that there was anything wrong with who they were."

Remi swallowed past a lump in his chest. His kingdom was one of the most tolerant on the continent—except when it came to him and his family. No one had ever been so kind as to think of his or his siblings' feelings when it came to their heritage. "Well, they seem like they've really enjoyed being here."

Caspian nodded, then glanced around at his Hoard milling about. They all looked so different from each other—one was covered in tattoos, another had grease all over his hands like he was a mechanic, and still another was shrugging off a chef's jacket. But obviously, they fit. Remi could actually feel the connection between them all.

"Are you sure you want to take them back?" Caspian asked, grinning.

Remi sighed. "It's not really in my hands. I'm heading back to campus."

Caspian's eyes narrowed. "Alone?"

Remi laughed. "Jeremiah's coming with me. I don't think he's overly thrilled with the idea, but I can't put my entire life on hold indefinitely, and I trust him."

"That much is obvious," Caspian said with a tiny smirk, then leaned his head in close. He reminded Remi of Oz a little bit, putting Remi at ease so quickly and teasing him mercilessly. "It must be something—being mated to a Hellhound."

"Oh. W-We're not mates," Remi said quickly.

Caspian snorted. "You might want to come up with a different cover story, then. Not only is his scent all over you, but he's bitten you."

Remi's hand flew to his neck, shock rushing through him. He felt a strange, echoing sensation, and he looked at Jeremiah, finding him staring at them from across the room. "That was just… you know. Fun."

"I certainly know how much fun a mating bite is," Caspian said with a laugh. "But he's a Hellhound, and you're a Siren."

"I… but I'm mostly human."

Caspian stared at him. "Darling, I'm afraid that's not how genetics work. You can't be mostly one thing or another. You're your own thing. And I say this as a geneticist. Literally. You can have dominant genetic markers, but those have no bearing on who and what you are."

Remi didn't know what to say. He didn't know how to feel. His entire life, he'd been ridiculed and mocked for what he would never have, thanks to him not being Siren enough, but this Dragon seemed so… so *certain*.

"Can we staaaaay?" Percy cried out.

Remi blinked out of his thoughts and shook his head. "No, but I bet Mom and Dad will let you come back for visits."

"We would love that," said one of the larger Dragons with a massive tattoo on his neck. He picked them both up like they weighed little more than river pebbles. "We can go hunt deer again."

"I'm gonna catch one with my fangs!" Percy said, baring his teeth.

Remi didn't have it in him to tell his brother he didn't have fangs. Instead, he smiled at the Hoard and stepped a bit closer to his siblings. "I bet you'll be really good at it."

"The best hunter ever," Percy said.

Jeremiah came close and wrapped his arm around Remi's waist as the Dragon let the twins down to gather their things, and he tipped his head close to Remi's ear. "You're not okay."

"Nope. But we can talk about it later," Remi said. He fought the urge to touch his neck again, but he was shit-scared if he said anything now, Jeremiah would reject him, and he wasn't sure he'd survive that.

No, all of it could wait until the threat was neutralized and they could all think straight. His gaze searched the crowd, and he found Storm in the corner of the room talking quietly with a Dragon several inches taller but with almost the same face and umber skin tone. Storm seemed tense, but the other Dragon was squeezing the back of his neck, and he looked surprisingly kind.

"Is he going to be okay?" Remi asked. "They all seem really great."

"This Hoard is," Jeremiah said, then smudged a kiss against Remi's jaw. "I wouldn't have suggested them for the twins otherwise, but he's not ready to completely forgive his family just yet."

Remi could understand that. Luckily, he'd never been through it, but he didn't think he'd be so eager to forgive anyone who had said horrible things to him over the years, even if they tried to be better. "We should probably get going, yeah?"

Jeremiah frowned at him, but after a beat, he nodded. "We have a long journey home and then a long journey back to Hillsland. Are you feeling ready?"

Remi had no idea what to say to that. He was already a freak on the human campus, being who he was, and he'd spent his entire time there trying to fit in and be more like them. But now he was going back with a Hellhound bodyguard that might be something more than just a lover to him, and he wasn't sure he was ready to burn everything he'd worked for to the ground.

But at the same time, when he looked at Jeremiah, he knew he wouldn't give him up for the world. It would be like asking him to cut off a limb. He rubbed his neck, and when he saw Jeremiah's eyes go hot, he leaned in and stole a kiss.

"I'm ready as long as you're with me." And as terrified as he was, he meant those words.

Jeremiah cupped his cheek. "I'm not going anywhere. Ever."

Remi believed the truth in those words. He was falling—maybe they both were—and try as they might, there was no way to stop the crash.

16

REMI

Saying goodbye to the twins right after they returned to the palace was excruciating.

They'd both started to cry, clutching at his hands and pantlegs, begging him to stay and telling him how much they didn't want him to go.

It had taken everything inside him to put on a smile and gently peel them off, handing their squirming bodies over to Priest. He'd promised to call as soon as he was back at his apartment and to come home for a visit as soon as he could.

Tears were burning his eyes as Jeremiah led him out to the waiting SUV, their things already loaded in the back. The ride to the airport was silent, the guards in the front keeping their eyes forward and Jeremiah giving him space.

It wasn't until they were back on the plane and in the air that Remi finally cracked. A tear slipped down his cheek, and he swiped at it angrily, pushing to his feet and storming back to the private bedroom. The bed was freshly made despite the fact the flight to Hillsland was only a couple of hours. He appreciated it, though, when he flung himself onto it face-first.

He never heard the door open, but when a familiar heat

settled next to him, causing the mattress to dip, he turned and curled around Jeremiah, craving his touch and comfort.

"They'll be okay," Jeremiah said, raking his fingers through Remi's hair and down his neck. "Unlike some people, they won't mind being confined to the palace grounds since that's where they spend most of their time anyway."

"It's not that—well, it's not *just* that," he corrected, then sniffled and wiped his face dry. "I miss them so much. It's just... really difficult being so far away from my family."

Jeremiah kept stroking his head for a minute, not saying anything, and then asked softly, "Why did you choose to go to Hillsland University? There are several schools a lot closer..."

He let out a shaky breath. "It seemed important."

"What did?"

"Getting away," he whispered. "Standing on my own two feet, away from the shadow of the throne and my birthright. Proving I could be independent. I could just be... me."

"I see."

Remi hoped he did, even though most of him didn't feel that way anymore. Especially after everything that had happened in the last few weeks. Sure, the idea of being king one day was still terrifying as *fuck*, but it was getting harder and harder to justify—even to himself—why separating himself from his family was so important. The complications of royal life aside... sometimes he just really wanted a hug from his mom, and that was pretty difficult when he was hundreds of miles away.

Jeremiah ran his hand over his back slowly, staying quiet, and Remi let his heat and scent soothe him. He had less than a year left before he graduated, and then he'd... Well, he'd have to figure out the rest of his life. Maybe without Jeremiah.

His fingers clasped harder on his soft T-shirt reflexively, and Jeremiah tightened his arm around him, humming in question. Remi shook his head and pushed his face into Jeremiah's neck, clutching at him. He knew he was being needy and annoying but couldn't bring himself to care. If he'd only have Jeremiah's strength and steadiness for a little while longer—he'd soak up every ounce he could get.

"I'm trying to remember," Jeremiah said slowly, voice quiet in the peaceful room, "but I'm not sure your major was included in the information we put together on you. What are you studying?"

Remi bit his lip. "Promise not to laugh?"

Jeremiah threaded his fingers through Remi's hair and gave him a tug backward so they were face-to-face. His beautiful eyes were serious and captivating. "Never."

Heart flipping in his chest, he admitted softly, "Well, since I'll learn everything I need to about… being king from my mom, I chose something that interested me, not something I needed to know."

"Okay…"

"Literature."

"Oh. That's not what—"

"With a concentration in folklore and mythology."

Jeremiah's eyebrows climbed up his forehead. "That's… specific. And not at all what I was expecting."

Remi waited for Jeremiah to make a joke or tease him, but he just stared back at him expectantly. "What?"

"Tell me a folklore or myth," Jeremiah urged, tucking his free hand behind his head. "Your favorite story. Or one you've read that was surprising."

"Oh, um." He glanced away, thinking. No one had ever asked him something like that before. He and his dad talked about books quite often, but his dad preferred biographies or historicals. He'd told stories to the twins before, but he usually had to change things to make them less scary.

Resting his chin on his hand, he thought about what he could share. He considered a Siren folktale but decided against it quickly, not wanting to focus on his history or people.

He could tell Jeremiah about the myth of a Hellhound's fated mate being immune to their hellfire, but that seemed cruel to them both.

"I didn't think it would be this hard," Jeremiah rumbled at him, amusement clear in his tone.

"Hush, you." He poked at Jeremiah's bristly cheek, laughing when he pretended to bite his finger. "Oh, I know. Have you heard the story of how the first Hellhound came to be?"

Jeremiah stiffened beneath him. "Everyone knows Demons kidnapped and impregnated female werewolves against their will to create an army of—"

"Okay, yeah, no." Remi pushed up to see Jeremiah's face better. "That's propaganda bullshit."

"Remi—"

"For real, the first records of that story are only like a hundred years old."

"Really?"

"Yup. But there are other stories—thousands of years old —that don't mention anything like that. Now, do you want to hear this or not?"

The corner of Jeremiah's mouth tipped up. "Alright, little princeling. Educate me on my people's folklore."

"Well, smart-ass, according to legend, the first Hellhound was a product of *love*, not violence."

"Love?" Jeremiah looked skeptical, but there was a lightness in his eyes. A hope.

"Yes, love. A Demon of great power and stature rose from the Underworld with the intent of conquering all the kingdoms of the land."

"Not sounding super promising…"

"Just listen, Sunshine," he murmured, settling back onto

Jeremiah's chest and tracing patterns on his pecs as he told the story of how a Demon fell in love with a beautiful Werewolf, defeated any who challenged their mating, and then used magic to create an entirely new species to please his new mate. Something wonderful and unique that was a mix of them both.

And he held Jeremiah tighter when his sweet hellbeast's breaths turned shaky.

"Oh fuck, that's so good, little princeling," Jeremiah groaned above him, one of his big hands on the back of Remi's head guiding him up and down. "Gods, you were made for sucking my cock, weren't you?"

Remi whimpered and squirmed where he knelt between Jeremiah's splayed legs, his satisfied dick trying to come back to life at those words despite Jeremiah having edged him for over half an hour before letting him finish.

The veins on Jeremiah's cock were pulsing against his tongue, and he squeezed the base, heat pooling in his belly at the fact that Jeremiah's knot was starting to grow just from Remi's mouth. Nothing made him feel sexier or more wanted than the visceral evidence of Jeremiah's desire for him.

He hummed as he pulled up to the tip and lapped at the smoky and salty precome streaming from his slit, not wanting to waste a drop.

Jeremiah grunted, and his fingers tightened in Remi's hair. "*Fuck*. I'm so close. Wraps your lips around me."

Remi complied, sucking hard and using his hand to stroke the rest of Jeremiah's shaft. He was rewarded with a mouthful of slick come a minute later, and he moaned at the thick, smoky taste.

Gentle fingers stroked his face and neck as he caught his breath, leaning against one of Jeremiah's strong thighs. When he raised his head and caught the happy, sated look on Jeremiah's face, warmth bloomed in his chest. Gods, sometimes he was sure he got more pleasure from pleasing his Hellhound than from his own orgasms.

"Come here," Jeremiah said, tugging at Remi until he was on the couch with him, sprawled across his bigger body.

Two weeks of sex and cuddling and classes. Of making meals together and watching crappy TV shows. Of just being… them. Remi hadn't known he could be so content.

It was a glimpse of a future that felt just out of reach, but Remi refused to give up. Jeremiah had offered to sleep in the second bedroom of his apartment to keep up appearances or some such nonsense, but Remi had put his foot down.

If these weeks were all he'd get… he was going to wring out every last drop of happiness.

Instead, Jeremiah had turned Greg's old room into an office and used it as a command center of sorts, touching base with the rest of Alpha Team and the investigation but also staying on top of the other teams who worked for him. Bravo Team had just wrapped up after spending the last month tracking a group of cybercriminals, and Charlie Team was starting a new assignment, protecting a famous Dragon actress and her Hoard from a crazed stalker sending her threatening texts. Remi was more than a little excited that he was tangentially connected to that one—he loved her movies.

Jeremiah had laughed at him when he told him but then said he'd introduce Remi to her if he could, so he'd forgiven him. And given him a preemptive thank-you blowjob.

"How was your meeting earlier?" Remi asked as he played with Jeremiah's chest hair. He'd had to go to one of his classes with extra protection because Jeremiah had needed to stay at the apartment to talk to the entire Alpha Team. He hadn't minded too much—Jeremiah tended to garner a bit more attention than Remi was used to. Most of the humans on campus didn't even know what he was, but they could tell he was *something*.

"Had to postpone," Jeremiah grunted, sounding less relaxed than he had a minute ago. "Priest had a jam emergency, apparently."

"A what?" Remi laughed.

"I don't even fucking know. I should have known leaving him in charge of the twins would be chaos. He came on the call for three seconds, covered in some red substance, and yelled, 'They jammed me! I have to retaliate.' Then he hung up and ignored my texts and phone calls."

Remi *cackled*. "They jammed him? As in, the twins—who are *four*—covered a *Demon* in strawberry preserves?"

"Maybe raspberry. Definitely something red."

That just made Remi laugh harder.

It took him a while to get himself under control, having to wipe tears from the corners of his eyes, but he finally managed to compose himself. "Should I be worried about his ability to actually keep the twins safe?"

He was mostly joking, but a small part of him was a smidge worried the Incubus was a little too immature to be effective protection.

"Oh, no. He'll keep them safe," Jeremiah assured him, rubbing down Remi's back and then cupping his ass. "The thing about Priest is he's got very little impulse control, but he's the most loyal asshole ever, so he makes up for it. He would die for those kids, don't worry."

"Has he ever… you know."

Jeremiah raised a brow. "What?"

"You know… fed on you?" Remi's stomach cramped uncomfortably just at the idea, so he wasn't sure why he'd asked except that once the thought popped into his head, he had to know.

"No." Jeremiah shook his head and kneaded Remi's cheeks, though he wasn't even sure the Hellhound was aware of it. "When we first started the Trident Agency—me, him, and Knight—I offered once, but he and Knight already had an arrangement to feed on each other. As far as I know, that ended a while ago. Knight… He has a hard time being touched, even by us, and that's Priest's preferred method, not dreams."

"Not liking to be touched must make it hard for him to get enough blood," he mused, too afraid to ask what had happened to make the Vampire so averse to it. He knew from Jeremiah that he and Priest had grown up in foster care and ended up on the streets together when things got too bad for them. They'd found Knight a few years later, not long after he'd been turned against his will.

"He uses Vamp banks." Jeremiah shrugged, his whole body moving Remi with the motion. "Luckily, he can afford the insane prices they charge."

Remi considered that, stacking his hands on Jeremiah's chest and resting his chin on them. Like Hellhounds, Vampires didn't have their own kingdom. They were considered inferior Supes because they were made from humans, infected with a virus from another Vamp, and then were forced to feed on others to survive. But unlike Demons like Priest who did the same, Vamps were looked down on for not being born as Supes.

It was all pretty ridiculous, in Remi's opinion.

"Who does Priest feed on now?" he asked absently, still preoccupied with the idea that Knight had to pay an exorbitant fee to get bags of blood because of his past traumas. It just didn't seem right.

"Mostly dancers at the Pearly Gates. He pays them well and always does it in a private room so Azriel doesn't get in trouble and other customers don't see."

Remi gaped at him. "The strip club in Midlona?"

"You've been to the Pearly Gates?" Jeremiah's eyes glowed, his fingers tightening where he still held Remi's ass.

He snorted. "Yeah, the crown prince could totally just waltz in without being noticed. I've heard about it though.

It's right near the border by Averna—oh, and my favorite bookstore is, like, next door. The owner, Oliver, can get his hands on anything. First editions. Out of print. Doesn't matter."

"Oh, I'm familiar with Oliver," Jeremiah said, rolling his eyes.

Jealousy ripped through Remi. The human was incredibly pretty and sweet—much nicer than Remi. Before his mind could run away with the idea, Jeremiah cupped his face and smiled gently at him.

"Gods, I can feel how upset you're getting. I've never even been to the bookstore, but Priest… Let's just say it's a good thing Oliver isn't a Supe, or he definitely would have noticed the light stalking."

Remi's eyes popped open. "Seriously? He's got a thing for a human? Can he even, like, feed on humans?"

"Sure, but he doesn't get as much strength and would need to feed more often."

"*More* often? Aren't Incubi already pretty insatiable?"

"Yes and no. If they bond—" He stopped and cocked his head. "Is that my phone or yours?"

Remi leaned over and found their pants on the floor, digging out their cells, and made a face when he saw Thad was calling him. "Ugh. I should take this. I haven't really talked to him since I got back, and there's some party coming up that he wants me to go to."

Jeremiah's face pinched in dislike, but he nodded and pressed a kiss to Remi's temple as they sat up. "Okay, I'll be in the office. Our postponed meeting starts shortly."

Pushing to his feet, Remi stole one more kiss to try and erase some of the tension Thad's name had caused. "Alright, Sunshine. Come find me in bed afterward."

Jeremiah's heated, glowing eyes followed him as he walked naked from the room, answering just before the call dumped into voicemail. "Hey."

"Fucking finally!" Thad exclaimed, sounding pissed.

Remi frowned and softly shut the bedroom door behind him, ignoring Jeremiah's low growl. "Excuse me?"

"I've been trying to get ahold of you for a week, asshole. You can't ignore calls from brothers like that." Thad's scolding was like nails down a chalkboard and made him feel about three inches tall. "Unless you're *trying* to get expelled from the fraternity…"

"No, of course not," Remi said quickly, then grimaced. He'd joined Kappa Alpha Chi for the same reasons he'd decided to attend Hillsland: to forge his own identity.

But things had changed, and he was more and more sure the fraternity—and the friends he'd made there—weren't the right fit for him anymore.

"I've just been super busy getting caught up on my classes." Which was partially true. He'd been able to keep up with a lot of things remotely, but there had been a couple of projects he'd fallen behind on.

Mostly, he'd just been prioritizing getting off as much as he could with the sexy Hellhound sharing his apartment instead of Kappa stuff.

"Whatever," Thad said, sounding unconvinced. "You're coming to the meeting tomorrow, right? The party is this weekend, and we need to make sure everything's in place."

"I'm not sure…" Remi said, chewing on his lip and sinking onto the edge of his bed. "My, uh, head of security—"

"Oh god, that's right. You brought that *thing* back to campus with you."

"Don't call him that," Remi hissed, eyes on the closed bedroom door. He prayed Jeremiah was already in his meeting and hadn't heard that.

"Oh, come on! Hellhounds are barely more than animals—"

"We're together." He wasn't sure how he got the words out through his gritted teeth, but they shut Thad up.

At least for a second.

"Man, he's smarter than I thought they could be," Thad said, laughing.

"What's *that* supposed to mean?"

Thad sighed, and his voice softened. "Look, Rem, I know you aren't real experienced, but even you have to see what he's doing, right?"

A knot of bad feelings began to grow in the pit of his stomach. "I don't... What..."

"Alright, bro, so it's like this: you're a prince. He's scum of the Supe world. Hooking up with you only benefits him. I mean, come on." When Remi just sputtered, indignant at the *scum* comment on top of the implication that Remi was somehow better than Jeremiah in any way, Thad said, "Plus, didn't you say he was, like, really good-looking?"

Remi made a noise that was barely more than a squeak.

"So... why else would he be fucking someone like you? No offense," Thad added as an obvious afterthought.

But offense was very much taken.

The words were creeping in on him though, burying in his brain and planting seeds of doubt. He didn't think Jeremiah was using him for status necessarily, but maybe... maybe something else? Maybe Remi was just conveniently there and inexperienced enough to think great sex meant more than it really did. Maybe he was just imagining the feelings growing between them.

There was some laughing in the background, and Remi's face flushed. Was he on speakerphone?

Before he could ask, Thad continued decimating all the good feelings Remi had managed to gather inside himself in the last few weeks. "I wonder if your parents told him to use whatever means necessary to keep you in line." The laughter grew louder. "I have to admit it's fucking effective—we haven't seen you at all in the two weeks you've been back. Must be a nice dick."

Humiliated and confused, Remi wrapped his arm around his middle and squeezed. "It's not like that."

"So you are coming tomorrow, then? The beast isn't the one calling the shots?"

Feeling like he might vomit, Remi forced the words out in a steady voice. "I'll be there."

17

JEREMIAH

"I don't like this."

Remi rolled his eyes at him, and Jeremiah resisted the urge to drive them back to the apartment and lock him in the bedroom. Permanently.

His instincts were on edge, his beast barely staying tucked under his skin, even with his scent fresh on Remi's skin. It felt like the answer to the question of who the fuck was after the royals was right in front of him, but he couldn't see it. He was too close.

He glanced at Remi, his eyes lingering on the patch of skin on his neck where he kept biting.

Way too close.

But he wasn't backing away anytime soon.

"Yes, you've made that *abundantly* clear," Remi sassed him, reaching for the door handle of the SUV. "But it'll be fine. I'll be just inside, and as soon as the meeting is over, you can escort me to class."

There was an edge to his prince's voice he didn't like. It had shown up after his phone call with the rude frat brother last night, but when he'd pressed, Remi had just clammed up, refusing to tell him about what was said. Jeremiah really didn't get the whole fraternity thing. Remi was a brat at times, sure, but he was mostly just a scared and kindhearted young man. Afraid of his future but loyal to his family.

What could he *possibly* have in common with the douchebag humans in Kappa Alpha Chi? As far as Jeremiah could tell, they were all entitled assholes.

What was his sweet prince doing with them?

When he'd tried to get Remi to explain why staying active in the frat was so important, he'd gotten huffy and shut himself in the bedroom all morning.

Jeremiah wasn't a fan of being ignored by his mate.

He cleared his throat. Not his mate. The crown prince could *not* be mated to a Hellhound.

Following Remi out of the SUV, he raised his brow at the stink eye he got. "What?"

"You can't come in," Remi said under his breath, pausing at the bottom step of the front porch. He glanced warily at the door and bit his lip. "They only allow… members inside during the day."

Jeremiah ground his teeth together. He had a feeling Remi meant they didn't allow *Supes* in the house and changed his mind at the last minute. The only reason he could think of for why they'd let Remi join when they were clearly anti-Supe was because of the clout a prince gave them.

His hound rumbled in his chest, infuriated at the idea of their ma—of *Remi* getting used like that.

"I need to at least clear the hou—"

"No, absolutely not," Remi said, eyes wide. He glanced at the door again before turning fully toward Jeremiah, who caught movement in the large picture window.

Jeremiah narrowed his eyes. *You should hide in there, humans.*

"There's nothing in there you need to keep me safe from—except maybe Deke's jungle juice, but I won't be having any of that at noon. It will be *fine*."

"I don't—"

"Like it," Remi finished, smiling more naturally and taking a step toward Jeremiah. His face softened, and he looked like the sweet boy Jeremiah had known the last two weeks. "I know. Hey, do you want to get sandwiches from that place around the corner tonight?"

Jeremiah stared at him blandly. "You can't placate me with steak sandwiches, princeling."

"Sure, I can." He winked, then turned and jogged up the steps, calling over his shoulder, "See you in a bit."

Grunting, Jeremiah watched until he disappeared from sight, eyes narrowing when some redheaded human sneered at him before closing the door. The whole frat gave him a bad feeling.

He glanced back at the two additional guys who'd been following and stopped half a block down the street. When they saw him gesture, both hopped out and hustled over.

They were part of Remi's new detail, and Jeremiah had been impressed with their willingness to follow his orders and take his precautions seriously. Neither ever batted an eye despite the fact the whole detail had to know by now what he and Remi were getting up to in his cozy little apartment. "Cover the perimeter and keep eyes on the exits. Ears open, gentlemen. If His Royal Highness so much as sneezes too hard in there, we're going in, rules be damned."

They both nodded and got to it.

Keeping his own gaze on the front of the two-story house, Jeremiah pulled out his phone and dialed Knight. Maybe he was being paranoid, but he had to be sure.

"What's up, Sunshine?"

"Maybe nothing," he said, shoving a hand into his hair and scratching at his scalp. "But this fraternity Remi is mixed up in… Something's off."

Knight hummed. "Off how? Like you think they're into

something illegal? I've heard that's pretty common for human frats."

"No, but the name sounds familiar, and the place is giving off bad vibes."

"Bad vibes." Knight's unimpressed voice wasn't appreciated. Not being born a Supe meant he trusted his advanced senses and instincts less than the rest of them did. But he always had a level head, staying calm even when he or Priest were flying off the handle, and he needed that right now.

"Can you just run a damn check, please?"

"Sure thing, boss."

Jeremiah rolled his eyes. He was the face of the agency and led Alpha Team, but he, Knight, and Priest had founded the company together. The two of them were just as much in charge at the end of the day as he was, and they both knew how he felt about getting called *boss* when it was just them.

He waited, listening to Knight type on his computer off and on as he checked the different databases and sources they had. While Jeremiah and Priest were stuck off-site, Knight was spending most of his time at HQ, making sure nothing got overlooked and the lights stayed on. It was his preference to being in the field, and considering his skills with tech, Jeremiah was just fine with letting him stay hidden behind his bank of computer screens.

"Huh, that's interesting."

Jeremiah's hackles rose. He knew it. "What is it?"

"We did a brief check on anyone Remi regularly came into contact with back at the beginning, right? And nothing popped, but digging a little deeper, I just found a well-buried article about the Kappa Alpha Chi house being threatened with probation from the university after some fucked-up hazing shit last year that involved three freshmen who were rushing the frat." There was some more typing, and then Knight let out a soft, angry hiss. "All three were Supes."

"All three? That seems—"

"Significant considering we make up less than ten percent of the student body at Hillsland. And as far as I can tell, Remi is the *only* Supe in this chapter's history to ever receive his letters."

"What did they do to the three freshmen?" Jeremiah said, half tempted to rush inside and grab Remi regardless of the kicking and screaming that would ensue.

"Not sure…" Knight said absently. "The article doesn't get into specifics but hints that it was pretty bad. Two out of three of the students dropped out and returned home, it looks like."

"Damn it. They left campus it was so bad?"

"Apparently. There's more though," Knight said, voice tight. "You know Remi's friend, Thad?"

Jeremiah gritted his teeth. "I know him."

"His dad is Senator Mick McCornal."

Gods *fucking* damn it. "The guy who just tried to push through that anti-Supe legislation? The one where all supernaturals would have to register with the Hillsland government to enter the country?"

"Bingo. When it failed to get enough votes, he said he'd be forcing the issue again. He's also made noise about reducing travel in and out of Hillsland by non-humans. Last week, he suggested any Supe from another kingdom or nation who wanted to enter Hillsland should be tracked while they were there."

"This guy is trying to take ignorant bigotry to a whole new level," Jeremiah muttered, muscles tensed. He never liked visiting this godsforsaken country, but having Remi so close to the son of a man like that?

Made his fingertips itch to extend his claws.

Maybe he could throw Remi over his shoulder and take him to the Trident Agency's safe house in the mountains. It was safe and isolated from humans and Supes alike. No one would get near Remi without Jeremiah knowing immediately.

"I don't like this," he muttered, moving closer to the house. He couldn't stop himself. He hated the wood and glass and insulation between him and his prince.

"Me neither. What should we do with this information though? I can't imagine the queen doesn't already know about the senator..."

Jeremiah grunted. "Add it all to the file and forward me a copy. I'll talk to Remi tonight. I can't imagine he knows the extent of things."

"He would have been there during rush week last year," Knight pointed out. "He was a member—"

"You don't know that. You said the article was sparse on details. There's every chance he has no idea, that the others hid it from him," he snarled. He knew Remi wasn't perfect—gods, did he ever—but he knew deep in his black soul that his little princeling would have never stood by and allowed other Supes to be tortured or brutalized right in front of him.

"Sunshine—"

"You don't know him, Edward." He used Knight's real name to emphasize his point.

Knight didn't say anything for a minute, just breathed over the line lightly. "You're right. I'm sorry for insulting your mate."

"He's not—"

"Don't lie to me or yourself," Knight said softly. "Not about this. The rest of us..." He cleared his throat, and Jeremiah wished they were together so he could wrap an arm around his friend for as long as he could handle the contact. "We'll probably not be so lucky. The bond between fated mates isn't something to ignore."

Jeremiah shook his head, his heart racing behind his ribs. "We both know Hellhounds don't get fated mates."

"We both know we don't know jack shit about Hellhounds," Knight shot back, sounding annoyed. "No one really does anymore. There aren't enough of you left. It's all misinformation and ridiculous stereotypes."

That was true. There were things he'd learned about himself growing up that had completely contradicted the insults his foster families would throw at him and accuse him of.

But even still…

"He's a prince, Knight. He'll rule Midlona one day."

"And? You got a problem supporting your man's career?"

"It's a birthright, not a career, and of course I don't. But having me standing at his side will make his life harder, not easier. I couldn't do that to him. I won't. He deserves every advantage, not a fucking liability."

"Such a fucking martyr," Knight huffed under his breath. "How about you stop assuming the worst and just give you both a chance to see what could happen?"

"How about you bite me?"

Knight laughed lightly. "I doubt your prince would like that, but I'm game if you are."

Jeremiah rolled his eyes. "Goodbye, Knight."

"Later, Sunshine. Keep your head on a swivel out there."

He grunted an acknowledgment, then shoved his phone away and planted his hands on his hips. He ignored the shit Knight had said at the end and focused instead on the news about Thad's dad and the hazing. Neither was enough to give him cause to force the issue of leaving the frat with Remi, but he didn't like the picture that was being painted.

18

JEREMIAH

Jeremiah supposed the one good thing about the fact that he was a Hellhound was that it was easy to blend in with humans. They lacked scent receptors and any other ability to sense Supes if they weren't either partially shifted or belonging to a race that had obvious physical markers. He'd gotten a couple of looks once or twice when he was out and about, and the barista who had served him that morning gave him a side-eye when he'd gotten a text from Remi and couldn't help the smallest purr in his chest.

But she hadn't asked, and Jeremiah had offered her a smile, which seemed to smooth the situation over.

Now, as he wandered through the quad, he was just another guy looking slightly out of place with his flecks of gray hair and leather jacket, more likely to commit violence than take a final. But there were plenty of humans like him. It meant that he could give Remi the space he needed to feel somewhat normal as he attended his lectures while also being close enough to the buildings that he'd be able to get there if he needed him.

It also helped that Jeremiah could sense him. He'd stopped trying to deny that there was a bond between them.

He just wasn't convinced that fated mates was it. Remi was reluctant to talk about it—not that Jeremiah could blame him. He couldn't imagine a single species that walked the earth who'd want to be bound to a Hellhound.

Not even other Hellhounds.

It was why they were rare. It was why they were a dying species.

Pushing that thought away, Jeremiah did a scan of the area, sniffing the air for anything off, but all he caught was overuse of body spray, weed, and human hormones. The thought should have made him laugh, but instead, it hit him like a punch to the gut.

This was Remi's life. This was what he was supposed to be doing. He was young and rich. He should be having fun and playing the field. He should be having his heart broken and then mended rather than tying himself to some bitter, angry beast that would only ever bring him more ridicule and pain.

If Jeremiah had been anyone else—any*thing* else—he could have found a way to make them work. But Remi was suffering enough as it was.

Taking a deep breath, he moved toward a bench in the shade of a lush willow, and just as his knees bent to sit, his phone began to buzz. He let out a quiet growl as he fished the device out of his pocket and tried not to feel a little burst of panic when he saw Priest's name on the screen.

"Tell me nothing's wrong," he said by way of answer.

"Nothing's wrong."

Jeremiah rolled his eyes. "Okay. This time, mean it."

Priest laughed. "Nothing's wrong. The palace is quiet, and the Bravo Team arrived last night and set up a perimeter around here and several spots in the city where the queen and king have appointments."

Jeremiah understood that the royal family couldn't just go

into hiding, but it drove him up the wall when they were out and vulnerable. "What about the twins?"

"Hellions," Priest said, and Jeremiah could all but see the grin on his face. "They're fucking great. They're so weird."

Unable to help a small laugh, Jeremiah shook his head. "Yeah, they are."

"How's lover boy?" Priest asked, and Jeremiah growled, loud enough for Priest to hear him but soft enough he didn't scare the shit out of any passersby.

"How about you shut the fuck up?"

"Touchy," Priest said. "I'd think you were part Incubus with how intense you are."

Jeremiah closed his eyes and took a calming breath. "This isn't up for discussion right now."

"He's not going to die, you know," Priest said. His words felt like a stab wound, forcing Jeremiah to think about the one scenario he couldn't live with. "You don't have to be afraid to love him even if he's—"

"That's not the issue," he snapped, and Priest just laughed. "It isn't. He's a crown prince, and I'm a goddamn hellbeast. He already deals with enough, thanks to his father. When this whole thing calms down and the reality of what it would truly mean to be with me hits him, he's going to end it. And the worst part is he'll probably be kind and gentle about it."

Priest sighed. "Knight's right—your pessimism is seriously such a bummer. The first one of us to find a fated mate, and you're acting like it's a prison sentence."

Jeremiah fought the urge to bare his teeth. "He's not…" He stopped, realizing those words tasted like the most bitter lie. Remi was more than just a lover. He was so much more than a good time, or a quick fuck, or even a longer fling. He had burrowed deep into Jeremiah's soul, and the only way to get him out would be to flay himself open. But even if it were true… it would only make everything worse. "I can't do this right now."

"Alright," Priest told him, sounding kinder than he had a minute ago. "I don't blame you for freaking out. If I got to have a fated mate…" He let out a loud, vocal shiver. "I think I might lose my mind."

Jeremiah wanted to tell him that he wouldn't, thinking about the soft-spoken bookstore owner Priest liked to watch from the café across the street. If anyone deserved the soul-deep bond of a fated mate, it was the men on their team. But he didn't say anything. Priest would only try to turn that around on him, and Jeremiah was far too fragile to get his hopes up.

"When is your first outing?" he asked instead.

"Uhh… I'm taking the twins on an excursion tomorrow afternoon. They're getting restless since their little vacation with the Dragons, so I thought I'd take them to the beach."

Jeremiah felt his hackles rise, though it was more the trauma of their last trip than any real danger. "I hope you'll have more than just palace guards with you."

"A half dozen palace guards and three from the Bravo Team," Priest said. "And we're going to a different area this time. Knight put together a map of spots he thinks are the safest."

Jeremiah trusted Knight with his life, but he didn't trust whoever it was that had access to the family. He hated not being in two places at once. The whole thing felt entirely outside of his control, and it made him want to put his fist through a wall.

"You're growling again. You're gonna scare the fragile humans," Priest teased.

Jeremiah pressed his hand against his throat and cleared it until the urge passed. "Keep me informed of everything."

"You know I will. Be safe and have fun. Enjoy using your dick the way it was meant to be used!"

Jeremiah hung up before he said anything he regretted. Leaning back, he finished his coffee, then crushed the cup in his hand. It was a pathetic show of strength, but it made him feel a little better as he closed his eyes and turned his face up toward the tree cover. Bits of light filtered through the leaves, and he let out a soft breath.

He wondered what life might have been like if he'd been someone else. Who would he be with a family who loved him instead of having parents who abandoned him? Would he have gone to college? Met someone, gotten married, popped out a litter of pups?

The thought was strange and foreign, and it hurt when he realized he'd have never met his little family. The idea of living without his team felt like someone threatening to rip his heart out.

"Is this seat taken?"

Jeremiah's eyes flew open, and he caught a growl in his chest before letting it out. His hackles rose as he felt the power radiating off the man in waves, and his claws extended, so he curled his fingers into fists. "Who are you?"

"Ozias," the man said. He stepped fully into the shade, and Jeremiah could see him better. He was tall, broad, and aesthetically gorgeous, though he wasn't really Jeremiah's type. He had the sort of college-professor look with slacks and a button-up, and he was carrying a laptop bag over his shoulder.

He was smiling kindly, and he looked completely human apart from his eyes. Jeremiah couldn't put his finger on it, but he'd definitely seen that indigo before.

"You're not human," he said.

"Nephilim," Ozias offered, his smile going wider.

Jeremiah bristled. Also a pariah among his kind. A half-angel, half-human abomination, only instead of making him weaker, the human side enhanced his powers enough that his kind were considered threats to the Heavenly Hosts.

And it took only a second more for Jeremiah to recognize his name. "You're Remi's ex."

Ozias's face fell a little, and Jeremiah felt a wave of possessiveness threaten to take over as the man sat. He sat his laptop bag down and crossed his legs, his ankle hooked over his knee. "He talked about me?"

"Briefly," Jeremiah grunted.

Ozias laughed very softly. "I imagine he did. I saw you with him the other day when he got back to campus."

"Is this where you attempt to threaten me, because I can assure you, that will not go well," Jeremiah warned.

The Nephilim held up both hands in surrender. "Not at all. Remi and I aren't on bad terms. I know I hurt him, but I didn't exactly have a choice."

Jeremiah raised a brow. "His parents?"

Ozias barked a laugh. "Gods, no. They don't care who Remi dates as long as he's happy. But Remi and I are not meant to be."

Godsdamned right they weren't meant to be. But he didn't say that aloud. He rubbed a hand down his face, then looked over at the Nephilim. "What do you want?"

"To ask if he's okay. Not emotionally," Ozias hurried. "But I know something's been going on. I do my best not to listen to student gossip around campus, but I hear things. Everyone was talking about the kidnapping attempt at the club, then he disappeared for weeks. Now you're here, and I know who you are."

"Do you?" Jeremiah asked.

"Trident Agency. You're not just Alpha Team—you founded it."

"And apparently, you're good at doing homework," Jeremiah said.

Ozias laughed again, the sound melodic and soothing, and gods, he hated it. He hated that this man put him at ease. He could see Ozias calming all of Remi's anxieties and fears without even trying. A Nephilim was dangerous, but they were far less hated by humans. It was likely why he was allowed to be on campus.

So why didn't they work?

"Because he wasn't mine," Ozias said.

Jeremiah blinked. Had he said that aloud?

"No," Ozias answered again. "Normally I can put up a block, but Hellhounds are notoriously difficult to shield, and you're kind of… projecting."

Jeremiah flushed. Hard. "That's fucking fantastic."

Ozias shook his head, his grin going a little softer. "It's nothing to be worried about. I just get bursts of active thoughts. I can't see anything. But I had to answer your question because I can tell the two of you have already started a bond, and that's the exact reason Remi and I would never work."

"Because of me?"

"Because the two of us belong to other people." Ozias glanced away, his gaze far-off and almost dazed. "I really liked him. He's so… kind, even when he's being a little shit. And he's so hurt by all the fucked-up people who act like it's their mission to tear him to pieces."

Jeremiah nodded, uncurling his hands and swiping them over the sides of his jeans. He wanted to claw the throats out of anyone who ever made Remi feel small. "It's obvious his parents tried, but…"

"There's only so much anyone can do," Ozias said. "And Remi was hurt because he's spent his whole life afraid to believe he's capable of having a fated mate. And he still thinks I used it as an excuse to dump him when I got bored of him. I didn't know how to tell him that I cared about him but that I wasn't capable of loving him the way he deserved to be loved. It seemed cruel."

Ozias was telling the truth. It was brutal and cutting, and Remi would have been destroyed by it. "So you just left him."

"I told him the truth as much as I could. I think he believes that I thought he just wasn't good enough for me, and I hate that. But it's easier to let him resent me. And it feels better knowing he found you."

Jeremiah couldn't bring himself to say that he had no faith that this would last. Even if he and Remi were somehow blessed enough to be fated mates… It didn't change who and what he was. No matter how much they both wanted it, Jeremiah couldn't sit on a damn throne next to him.

"Do you think you'll be able to keep him safe?" Ozias asked after a beat.

Jeremiah blew out a puff of air. "I want to say yes. I'm trying my damnedest, but he's not making it easy. He wants things to feel normal, but they're not, and we're coming up short on leads."

"I could… give you some suggestions on where to look," Ozias said carefully, eyes averted.

Jeremiah bristled. "What do you know?"

Ozias shrugged. "Like I said, I try not to listen, but sometimes I can't help it. It's not safe to talk here though."

Jeremiah bit his lip, then glanced around before nodding. "Give me your number. I'm going to put you in touch with a member of my team, and you can speak with him when you're certain you're safe."

Ozias nodded, and it was clear from the expression on his face that he was taking Jeremiah seriously. "Whatever you need. I really care about him, but more than that, he's being targeted because of who he is. And if they can get to a crown prince…"

He didn't finish the sentence, but Jeremiah didn't need him to.

None of them would be safe.

Jeremiah was reeling from his meeting with Ozias, but he'd sent his contact info to Knight, who promised he'd follow up on any leads the Nephilim gave them. It wasn't much, but it was something, and Jeremiah could only hope that Ozias knew something they didn't.

He sent a text to Remi when he finally got to the building where his prince's last class was, but he waited fifteen minutes for a reply before getting something he wasn't expecting.

Remi: *Left early. See you at home.*

Jeremiah's heart started pounding in his chest, and he knew his speed was terrifying to humans, but he stopped giving a shit as he raced for the apartment. He fumbled with the key to get in but eventually made it to their floor and burst inside, only to find it empty.

He grabbed a pillow from the couch to muffle his roar before he calmed himself and dialed Remi. It rang three times, and he was half expecting it to go to voicemail before the prince picked up.

"I said I'd meet you at home." His voice was calm, but Jeremiah knew him well enough to tell it was faked. He could also hear what sounded like that dickbag Thad in the background, egging Remi on.

"What the fuck do you think you're doing?" Jeremiah demanded. "Where are you?"

"Out with friends," Remi said, voice firming, but there was a shaky edge to it that was setting off Jeremiah's instincts. "W-without my leash."

Jeremiah swallowed heavily. He knew this was a lot for Remi, but that didn't sound like him. At least, not the Remi he was falling for. The one who'd spent the last two weeks pressed as close to Jeremiah as he could get, smiling at him and constantly kissing him and sharing his thoughts and fears. "I don't know if you think this is some kind of game, but you're not going to waste your time or mine by trying to disappear on me. I can find you, and I will, but you're the one who said you don't want a scene."

"Are you trying to threaten me?" Remi asked softly, the noise in the background growing fainter.

"Oh no, princeling. This is a fucking promise. Either I see your ass walk through this apartment door in five minutes with an apology and a promise that you won't ever pull this shit again, or I'm going to treat you like a toddler in front of all your big-boy college friends."

"You're being a dick," Remi spat.

Jeremiah laughed harshly. "No, I'm doing my job. Timer starts now."

He hung up before he could destroy what fragile threads were left connecting them and started pacing, which was the only thing he could do to keep from flying out the door and tracking Remi down. He knew his prince by scent and could easily catch it on a breeze, but he didn't trust himself to stay calm in front of all the humans.

He would make good on his promise, but if he had to go search his little brat out, it could ruin everything between them. He'd do it though. He'd do just about anything to keep him safe.

Three minutes passed. Then four.

At five, Jeremiah started to pull his jacket on, but just before he reached the door, it opened. Remi walked in, slamming it behind him, and something inside Jeremiah sparked.

One look at his frustrated, pouting face, and it began to burn like a raging wildfire.

He was on Remi without thinking, hand to his throat, pressing him against the wall. He buried his nose in Remi's neck, taking in huge lungfuls of his coconut-and-ocean scent before letting his fangs drop to drag them over his favorite spot.

"The fuck?" Remi gasped, but he didn't sound angry. He

sounded horny, and Jeremiah was struggling not to give in to what his hound wanted.

To mark and possess and *own*.

"You don't get to do that again," Jeremiah growled.

Remi shoved at him, but it was half-hearted, and Jeremiah didn't budge. "You don't get to tell me what to do."

He laughed humorlessly and gripped Remi by the jaw, the grip probably painful, but he struggled to care. "Yes, I do. Your parents are paying me a fuckload of money to keep your ass alive, and I don't think they're going to thank you if they find out you wandered away from your goddamn bodyguard."

Remi's lips trembled. "They were right. You're in this because of the money. You don't actually give a fuck about—"

Jeremiah slapped his hand over Remi's mouth, his body blazing hot. His free hand was fisted at his side and encased in hellfire. It took all of his self-control not to shift. "Do you seriously think that? Look me in the eye and tell me that you think everything that's happened between us is because of money. Do you know how rich I am, Remi? Do you want to see the statements?"

Remi swallowed heavily, and he said nothing for a long while after Jeremiah pulled his hand away. "Why are you really here, then?" he whispered.

Jeremiah pulled himself together, extinguishing his fire, and then cradled Remi's face between his palms. He knew his skin was probably too hot, but Remi just sighed and leaned into the touch. "You know why I'm here. You and I are entirely wrong for each other, but everything in me doesn't give a single fuck. I have no idea what our future looks like, but I will not walk this earth if you're not in it. If someone got their hands on you, Remi…"

"I was fine," he tried to argue half-heartedly.

Jeremiah shook his head. "The last time you said that, you were almost killed. And you have been nearly taken from this campus. This is not a game," he repeated. "You don't get to walk off without me because you're having a crisis of self-esteem."

"That was mean," Remi said, his voice shattered.

Jeremiah hated himself for causing the pain, but he had to be honest. "It was mean, but it was the truth. You were reckless, and you let people who don't even care about you get to you. I thought you trusted me."

Remi winced. "They just... it's so..." He squeezed his eyes shut and turned his head to the side. "They had no idea what you'd see in someone like me, and it's not like they're wrong. I've thought about that since you first kissed me."

"You're smarter than that," Jeremiah told him. He gave him a gentle shake and waited for Remi to meet his gaze. "I get paid so I can take care of my team. So they can live better lives than the ones we had before I founded this company. But you are more than a client, and if I've failed to show you that before now—"

"No. It wasn't you," Remi said. His jaw started to tremble. "I don't know what's wrong with me. I'm so fucking stupid sometimes. I—"

With that, Jeremiah leaned in and captured his lips in a slow, pressing, searing-hot kiss. Remi melted under his attention, sagging in his arms as Jeremiah wrapped them around his waist, and he pulled him away from the wall and walked him to the couch without breaking apart. He laid him out, then pressed his knee to the cushion and eased back with several soft pecks.

When Remi's eyes were back on his, Jeremiah let his fangs slide out, then sank them into Remi's neck. He gasped, arching against him as the tang of blood hit Jeremiah's tongue, and he laved it over the wound until it was closed.

"I don't know what the future holds," Jeremiah whispered against his skin. "But I know that I won't just die for you, Remington. I will live for you, and I will fight for you. And I have never made that vow to anyone before in my life. Do you understand now?"

He pulled back, and Remi reached up, tracing a touch over his lips. "I get it."

Jeremiah nodded. "Good. Now, promise me, princeling. Never again."

Remi nodded, and Jeremiah felt a pulse of truth in his words. "Never again."

19

REMI

"Is the warden going to let you come to the Pimps and Hoes party tonight?"

Remi didn't look up from his notes. He wasn't actually reading anything—and not just because he'd been schooled in archaic Midlonian since he was learning to read, but because it was easier than looking Brendan and Thad in the eye.

The Pimps and Hoes party was something their frat threw every year. In the public eye, the party was for charity. In reality, the party was a good way to humiliate future pledges and brothers who were hoping for a spot in the frat house and a good way of getting people drunk enough to say yes to things they normally wouldn't.

The whole thing had always made Remi feel sick to his stomach, and he avoided events like it as much as he could. And it was somehow worse now that he and Jeremiah had connected in ways that no human would ever be able to understand.

"I know that look," Brendan said, leaning forward and dropping his voice. "Someone's getting some regular dick. Is that a bonus part of the package? Do you get to tell him what to do because you're paying?"

"Fuck off," Remi hissed.

Brendan sat back, laughing his annoying, high-pitched laugh. "What's it like? Does he have a dog dick?"

"Don't be an ass," Thad snapped, then clapped Remi on the shoulder. "He's high."

Remi didn't think that was the problem, and he was pretty sure Thad would have gone along with the shit Brendan was saying if it wasn't a social event he needed a crown prince for. "Whatever. It's fine. I probably can't come."

"Dude," Thad said from behind a sigh, "you can't let this guy dictate everything you do. Like, I get there's shit going on, but this is your right. You're a high-ranking member—"

"I know," Remi interrupted. "But it's complicated."

"You're also a fucking prince," Thad told him. "And he's literally staff. What the fuck is it going to say to everyone watching when some mutt starts telling you what you can and can't do? You know some reporter's going to ask you what was up with this semester. They're going to want to know why the royal family of Midlona sent the heir to the throne back to college with something that spawned from a dog and a Demon."

Remi felt a sudden urge to put his fist through Thad's face. Literally. The very idea of calling Jeremiah anything but a godsdamned miracle that made Remi's life worth living made him want to drop claws and tear the room to shreds. And the terrifying thing was, the more he and Jeremiah were together, the more that felt like a possible scenario.

Remi had been avoiding the campus pool since they got back for the simple fact that he could apparently shift now, and he was shit-scared of not being able to control it.

"Can you just drop it?" he finally asked.

Thad shook his head. "No. I literally can't. I don't care what you say to him, but you either show up, or you can kiss your letters goodbye. I might have power, Rem, but I can't work miracles. Rules are rules for a reason."

Remi narrowed his eyes. Gods, he was so fucking tired of this. Let the fucking frat boot him. What did he care anymore? He'd been holding on to his old life with the tips of his fingers, and why? What was so great about being around people like Brendan and Thad who made shitty comments about Supes but then added a "except you, dude" to the end, acting like that made it better.

He'd made so many damn decisions in his life because he was scared. Maybe it was time he chose what he actually wanted, and that was Jeremiah. Maybe the Hellhound would leave him in the end—gods, the thought alone made his chest *ache*—but would he throw away what they had just for some dumb party?

But he couldn't say all that five minutes before class was set to start, knowing it would cause a huge fight. Thad hadn't exactly been subtle about wanting to parade Remi around at upcoming events, and despite his threats about Remi losing his letters, he had a feeling the guy would lose his shit when he found out Remi was done with the frat.

"I'll do my best," he said, forcing a smile.

Thad's face relaxed, thinking he'd won. "Fuck yeah you will."

The classroom door opened a second later, and Remi felt something familiar shoot up his spine. His eyes lifted and fixed on someone he hadn't seen in a while. Oz had been avoiding him since their split, but his gaze sought and found Remi's like maybe he wanted to come over and talk to him but changed his mind when he spotted Thad and Brendan.

Oz changed direction, walking over to the professor's desk, and leaned over, speaking too quietly for anyone to hear.

"Freak alert," Brendan said with another high-pitched laugh. "I bet he's here scoping undergrads."

Remi watched the way Oz's back tensed, but the Nephilim didn't look over, even as Thad laughed loudly and added,

"Guard your dicks, boys. I heard his kind can touch you without being near you."

"Stop," Remi hissed, horrified.

Thad gave him an incredulous look. "You're fucking defending that asshole after what he did to you?"

"Dumping me isn't exactly a crime."

"He hypnotized you," Thad said, his voice rising. "Everyone knows creatures like him are capable of it. They get off on it. They prey on humans because they think we're lesser. He thought you were an easy target because you're a…"

Halfbreed.

But Thad didn't say it. Not that he needed to.

Remi gritted his teeth. "It wasn't like that."

"You just need to embrace the fact that he was able to trick you because you're more human than the rest of them. It's why we let you pledge. It's why we can call you brother. And it's why we want to protect you from the freaks your parents keep sending with you to this school."

Remi opened his mouth to argue, but Oz swiftly left the room, and Remi felt guilt filling his stomach like a ten-ton boulder. Oz had left him because they weren't meant to be. Because he was a Supe with a fated mate out there somewhere, and it wasn't Remi. Remi understood that now, even if he hadn't before.

But he knew what they'd had was real. It hadn't been some magical or mystical mind manipulation.

He couldn't wait to separate himself from these people he thought he could be friends with. It made him queasy to sit there and act like everything was fine through class, but he promised himself he'd tell Thad things were changing as soon as he could.

Thad: *Waiting outside. How much longer?*

Remi: *I'm trying to get out. Just give me a few.*

Pocketing his phone, Remi walked into the kitchen and saw Jeremiah cleaning up what was left of their little dinner. It was a far cry from campus takeout and microwaved commissary burritos that Remi had been surviving off the last few years. He hadn't expected Jeremiah to be able to cook, but the Hellhound had many talents, and Remi would have married him for his carbonara alone.

And that only made the guilt worse because he was about to trick Jeremiah. He was going to break the only promise Jeremiah had asked him to make because of some misplaced loyalty. Sure, he wasn't actually planning on attending the party, but he hadn't had a chance to talk to Thad alone, and he'd been blowing up Remi's phone all day, making sure he was coming.

He'd go down and talk to him face-to-face, and that was it, but he felt like he owed him that much. Thad may be a lot of things, but he'd also befriended Remi when no one else had. Under all his douchebaggery, there was a little bit of a good guy.

Maybe…

But he knew Jeremiah wouldn't like it, so he needed to employ some sneakiness. Hopefully, his Hellhound wouldn't be too upset when he found out he left the apartment alone.

"What's wrong?"

Jeremiah's rumble hit Remi right in the center of his sternum, and his resolve almost broke. He knew he was taking a risk, but he was only going to go as far as Thad's car. He'd be perfectly fine. He took a breath, then shrugged and stepped close to Jeremiah.

He could do this.

"I'm feeling low."

Jeremiah set down the bowl he was holding and tugged Remi into his arms, kissing over the bite mark he'd made not even an hour ago. The wound had healed, but there was starting to be a faint scar that made Remi shivered when he touched or looked at it. "What can I do?"

Remi groaned. His resolve cracked a little harder, but it didn't shatter. "Would it make me a giant asshole if I asked you to go out and get me a little comfort food?"

Jeremiah kissed him again, then pulled back and pinched his chin between fingers and thumb. "Depends. If you want me to fly home to get you some Siren delicacy, my answer is going to be fuck no."

Remi rolled his eyes. "No. There's this little dessert shop over by the bookstore that's always open late for the stoner kids. They make these amazing beignets with chocolate sauce, but they don't do delivery."

Jeremiah sighed, staring up at the ceiling like it was the worst task Remi could have asked him, but there was a smile playing at his lips, telling Remi he'd won. And fuck, how could be not fall in love with this man?

"Kiss me," he said, knowing there was a chance—even if it was tiny—that Jeremiah wouldn't forgive him for lying and it would be the last time.

Jeremiah just smiled, cupped his cheek, and obeyed. "Okay, my little princeling. But if you tell anyone I've become some dessert errand boy..."

"Never." He lost himself for just a moment, kissing Jeremiah again until he was forced to break away or fess up. "Thank you."

Jeremiah nodded and leaned in, rubbing his nose over Remi's neck, scenting him, before finally turning away to grab his keys. "Why don't you pick a movie? We can cuddle and eat your gross treats."

Remi laughed, hoping the sound didn't sound as forced as it was. That sounded perfect, and he just hoped Jeremiah would still want to when he found out what Remi had done. Sneaking around behind his back was making him feel like he might throw up, but he forced himself to pull out his phone and text Thad.

Remi: *Coming down now.*

There was a ball of anxiety in his chest at the idea of blowing up his life without the certainty of a future with Jeremiah, but he had to do it. Even if he ended up without his Hellhound, he couldn't keep pretending he was okay with the things the frat said and did. It was time for him to stand up to their bigotry and become the man he'd been scared to be for so long.

He sighed and tossed his phone on the couch, not bothering to read Thad's exuberant responses. He rolled his shoulders and hyped himself up, then headed out the door.

Taking the stairs three at a time, Remi made it to the building's back exit and immediately spotted Thad's little sports car waiting for him. The trunk popped as he got closer, and he simply closed it again, not having a bag with his change of clothes in it.

He opened the passenger door and slowly lowered himself into the seat.

Thad took one look at his face and made a disgusted sound. "Fuck, dude. Is the leash really that tight?"

Remi's cheeks reddened. "It's not like that. I'm… Listen, I appreciate you taking me under your wing freshman year, but I don't think the frat is for me anymore."

Thad stared at him, mouth gaping open. "Are you shitting me? Because that *thing* doesn't want you to go to a party? You're just going to ruin your whole life?"

"This isn't my whole life," Remi said furiously. "My people and kingdom are my life. This has just been… a nice diversion. And Jeremiah isn't a *thing,* Thad. I can't believe you let your dad's hatred sour you so much."

Thad's face twisted. "Don't bring my dad into this."

Remi took a deep breath and let it out, reaching into his pocket to pull out the pin with his Greek letters on it. He dropped them in the cup holder, and Thad stared down at them in the dim light. "You're right. This isn't about him, not really. Have a nice life, Thad."

He pulled the door handle, eager to get back upstairs and wait for Jeremiah so he could apologize and beg for his Hellhound to hold him until he stopped shaking. As he swung a foot out, he felt Thad grab his arm.

"Remi, wait."

Sighing, he turned to tell him not to bother trying to change his mind, but there was a sharp prick on the side of his neck before he could say anything. He gaped at the syringe in Thad's hand as he watched impassively as Remi slumped against the seat, losing control of his muscles and vision dimming.

"The party's just getting started, freak."

Remi woke in little bursts, his head heavy and so full he was afraid it was going to explode. He couldn't see, and he had no idea where he was, and terror crept up his spine as he gained more awareness. Wiggling his hands, he realized he wasn't tied, but his arms felt like they were made of Gargoyle stone.

"Remi?"

A voice spoke—small and trembling and so familiar it filled Remi with the worst sense of dread he'd ever experienced. He forced his head to turn, and he saw two small figures sitting on a stained mattress on the floor over in the corner of the room.

"Is he alived?"

"Remi?"

It was the terror in his siblings' voices that filled his limbs with strength, and he pushed himself halfway up before a heavy boot kicked him back to the ground. Remi let out a rush of air, pain exploding through him, then turned his head to see Thad looming over him with a sick grin on his face.

"What… the f-fuck?" he managed.

Thad snorted. "You seriously have to ask that?"

Remi attempted to swallow, but his mouth felt like it was filled with cotton. "Yes. What the fuck?"

Thad rolled his eyes and kicked Remi again, sending him sprawling onto his back. The twins began to scream, but Remi held up his hand before Thad could get pissed and take it out on them.

"Gods, it was you the whole time, wasn't it?" Remi finally said. His brain was a foggy mess, but it was still connecting the pieces.

Thad shrugged when Remi forced his pain-filled head to look at him. "It wasn't just me. I have friends in high places, but they couldn't get their hands dirty. It was easy for me to volunteer, considering what you fucking did to my family."

Remi blinked and pushed himself halfway up. He tried not to make eye contact with the twins. If he did, he'd panic, and then they'd panic. "I didn't do anything to your family. Thad, what the hell are you—"

Thad kicked him in the face, sending him flying back, and he hit the floor as white-hot pain burst across his jaw, and the twins began to scream. Stars burst behind his closed eyes, and he was positive if he'd been fully human, Thad would have just broken something.

"Shut the fuck up!" Thad shouted, stomping across the room, and then there was silence.

Panicked and panting, Remi forced his vision to clear until he could make out what was happening, finding the twins gagged and bound where they were huddled together against the wall. Remi felt rage like he'd never known in his life course through him, but before he could do anything more than flip onto his stomach and push up on his shaky arms,

Thad landed on his back and grabbed him by the throat, shoving something sweaty and gross past his teeth.

"Don't you get any ideas, *Siren,*" Thad sneered.

He secured the gag behind Remi's head with something hard that cut into the corners of his mouth, then grabbed him by the arms and hauled him to his feet, marching him over to the twins. The world spun, and Remi's weak legs collapsed the moment he was near the mattress. He had no strength to fight when Thad began to tie his arms behind his back. Dizziness was swamping him, and nausea was building in his belly. It was all he could do to stay conscious, too worried about the twins to let the blackness creeping at the edge of his vision take him over.

"See, you think we're all stupid, but the fact is humans have been studying you things for generations. Learning where you're weak. Learning how you operate. Learning how to hurt you the most." He leaned into Remi's face, grinning in a way that made him question the guy's sanity. "Imagine my happiness when you started parading your disgusting mate around campus for everyone to see. I knew exactly what to do as soon as I realized who he was to you."

Remi met Thad's crazed eyes and shook his head, but Thad just laughed.

"Don't play stupid. It won't work. I've had eyes on you since your parents dragged you back home. I know who he is —and what he is. I know he's bitten you and fucked you, and I know what that means." Thad pressed his thumb to Remi's bite mark before he could jerk away, and something primal took hold of him.

Remi snarled around the gag, feeling blistering hot all over, and lunged at Thad, landing his shoulder square in Thad's chest and sending him flying back several feet away.

The heat began to ebb, but the pain and dizziness had lessened too. Remi felt stronger than he had since waking. He knew what that was, even as his brain tried to deny it, had been denying all the clues around him since he'd met Jeremiah.

Thad straightened up, then laughed as he tugged on the hem of his shirt. "Cute. But it doesn't matter. The world's going to know what monsters you all are soon enough. Your fucking mutt of a mate is going to lose his shit and go feral when he realizes you're dead, and he's going to tear everything in this room apart. Including the children."

Remi heard the twins whimper, and he reached for them as best he could. He felt two tiny hands grip his, and he held them as tight as he dared. His gaze found Thad's again, and he glared at him, wishing he could gouge his eyes out with the power of his mind.

"Don't look at me like that. You're all the fucking same. Home-wrecking whores who think they can have whatever they want. I watched what that bitch did to my family. She seduced my father, ruined his marriage, and left with everything. And somehow, our government expects everyone to just accept having you *things* living among us?"

Remi wanted to laugh. Yes, there were probably Sirens who would stoop to such tactics, but he knew what Thad's father was like. He was a bigoted asshole that was likely fucking a collection of Supes on the side. It wouldn't have surprised him to know that he had mistresses in every kingdom. Hell, on every continent.

But the fact that Thad was willing to go this far over his parents' divorce? He didn't understand.

He was scared though. With his hands bound and his mouth gagged, he had no power. He wasn't sure how he'd protect the twins. He couldn't even protect himself. And because he'd left his phone at the apartment and been brought here in a car, Jeremiah had no way of finding him by technology or scent.

Only… there was an almost shrill pulsing of panic at the base of his spine that didn't *feel* like his own. It was wrapping around him, growing stronger by the minute, and he knew what it was. He knew why it was there.

All the lore he'd ever read about the strength of the bond between fated mates came back and smacked him in the face.

No matter how hard he protested, he couldn't deny it any longer. He wasn't too human for his birthright, and Jeremiah was his. He was his *mate*. The fates had given him the Hellhound as his own.

He breathed and closed his eyes, following the threads of their bond out and out and *out* until he felt something snap into place. He could feel it in his gut when Jeremiah's awareness locked in, like a sharp bolt of lightning.

His fear melted away as his mate's rage and determination flooded him. Tears filled his eyes, his breath catching in his chest, when Jeremiah's deep, dangerous rumble filled his head.

I'm coming for you. Just hang on.

Remi had no idea how it worked, but he knew—without a shadow of a doubt—that his mate would keep him safe. All he had to do was hold on until Jeremiah found him. And then it would all be over.

I'm waiting, he sent back. *I need you.*

I'm on my way.

20

JEREMIAH

"I hope you're hungry," Jeremiah called out as he unlocked the apartment door, juggling the three Styrofoam boxes. "I got a little of pretty much everything. The place smelled so fucking good I couldn't resist."

He kicked the door shut behind him and set the boxes down on the counter in the kitchen. Shoving his keys into his jacket pocket, he shrugged off the leather and frowned, glancing toward the bedroom.

"Remi? Did you pick a movie?"

The silence that greeted him had the hair rising on the back of his neck. Lifting his head, he scented the air, and trepidation rippled down his spine.

"Remington?" He stormed toward their bedroom, even though his nose and ears were telling him there wasn't another person in the apartment. Fear choked him as he threw open the door to the tiny closet and then the bathroom before rushing across to the other bedroom, nearly pulling the door straight off its hinges and being greeted by nothing but his computer and forgotten coffee mug from that morning.

Remi was gone.

Remi was *gone*.

He became aware of a vibrating noise as he stood in the middle of the living room, the scent of chocolate and sugar mocking him, and tried to get his brain to reboot. The noise stopped but then almost immediately started up again.

Snarling, he ripped his phone out of his pocket, but his surge of anger was snuffed short when he saw Priest's name, a shiver of premonition working through him. "Priest?"

"They're gone," Priest said, voice hard and inflectionless. "The twins have been taken, but I know where they are."

"How?" Jeremiah asked, lips numb as he stared at Remi's phone on the couch and stumbled over to it.

"Convinced the guard who was stationed outside their bedroom that it was a good idea to tell me everything he knew."

"He gonna be a problem?" Jeremiah turned Remi's phone over and punched in the security code without hesitation, pulling up the texts.

"Drained him," Priest said, his cold façade finally breaking on the words. "I'm sorry, Jeremiah—"

"I know. We'll get them back." He stared at the last text Remi had sent and felt like a hole was opening beneath his feet, dragging him down into darkness and pain. He'd promised him. He'd look Jeremiah in the eyes and promised he wouldn't run off again.

And he'd done it for a party?

"We're in the air already," Knight's voice came over the line, steady as ever. "We've got Stone on the line with us, but he won't get there until tomorrow."

"I'm stuck waiting on a commercial flight," Stone's deep voice rumbled.

"Storm is closest to you since he was checking up on some leads Remi's ex had given us," Knight continued. "He should be there any minute. The guard Priest… *interrogated*—" He said the word delicately, and under any other circumstance, Jeremiah would have chuckled at his discomfort for the messy stuff they sometimes had to do. For a Vampire, he was damn squeamish. "—seemed certain this Thaddeus McCornal will be able to get Remi away from you, so keep him close until—"

"He's already gone," he said flatly, locking Remi's phone and setting it down exactly where he'd found it.

There was a loaded pause where he assumed Knight and Priest were sharing confused looks, and then Priest said, "He was taken? Why didn't you call us?"

"He wasn't taken. He—" His voice broke, and he had to stop and clear his throat, the magnitude of what was happening hitting him and causing him to curl over. His heart was thudding in his ears, and he wasn't sure he wasn't going to be sick all over the floor. "He lied to me," he croaked out. "Sent me off on a dumbass errand and then left to go to a fucking *party*."

"Take a breath, Sunshine," Stone told him, audibly sucking in a breath in example. The Gargoyle was the newest member of their team, having joined a few years ago, and fit right in. He was smart and lethal, a real asset in the field. But in that moment, Jeremiah kind of hated him. His mate was out there somewhere enduring who knew what, and Stone wanted him to— "You can paddle his ass once you rescue him."

Jeremiah choked on a laugh, breaking out of his spiral and shaking his head. "Fuck, I think I might. He's so… I can't believe he did this."

"He couldn't have known they'd make a play for his siblings," Stone said. "His priorities may have been skewed, but I hear he really dotes on those two. He's probably panicking right now, which means you need to be steady for the both of you."

Even as Stone said it, Jeremiah became aware of the fact that he was jittery with terror—and it wasn't coming from *him*. He was scared and pissed and losing his mind with worry, but he was a fucking *professional*. He knew how to compartmentalize his emotions and focus on what needed to be done.

Except in that moment, he was overwhelmed, getting sucked under by feelings so strong he could barely stay upright.

The door burst open, and Storm was there, wrapping an arm around his back and helping him to sit down on the couch. The familiar scent of the Dragon helped ease the stranglehold the fear had on him, and he let himself lean into him.

"I can… I think I can feel him," Jeremiah muttered, sagging against the couch and squeezing his eyes shut to concentrate.

He heard Storm drag the coffee table closer and sit on it, their knees knocking together. "That's great. We'll find them faster that way."

"Wait, you can *feel* him?" Priest asked, sounding awestruck and maybe a little jealous. "I thought only Dragons could feel their mates?"

Jeremiah peeled his eyes open to peer at the apparent expert among them.

Jaw tight, Storm shook his head. "No, anyone with a strong bond to a fated mate can develop the ability. It's just more common among Dragons because their bonds are strengthened with each additional mate."

"But that's—"

"Later." Jeremiah cut off the chatter before Priest could really get going. Eyeing Storm, he asked, "I can use the connection to find him?"

"Yes. Depending on how developed it is, you may be able to communicate too."

Determination growing inside him, Jeremiah sat forward. "Show me."

"Are you sure this is where he is?" Storm murmured next to him as they stared at the overflowing Kappa house. The music was so loud it was hurting Jeremiah's sensitive ears even from across the street, and the stench of human sweat and beer and weed was making him queasy.

"He's… close. Knight, how far's the plane?"

The high-tech communication device in his ear was barely noticeable and delivered the others' voices as clearly as if they were standing in front of him.

"Another half an hour and then twenty minutes from the airport—"

"Fifteen if I drive," Priest interrupted.

"Don't wait for us," Knight finished, ignoring the Demon. "We know from the palace guard Thad doesn't plan on trying to ransom them."

Jeremiah's stomach curdled. Priest had told him and Storm everything he'd been able to extract from the guy before killing him as they'd driven through campus, Jeremiah doing his best to let the thread connecting him to his mate guide them. The handful of guards who'd been persuaded to help had apparently done it because they'd been promised a part of the money Thad had planned on demanding from the royals to get their kids back.

But Jeremiah knew that was bullshit. The guards might have told themselves that was the plan, but each attempt on Remi's life proved the group's intent was a lot more deadly. The guard Priest questioned had apparently cried and said he hadn't actually wanted the prince to die—just be too scared to take over the throne.

Jeremiah was almost sorry Priest had already killed him, but he figured he'd have his chance when they hunted down the rest of the complicit guards.

"Make sure you have the lawyer on standby," Jeremiah muttered as he and Storm moved closer to the house, eyes peeled for any sign of Remi and the twins. "With who Thad's dad is—"

"She's been briefed," Knight assured him. "The queen said to tell you she'd cover any legal fees but to make sure the threat to her family was eliminated."

Jeremiah grunted. "Yeah, that won't be a problem."

Just as they were going up the stairs to the front door, Jeremiah felt the connection to Remi pulling him to his right. He followed the instinct, trusting it to help him find his mate in time, and Storm stayed close behind him as they stepped around the occasional drunk person or couple making out.

The porch wrapped all the way around the frat house before dumping them in the backyard. Jeremiah growled under his breath at the number of partygoers, tempted to shift and terrify them into leaving. Storm's hand on his shoulder stopped him.

"What's that back there?" Storm pointed to a darker area of the yard, shrouded in shadows from the tall trees and some overgrown bushes. "Is that a shed?"

"It's always a shed," Priest said over the comms. "Sheds or basements."

"Or both," Jeremiah said softly, exchanging a look with Storm. The bond pulling at him was definitely coming from the dilapidated building, but it was too small and unsecure to hold people against their will.

"That's a twist," Priest said. "If there's anything stronger than a human in there, can you leave them for me? I'm still hungry."

"You're always hungry," the rest of them said as one.

Jeremiah strode forward, eyes locked in on his target. He knew Storm would protect his flank if any of the humans in the yard around them decided to try and stop them.

Gods, he sort of wished someone would. He wouldn't mind taking the edge off his aggression, but he also didn't want anything to delay them.

The few humans close by scattered as soon as they drew near, and Jeremiah could only guess what he looked like: eyes lit up with blue flames, fangs protruding from his mouth, and smoke rising from his shoulders.

Anyone with even just a few brain cells left would know to get the fuck out of his way.

Without even pausing, he kicked the padlocked door to the shed open. It was empty inside except for a guy who scrambled up from a lawn chair next to what looked like a wooden pallet on the floor except for the heavy-duty lock securing it to the ground. The guy stared at them with wide eyes as he scrambled to grab the weapon from his waistband.

Jeremiah leapt across the dingy space, landing on the human and taking him to the cement floor with a muffled scream. He laid a clawed hand on his throat and snarled, "How many are down there with them?"

"Please, don't kill me. I don't know anything," the guy begged, the scent of his fear sweat making saliva pool in Jeremiah's mouth.

"That's too bad for you," drawled Storm as he examined the pallet.

The guy glanced at the Dragon and then back at Jeremiah, mouth working wordlessly before he finally found his voice again. "Oh fuck. No, please!"

Jeremiah didn't bother saying anything. With a simple flick of his hand, he flayed open the human's throat and stood up, leaving him to bleed out on the filthy floor.

"Ready?" he rumbled as Storm stood, holding the melted lock in his hand as his skin slowly stopped glowing orange.

"Lead on, Sunshine. Let's get your mate back."

Jeremiah threw the wooden pallet aside and stared down into a dark hole, but he could tell there were lights on down there and probably a tunnel. He didn't bother using the ladder, just leapt the twelve feet into the hole and landed in a crouch, ready to fight if need be, but the space was clear.

He moved out of the way so Storm could join him, and then they made their way together through the roughly hewed tunnel. There were lights hanging every few feet, but even if it was pitch-black, he would have known this was the way to Remi.

He could have followed the scent of coconuts and sea breeze completely blind.

About forty feet farther away from the frat house, there was a solid-looking steel door blocking their way.

"I'd guess this is it," Storm murmured, stepping up next to Jeremiah and laying his glowing hand over the lock. They watched as it slowly began to melt, no match for the heat from a Dragon's fire.

They could hear Thad on the other side, cursing and screaming something, but Jeremiah didn't let it affect his focus. If his mate were already… Thad wouldn't be killed so quickly if a single hair was out of place on Remi's head.

The lock mechanism on the other side fell to the ground with a *thunk,* and Jeremiah turned the handle, swinging the door open and taking in the scene in front of him.

There was a filthy mattress shoved into the farthest corner, and Thad was kneeling on it next to Remi, a large knife in his hand pressed against Remi's bared throat. He could just barely make out the twins cowering behind his mate, their soft crying tearing at his insides.

"You got here faster than I thought, *dog,*" Thad sneered at him, and Jeremiah forced himself to meet Remi's eyes, braced for his panic.

But his mate was staring at him with determination, barely a speck of fear in his lavender gaze.

Gods, he loved this man. How could he not see how fucking brave he was?

"That's okay," Thad was saying, laughing in a way that said he wasn't really as sane as he'd been pretending. "This way, you can watch your precious little halfbreed die."

"How do you plan on getting out of here?" Storm asked, trying to play the voice of reason. "Huh? Why don't you put that knife down, and we can all walk out of here in one piece."

"I have two more tiny fishes to use as leverage," Thad said, reaching back with his free hand to poke at one of the twins until they screamed around their gags.

Remi's eyes began to heat, his fury pouring into Jeremiah through their bond.

Burn him.

Jeremiah took a step closer instinctively, cocking his head to the side. Had Remi just told him to *burn* Thad? He was too close to Remi and the twins—Jeremiah would kill them all with his hellfire.

It's too dangerous.

Thad was saying something, but Jeremiah stayed focused on his mate and the knife by his neck. It wasn't pressed against his skin anymore, Thad's inattention loosening his grip. Even as he was trying to figure out if he could close the distance between them before Thad slit Remi's throat, Remi took a deep breath, his chest rising and falling, and fell to his side, away from Thad.

Thad cursed and reached for him, but Remi was already slamming his foot into his junk and then throwing himself on top of the twins.

Do it! Now!

He was gathering his fire in his hands almost before he thought about it, his hound's trust in their mate complete.

"Oh fuck!" Storm yelled, sprinting back out into the tunnel and slamming the metal door shut behind him. "Are you crazy?"

Maybe, but he had to believe Remi knew what he was doing. Thad was already scrambling to grab onto Remi, knife still glinting in his hand, so he didn't have time to doubt him.

He released the flames, shooting them toward the mattress

and sending a prayer to any gods willing to listen. Thad didn't even have a chance to scream, the fire consuming him from one breath to the next, and Jeremiah quickly pulled it back inside himself and scrambled forward.

The mattress was burned and smoking under Thad's crispy body, but Remi looked… fine.

Completely unharmed.

Weak with relief, he untied Remi's hands and then unbuckled the belt wrapped around his head holding the gag in his mouth. They worked together to free the twins, who were crying hysterically and clinging to them both.

Jeremiah wrapped all of them in his arms as tightly as he could and rocked back and forth, barely able to believe it was over and they were safe.

Thank the fucking gods.

21

REMI

Remi was pretty sure he was in shock, his body feeling heavy and floaty at the same time as he looked back at the sleeping twins as Jeremiah led him out of the second bedroom. He was glad they'd left the bed in there so he could keep his brother and sister close until he could get them home in the morning. He met Priest's eyes, the Demon lounging in Jeremiah's desk chair, but his unwavering stare said he wouldn't be getting any rest until the twins were back at the palace.

He'd talked to his parents on the phone a little while ago, both of them so overcome he could barely understand them. He just reassured them over and over that they were all okay and that they didn't need to come to Hillsland.

He was coming home.

For good.

As soon as their bedroom door shut, Remi sagged against Jeremiah, wanting his warmth and comfort but finding resistance instead. For the first time in hours, Jeremiah didn't wrap his arms around him as soon as he leaned into him, his body stiffening against the door.

"What's wrong?" He peered up at him, trying to read his

tense face. "Are you worried about staying in Hillsland overnight?"

Jeremiah cleared his throat. "We need to talk."

Ice water rushed through his veins. "What?"

"Remi, I'm so glad you're okay. All of you," Jeremiah said carefully, stepping around Remi and putting space between them. "But you… You broke your word to me."

Swallowing, Remi nodded. "I know. I'm sorry. I thought it'd be okay since I wasn't going far."

Jeremiah narrowed his eyes. "Not going far? You were planning on going to a party full of people you didn't know without any protection. You sent me to get *dessert* while you put yourself in danger again."

"Wait—what?" Remi frowned, trying to catch up and then realizing Jeremiah didn't know what had actually happened. "No, that's not—"

"I love you, Remi, but I'm not sure I can trust you."

Remi sucked in a breath, warmth filling his whole body. Jeremiah *loved* him? Smiling, he took a step closer, wanting to hug his fucking mate, but Jeremiah moved back. "I didn't go to a party."

Jeremiah sighed and ran his hands through his hair, ruffling the waves. "Obviously, but I saw your texts with Thad. I know you were sneaking out to go to the stupid frat house when he kidnapped you."

Remi crossed his arms over his chest. "You read my texts?"

"You were missing!"

He rolled his eyes. "Yeah, well, you should probably know something, Sunshine."

"What's that?"

"I lied to Thad."

Jeremiah furrowed his brows. "About what?"

"Going to the party." Remi sighed and let his arms drop. He was so tired, but he knew they needed to get this straightened out before moving forward. "I let him believe I was going to go, but I went down to his car and told him I was leaving the fraternity."

"You did?"

Remi nodded, tentatively stepping closer, so damn relieved when Jeremiah didn't back up again. "I did. I thought I owed him a private conversation to tell him." He shook his head at his own naivete. "I was so dumb. I really thought he'd befriended me out of some deep-seated goodness his dad's bigotry hadn't touched. Instead, the guy fucking drugged me when I wasn't looking."

He scrubbed at his face, the tears he'd been holding back rushing into his eyes. Gods, he was exhausted. He wanted to sleep for a whole year.

"I'm so sorry I tricked you," he said behind his hands, voice muffled. "I understand if you can't forgive me yet, but maybe—"

"Shh." Jeremiah's wonderfully warm and strong arms wrapped around him, and the knot in his stomach finally eased. He threw his arms around his neck and held on tight.

"Please forgive me," he gasped, sobs shaking his body. "I promise to listen to everything you say the next time a psycho terrorist group targets me and my family."

Jeremiah huffed a laugh. "That's not funny, little princeling."

"I know." He sniffled and buried his face in Jeremiah's neck. "I really am sorry though. I was so fucking reckless. Thank you for saving me."

Shushing him again, Jeremiah carded his fingers through Remi's hair, soothing him. "I should stay mad a little longer, but you're breaking my heart."

"You forgive me?"

"Yes, my prince."

If anything, that made Remi cry harder. Relief and exhaustion and residual terror all blurred together inside him, and he just couldn't stop, big ugly sobs racking his body as Jeremiah scooped him up and carried him to their bed.

He wasn't sure how long it was before he finally caught his breath, but Jeremiah's T-shirt was soaked with tears and snot. "Oh gods, sorry. That's so gross."

Jeremiah chuckled and whipped it off over his head, then used the clean end to wipe Remi's face dry before tossing it away. "Feel better?"

He did, hollowed out and empty, but in a good way. Like now that he had gotten all the pain and sorrow out of him, he could fill back up with warmth and love. "Yeah… did you mean it?"

Jeremiah cupped his chin, not even pretending not to understand. "Yes, little princeling. I love you. I know being with me won't be easy—"

Remi silenced him with his lips, kissing him until he absolutely had to draw breath. "Shut up. I don't need easy. I just need you." He licked his lips and stared into Jeremiah's softly glowing eyes. "I love you too."

"Thank the gods," Jeremiah said, lips twitching into a smile.

Rolling his eyes, Remi leaned in and kissed him again, humming softly when Jeremiah took control, licking inside and rolling Remi onto his back. The heat and weight of Jeremiah on top of him should have been suffocating, but it made him feel so safe, so *loved*.

Jeremiah pressed wet, sucking kisses down his throat, and Remi arched against him. "What if… Oh gods… What if I decide to abdicate? Will you still love me if I'm not a prince anymore?"

Grunting, Jeremiah raised his head and stared down at him. "You don't have to do that for me. I'll stand by you no matter what."

His chest warmed as he cupped Jeremiah's handsome face. "I know, and I don't know if I can leave the burden to

Sadie or Percy. But… maybe when they're older and we can talk about what they want…"

"I'll support you, no matter your decision." Jeremiah leaned down and laid a lingering kiss on his mouth. "And you'll always be my prince."

Remi let out a soft breath, melting into the plush bed beneath him. "And you'll always be my second-favorite bodyguard."

Jeremiah raised a brow at him.

"What? Greg was really—" He broke off into peals of laughter as Jeremiah dug into his sides and growled against his throat.

"Such a fucking brat."

They rolled around on the bed for a while, laughing and kissing, until Jeremiah unzipped his pants, and things got heated in the blink of an eye. They were still smiling at each other as they quickly undressed and then came together once more, bare skin against bare skin. Remi ran his feet up the outside of Jeremiah's legs and wrapped his arms around his shoulders.

For long, languid minutes, they did nothing but kiss and press their bodies close, reveling in the feeling of being alive and together. By the time Jeremiah was pushing lube-slicked fingers against him, Remi's lips felt swollen and sore.

He spread his legs and pushed back against the intrusion, moaning as Jeremiah slipped inside.

"How'd you know?" Jeremiah mumbled, his gaze locked on where he was thrusting a finger in and out of Remi's body.

"Know what?" he asked breathlessly, throwing his head back and groaning louder than was probably advisable with a sex Demon in the apartment.

"My fire wouldn't hurt you."

Remi forced his eyes to focus and found blue, fiery ones staring back at him. "Folklore."

"Folklore?"

Remi nodded loosely, sinking his teeth into his lip when Jeremiah pushed a second finger inside him and began stretching. "Uh-huh. Pretty much every species has one."

"A folktale about hellfire?"

Remi chuckled, but it turned to a moan, his body flushing with pleasure and toes curling at how perfectly Jeremiah was rubbing against his prostate. "About fated mates being immune from each—ah, *fuck*—each other's powers. Gods, right there. *Harder*."

Instead of giving him what he wanted, Jeremiah pulled his fingers free and slicked his heavy cock. Remi stared at it, a little surprised every time when it all fit inside him.

And that was before the base swelled with his knot.

"That day on the beach…" Jeremiah said softly, pressing his large head against Remi's hole until he popped inside, and they both groaned. "You should have been killed, but you were fine. I thought I'd hallucinated from the holy water or something."

"It's why my Voice has never worked on you either," Remi panted out, gripping Jeremiah's massive biceps as he sank farther and farther into him. Once he was bottomed out, Remi let out a shaky breath and slipped his hands around to Jeremiah's back, the heat he was putting off all-consuming.

Or maybe that was the feeling of rightness growing inside him, the way his soul was reaching for and entwining with Jeremiah's as he slowly pumped in and out, holding Remi's eyes. Remi could *feel* how good it was for Jeremiah, his mate's pleasure fueling his own and driving everything up higher than he thought possible.

"You're moving in with me when we get back to Midlona," Jeremiah said, driving forward with more force as they both got caught up in how perfect the moment felt.

"Okay."

"And you're not going anywhere without me for a while. I'm not letting you out of my sight for at least a month."

Remi smiled up at him and smoothed his hands up and down on his Hellhound's strong back, trying to soothe him. When he gave a particularly strong thrust and Remi ended up crying out and digging his nails in instead, he wasn't sure how affective it was. "Gods… Um, yes, okay. Whatever you need. Be prepared for photo ops and hospital visits though."

Jeremiah grumbled and grabbed at Remi's hips, lifting to angle his cock better. "People will love that."

Remi grunted with each solid thrust, losing the conversation. Ecstasy built inside him, but it stayed just out of reach, even as Jeremiah worked his hips like a damn machine, driving him out of his mind with pleasure.

He grabbed at the back of his neck and yanked, scowling when he didn't move his mate at all. "Bite me, baby. Bite me while you fill me with your knot. Need to be yours."

"My prince," Jeremiah groaned, sinking down to smother him with his weight. It shortened his thrusts, but he still used his considerable strength to snap forward each time, hitting all the best spots deep inside Remi. "Never letting you go."

"I'll never want you to," he promised, then slapped a hand over his mouth to muffle his scream at the last second. Jeremiah's teeth bit into him, a sharp, *glorious* pain just as his cock began to expand, locking them together.

The heat from his release burned him up from the inside out, and if it was how he died, he'd go with a fucking smile on his face.

His whole body tensed, scales erupting across his body as their bond *snapped* into place, and come shot from his untouched cock, the pressure on his sensitive bundle of nerves so, so good he couldn't have stopped if he wanted. Gods, he wanted to have Jeremiah stretch him to the max on his knot every day for the rest of their lives. Nothing came close to feeling as good.

He rode a wave of blissful contentment, humming as Jeremiah licked at his neck and then nosed at a patch of shimmery purple scales just beneath his clavicle. His eyes were still fiery blue, and Remi realized with a jolt they would stay that way, now that they were completely and fully bonded. Sure, they'd dim a bit when he was calm, but their connection would keep them on full display.

Remi sighed, enjoying being tied so tightly together, and absently wondered if his scales would stay too. He hoped so. Not because he wanted to look more Siren, but because he wanted the world to know he was mated to his sexy Hellhound.

By the time Jeremiah's knot started to shrink, Remi was half-asleep, but he stirred and moaned at the sensation of Jeremiah pulling out and the mess of come they left on the bed beneath him. He barely stirred, though, as Jeremiah cleaned them up a bit before climbing back into bed with him and pulling Remi firmly against him.

"We'll teach them," he muttered against Jeremiah's salty skin.

"Hm?"

"The people of Midlona. We'll teach them about you. We'll teach them so they won't be afraid."

He wasn't sure if he said all that out loud, too busy sinking into unconsciousness, but he could have sworn he felt Jeremiah press a kiss to his temple and whisper, "Yes, my prince."

He wasn't sure how much time had passed when he jolted awake to someone pounding on the apartment door. It couldn't have been more than a couple of hours, his brain sluggish and barely comprehending what was happening. Jeremiah didn't have that problem though.

Growling, his mate got out of bed and pulled on a pair of

sweats and a new T-shirt. "Go back to sleep, princeling. I'll take care of this."

Murmuring an assent, he turned onto his stomach and pressed his face into Jeremiah's pillow, sucking his wonderfully smoky scent into his lungs and letting it lull him back to sleep.

Raised voices roused him before he could completely succumb. He frowned and sat up, trepidation rolling down his spine. Gods, what now?

"This is fucking ridiculous," he heard Jeremiah snarl. "It was self-defense."

"Stop resisting, or we'll tase you, Hellhound."

What the hell?

Remi scrambled out of bed, throwing open the door and taking in the scene in the kitchen with his heart in his throat. Two police officers were putting handcuffs on Jeremiah, who was bent over the kitchen island, face smashed into the countertop.

Priest was standing nearby, phone pressed to his ear.

As the officers grabbed his arms and raised him up, Jeremiah met his eyes and fucking *smiled*.

"It's okay, little princeling. Do what Priest says, okay?"

He didn't even have a chance to agree or demand to know what was going on before he was dragged out of the apartment.

Then he was just… gone.

22

REMI

Someone cleared their throat to Remi's left, and he looked over—mostly on instinct—and saw Priest attempting to avert his eyes while thrusting a ball of gray cloth at him. It took Remi's shocked brain a second to realize they were his sweats and that he was stark naked in front of the whole Alpha Team.

He wasn't sure when they'd all arrived, the last few minutes feeling like he'd been walking through molasses, but he was grateful the twins seemed to have slept through the commotion.

His face on fire, he grabbed the pants and did his best to get them on without falling on his face. He was trembling, and every instinct in his body said he needed to rush down to the police station and burn it to the ground so he could rescue Jeremiah from the ashes.

"Calm down." That was Knight, the sharp-dressed Vampire. Remi almost started laughing hysterically when he realized he didn't actually know their real names. "Your panic scent right now is a little powerful, and it smells like prey."

Remi scoffed, irritated that none of Jeremiah's team seemed even remotely worried that he was just arrested, probably for the murder of a human senator's son, and was being carted off to jail. "I don't give a shit. We need to get down there. He has a lawyer, right? I mean, you must have a lawyer. But if you don't, we can call my parents and—"

"We have a lawyer," Priest said, looking at Remi now that he was dressed. His eyes roved over Remi's chest, and he was about to get pissed when he realized he still had his scales out.

He swallowed heavily and tried to pull them back in, but he couldn't. He had no idea if it was his full bond with Jeremiah or if he was stuck that way because he couldn't seem to relax. He'd never done a partial shift like this before, and it just made him want his mate even more. "Then what are we waiting for? If you think we're just going to let him rot in prison—"

"Enough." Knight spoke one word with enough power to make Remi want to drop to his knees in supplication. That had never happened to him before, and it terrified him just a little. Gods, who was this guy? "Jeremiah is our brother in more ways than anyone could possibly understand. We aren't concerned because there's nothing to be concerned about. We have connections everywhere. This is what we do for a living. We have security footage from your building of your friend—"

"He is—was—not my friend," Remi spat and began to pace. He used his connection to Jeremiah to reach out to his mate, but all he found was mild irritation.

Priest gave him a look of pity. "He was your friend. No one's blaming you for not realizing the kind of person he was. But you're not going to assuage your guilt by trying to deny what was. Trust me. I've been down that road, and there's no ending to it."

Remi swallowed heavily and fought back a sudden and intense urge to cry. "I need him here. I don't want… I *can't* do this alone."

Priest and Knight exchanged a look, and then Priest glanced over his shoulder where Storm was standing, phone in hand. "Any word?"

"Not yet. It'll take a few hours for processing."

Remi dug his hand into his hair and pulled hard enough to make his eyes water. "Hours? Gods, can you even imagine what a human jail is like for Supes?"

"Yep," Priest said, sounding far too cheerful about that. "Trust me, we know how to make it fun. All of us have been exactly where Sunshine is right now. He's going to be fine. They're not hurting him."

Remi wasn't sure he could believe them. He'd never experienced it himself, but he'd been warned by more than one person before he enrolled at Hillsland about what it would be like for him if he ever broke the law. They'd dehydrate him to keep him weak, gag him to keep him separated from his Voice, shackle him to keep his claws retracted, and deprive him of sleep to keep him disoriented. And he was just half Siren. The gods only knew what they were doing to a full-blooded, extremely powerful Hellhound.

"You're panicking again," Priest said. He was closer now, and he draped his arm over Remi's shoulders. "Come on. We're going to order some takeout and watch some cartoons while we wait for word. Do you mind if Knight packs for you? Nah, of course you don't. You're used to servants going through your underthings, aren't you?"

Remi let Priest tug him to the couch, staring at him in fascination. He found every spare blanket from the apartment and put them in a massive pile right in the middle. Storm nodded encouragingly as Priest urged him down onto the little nest. He was suddenly exhausted and so lonely he wanted to scream. How had it been just a couple of hours since he was on his bed with Jeremiah deep inside him, their bond singing between them, making them both feel whole for the first time in either of their lives?

How had it turned into this?

"I know you're used to this," Remi said as he nestled into a particularly soft throw, "but what if this is the one time it doesn't work out the way you think? Thad wasn't just some guy."

"He wasn't, no," Priest agreed as he flopped down and snuggled close. Remi waited for a possessive feeling to overcome him, figuring Jeremiah would know now when someone got too close. But he just felt a small pulse in his chest telling him it was okay. He relaxed a fraction and let his temple drop down against Priest's shoulder. "But this isn't the first time we've had to deal with some high-powered government official. We have plans in place for when things like this happen."

Remi wanted to ask more, but he was exhausted. "I just found him. I don't want to lose him."

Priest reached up and stroked his fingers through Remi's hair. He felt a strange tug, like Priest was draining him of the will to stay awake, and he both hated and loved the sensation. "I'm just helping you relax. I used to do this for Jeremiah all the time when things got to be too much."

"What was too much?" Remi mumbled.

"Existing, sometimes," Priest answered, keeping his voice low and soothing. "We had very lonely childhoods. Painful at times. Jeremiah holds his in more than most of us, and sometimes those feelings overwhelm him."

"You love him," Remi said.

Priest stiffened against him. "Not like that."

Remi felt himself laughing, feeling floaty as he rolled his eyes. "I know. I can feel that. It's different. It's nice. I never… I mean, I have my parents, and they love me. But I'm a disappointment to them."

Priest's expression went sad. "Is that really what you think?"

"Dunno what else to think," Remi said, then yawned so

hard his jaw cracked. "Sadie and Percy are better than me. Stronger. More… everything." Gods, words were getting hard now. "M'only crown prince because I was first."

"Your parents adore you. All three of you. I wasn't there very long, but Remi…" Priest sighed. "All they do is worry they haven't been good enough. And they want you to be happy."

Remi's chest ached, and suddenly, he missed them with a fierceness he hadn't felt since he was a scared child. "I want to go home."

"Soon," Priest told him. His voice rumbled a little deeper in his chest, and Remi couldn't keep his eyes open. "Sleep for a bit. Things will be better when you wake up."

Before Remi opened his eyes, he tried to find it in him to be pissed that a Demon essentially cast a sleeping spell over him like he was some damsel in a fairy tale. However, he felt a little more clearheaded and refreshed, so it was hard to be angry at Priest for knocking him out.

He was on the couch, but he could hear members of the Alpha Team talking not too far away.

"You're up?"

Remi forced one eye open and saw Storm lounging in a chair near his feet. With a yawn, he stretched his arms above his head and sat up. "How long was I out?"

"Just a few hours. Looked like you needed the rest."

Remi wanted to say he'd only slept that hard because of Priest, but he wasn't sure if that was true or not. The bonding had drained him; then losing Jeremiah not too long afterward to the human police had ruined what should have been all-night cuddles with his mate. So there was every chance his body had decided to just shut down.

"You want some coffee?"

Remi looked over at the Dragon, who had dark circles under his eyes, and he had to wonder if the team had been getting regular sleep. "Has anyone heard from him?"

Storm leaned forward. "Yes. We're going to head over there in a bit, but Knight said you might want the chance to clean up. You, uh… smell a bit."

Remi flushed hard. He knew it wasn't offensive body odor from working up a sweat. He'd been marked by Jeremiah and probably smelled like raging pheromones. "Yeah. I'm, um… gonna shower."

Storm shot him a small grin and shook his head. "For the record, it didn't bother any of us. We're really happy for you two."

Remi wanted to say he was happy too, but it was hard to feel like the world wasn't falling out from under him now that he was bonded and immediately lost his mate. He wanted to trust that the team really had taken care of matters, but what if this was that one time they couldn't solve it?

What if whatever evidence they had wasn't enough?

He didn't want to let that thought cloud his head too much, and as he reached for the shower knob, he felt a sudden pulsing in his chest. It was like a steady second heartbeat, warm and comforting, and he realized it was Jeremiah calming him down.

Remi felt his eyes grow hot with tears. Fuck, he needed him.

I know, the heartbeat seemed to say. **Soon.**

He jumped under the spray and washed just enough to water down his scent, then immediately hopped out to dry off. He didn't really give a shit if he looked a mess. He just wanted to be with his mate. He wanted to call his parents and demand they figure out a way to free him.

He also needed to tell his parents about him and Jeremiah, but he didn't think they'd be anything other than happy for him. Even if he decided to also tell them that he was going to abdicate and leave room for his siblings to rule. He no longer felt like he wasn't Siren enough, but he would be the worst liar and an even worse ruler if he tried to say that his loyalty to Midlona came first.

He had a feeling Jeremiah wouldn't survive ruling at his side. He was not the sort of person who could be caged by a crown, but he also knew his Hellhound would do it for him. The moment Remi gave himself permission to think about a life alongside his mate and free of royal responsibilities, he felt… at peace. He just hoped if that's what he decided, it wouldn't be the one thing that his parents couldn't get over.

Throwing on a fresh pair of jeans and a shirt, Remi dragged his fingers through his hair and then headed for the living room. There was a strange mood shift when he walked in, and after a beat, he realized why.

Ozias was there, staring at him with an odd expression. "Remi," he said after a beat.

Remi swallowed thickly. "Hey, I—" Before he could finish his sentence, Oz was on him, hugging him tightly. It was more affection than the Nephilim had shown since the end of their relationship, and Remi heard a soft hiss coming from one of the team members.

Oz ignored the angry sound, holding on even tighter. "There were people on campus saying you were dead. Gods, I just… The team filled me in though."

Remi stepped back and rubbed the back of his neck, feeling like absolute shit. "I know you always hated Thad. I wish I hadn't been so blind to how awful he was."

Oz shook his head hard, grabbing one of Remi's hands and squeezing. "Don't do that. How could you have ever guessed he was capable of something like this?"

"Actually, Ozias was the one who pointed us toward some not-so-legal dealings the senator was involved in," Knight said, staring at where Oz was holding his hand still. "That information has been helpful in getting Sunshine released quickly."

Oz flushed a little, glancing at the Vampire out of the corner of his indigo eyes. Remi did his best to hide his surprise at the unusually shy behavior. "I'm glad I was able to help, and I've always told you I understood why you were friends with him."

"I still should have listened," Remi said, angry at himself. "If I'd pulled my head out of my ass…"

"Don't," Oz said softly. He squeezed Remi's hand once more before backing away. "I just needed to see for myself that you're okay. The only thing I wanted to say I told you so about was that new mate of yours."

Remi laughed and rubbed at his face. "Even as it was happening to me, I didn't believe it."

"But you do now, don't you?" Oz pressed. "I can sense you're bonded. Truly bonded."

Truly bonded. The words settled something in him, and he nodded. "I'm sorry I didn't believe you about that either," Remi told him very quietly, aware of their audience.

Oz smiled at him, glancing once more at Knight before clearing his throat and saying, "I wouldn't have hated if it was you. But I think the fates made the right choice. I don't know Jeremiah well, but it's obvious you'll never want for anything, including love, and you deserve a mate like that, Rem."

He had no idea what to say. Those were strange words coming from his ex, who had always been a little… standoffish. But now that he knew the truth, he understood. If he'd believed it when he met Oz, nothing between them would have ever happened because nothing could compare to what it felt like being with the person fate chose.

"We need to go," Knight broke in before Remi could decide how to respond. When Remi looked up, he saw his gaze was locked on Oz, a little unnerving in its intensity.

There was a strange feeling in the air, almost like static electricity, and then Oz dropped his eyes and took a step back, and the moment shattered.

What the hell?

"See you around," Oz said, and he was out the door before anyone could move.

Priest walked over a second later, but Knight shook his head, avoiding the arm Priest aimed to throw over his shoulders. "Do not."

Priest held his hands up and stepped back. "Hey, I wasn't—"

"No," Knight snapped. "Just… Just don't, Priest. Let's go."

Priest backed up, and Remi was far too tired and far too anxious to see Jeremiah to give a shit what was going on between them. He grabbed his phone and slipped into his running shoes without bothering to look for socks, and not two minutes later, he was in the back seat of one of their cars, speeding toward downtown and the police station.

Remi had about a thousand plans of how he was going to storm the building and rescue Jeremiah from the torturous clutches of humans when that second heartbeat started thudding wildly in his chest. He was sure something terrible was happening to Jeremiah.

Then they turned the corner, and the first thing Remi saw was his tall, gorgeous Hellhound in his gray sweats and bright white T-shirt just… standing there, leaning against the building column like he didn't have a care in the world. Remi found himself reaching for the door handle before the car had even pulled up to the curb, and Priest had to slam on the brakes so Remi didn't kill himself as he flung himself onto the pavement.

He might have actually fallen on his face too, but Jeremiah

was just *there*, wrapping him in his arms and mouth on his before Remi could draw in a breath. The moment their lips touched, it was like the world had righted itself again. It was like nothing had ever been wrong.

Jeremiah dug fingers into his hair and wrenched his head to the side so he could lick along the bond bite, and Remi shuddered, groaning softly.

"You're going to get arrested again, and we definitely can't save you from public indecency charges," Priest called out.

Jeremiah growled, but he pulled back, though he didn't let Remi go. "There's something to be said about being scolded by an Incubus Demon about public indecency."

Remi laughed. "A well-fed one too, considering how well his shit worked on me a few hours ago."

Jeremiah's eyes flared brighter. "He did what to you?"

His entire voice was nothing but a growl, and it went straight to Remi's dick.

Priest just laughed. "Demon Benadryl. I just put him to sleep. Relax. I didn't feed on him."

Jeremiah's body released some of its tension as he cupped Remi's cheek. "Tell me you're okay."

"I'm okay. Better now," Remi said. He licked his lips and let out a trembling breath. "I was terrified I wasn't going to see you again."

Jeremiah shook his head. "They wouldn't have been able to hold me if I was going to end up in any real danger. We do our best to keep to the law whenever we're in foreign territory, but we always have a plan B."

"And C. And D," Priest rattled off.

"H, I, J, K," came another voice that Remi didn't recognize, and he felt a pulse of something like jealousy when Jeremiah let him go and immediately rushed at the newcomer, throwing his arms around the massive man.

He was very good-looking—tall with deeply tanned skin,

dark hair, and light green eyes. He was wearing a T-shirt, jeans, and biker boots, and he lifted Jeremiah off the ground as he hugged him. Remi wanted to put his fist through the man's ridiculously handsome face.

Jeremiah must have felt that because he was genuinely laughing as he turned and beckoned Remi close. "This is Gray, but everyone calls him Slate. He's been on assignment for the last two months."

Remi felt some measure of comfort as Jeremiah linked their hands together, kissing his wrist before letting go so Remi could offer his hand.

"I heard Sunshine found his mate," Slate said, his voice a low rumble. It only took Remi a second to recognize the secondary traits of a Gargoyle. But he wasn't as stoic as Remi was used to, pulling Remi into a hug instead of taking his hand.

It was odd and comforting, and Remi understood now why Jeremiah was close to him.

"You missed all the action, bud," Storm said, clapping him on the arm.

Slate rolled his eyes. "I have a feeling something will make up for it. But I'm sorry I wasn't here before things got bad. How are the kids?"

The question sobered Remi almost immediately. He knew his brother and sister were fine, being looked over by the rest of Remi's detail until they could all get on the plane back to Midlona, but he also knew the trauma of being kidnapped and everything else would be lasting. And fuck, he'd missed them. He was so done with Hillsland and their bullshit bigotry.

"We're heading back to Midlona today," Jeremiah said, pulling Remi close. "You can hang out with them on the jet."

Slate's eyes were soft and crinkled at the corners as he smiled. "Awesome. I love kids. My family is—was—huge.

Full of kids, and I was always the uncle who volunteered to babysit."

Remi swallowed. "Are… did something…"

"No," Slate said before Remi could finish his question. "Not the way you're thinking. We had some disagreements, and we don't speak anymore." He bowed his head, but he smiled when Storm gripped the back of his neck, and Remi remembered from their trip to pick up the twins why the Dragon understood exactly how Slate felt in that moment.

"Let's get the fuck out of here before we turn into some melancholy folk ballad," Priest said, clapping his hands.

Jeremiah groaned, but he motioned everyone forward, and they all headed back to the SUVs. Before Remi could take more than a few steps though, Jeremiah pulled him back. His Hellhound gripped him by the chin, locking their gazes.

It made Remi feel some type of way to be looking in Jeremiah's eyes, now permanently changed thanks to their bond. Fuck, they were beautiful on him—a glowing blue that lit up whenever his hound was close to the surface.

"Tell me you're okay," Jeremiah said.

Remi nodded. "I am. Now, tell me you're okay. Tell me the humans didn't hurt you."

"No one touched me," Jeremiah said with a tiny smile playing at his lips.

Remi nodded, but he didn't feel comforted just yet. "Is it over, or are they going to come for you?"

Jeremiah sighed, and Remi's heart sank. "It's nothing we can't handle. Nothing we haven't done before. There's been unrest in Hillsland for a long, long time, and people like me are easy targets. But nothing is going to happen to me, my little princeling. I promise you."

Remi closed his eyes and surged up for a kiss that Jeremiah took gratefully, holding him close as he breathed a sigh against Remi's lips. "I love you," Remi said.

Jeremiah shuddered like the words were almost painful to

hear, and maybe they were. Remi knew Jeremiah had spent too much of his life unloved, and he wanted to spend the rest of his making up for that.

"I love you too," Jeremiah whispered. "Now, let's get you home."

Remi nodded. "I need to see my family, then I can't wait to see your place."

"Our place," Jeremiah murmured. "If you're sure?"

Remi cradled Jeremiah's face between both palms and looked him directly in the eye. "I have never been more sure about anything in my entire life. You are my home now. It's time for me to take charge of my future. So let's go, because now that I have you, not even the gods themselves can take you away."

Jeremiah grinned, then kissed him again.

EPILOGUE

JEREMIAH

"Come on, little brat. I think you can be a little nicer when you beg me."

"I hate you," Remi spat, his tail writhing in the water.

Jeremiah threw his head back, laughing at the sight of his beloved so needy, so tormented. He loved it because Remi loved it, and through their bond, he could feel Remi's pleasure and desperation as he sat with just the head of his cock pressed into Remi's slit. His cock was just behind that, pulsing, desperate to unsheathe, but Jeremiah kept him plugged.

"Hmm. That didn't sound nice at all. It seems like my pretty little Siren doesn't want my knot."

Remi groaned, his head falling back, tail thrashing and making waves against the side of the pool. His scales were more plentiful in his full shift and flashing in the sun. "I'm going to fucking die, baby. I'm literally going to die."

"You know I'd never let that happen," Jeremiah promised, his voice a low growl. He knew that Remi's words were spoken out of passion, but they were a little hard to hear after everything they'd been through.

They were safe now, having traded in Jeremiah's top-floor penthouse for a cozy house near the Trident Agency's headquarters. It was a bond gift from the queen and king, who had taken Remi not wanting to live at the palace remarkably well. They visited often, Remi not able to go too many days without seeing the twins. While they loved everything about their home and building a life together, the large saltwater pool in the private backyard was their favorite feature.

Extending his claws, Jeremiah dragged the edge of one over Remi's throat, then down his chest. He flicked at his nipples, then dragged them along his waist, where his skin turned to scales at the beginning of his gorgeous tail. He knew how sensitive it was there for him, and Remi moaned so loudly he was pretty sure his cries were heard all the way to the mountains.

"Jeremiah. Please. Please, I need you. I need your knot." His whine went a little high-pitched and melodic, like a gorgeous Siren Song attempting to drag Jeremiah under his spell.

His cock throbbed, and he could feel the base start to swell. Withdrawing his claws, he dug two fingers into Remi's slit, spreading it wide enough for Remi's cock to finally extend, and as it did, Jeremiah thrust his own in.

Remi howled. His head fell back, and his body trembled as Jeremiah thrust his hips fast and furious into his tight, slick heat. "Touch me. Touch me, baby. I'm so fucking close."

Jeremiah didn't need to be asked twice. He got his hand around Remi's wet, throbbing cock and stroked him with the same rhythm as he fucked him, and it wasn't long before he felt Remi's orgasm rising and cresting. His own followed almost at the same time, and he squeezed down on Remi's cock just as they both let go.

Feeling them both was still overwhelming for Jeremiah. His vision whited out as his knot swelled, locking himself inside Remi as his lover spilled in the water between them. The scent was overwhelming, and his fangs dropped seconds before he sank them into Remi's skin. His blood was sweet, the bond even sweeter, and he licked the wounds before burying his face in Remi's neck.

"Love you, love you, love you," Remi was whispering, drawing his own claws along Jeremiah's naked back.

Jeremiah let himself just exist, his knot pulsing and filling Remi, marking him from the inside out. Never in his life did he think he could be so content—so loved. So happy.

"I feel that," Remi said with a playful laugh, but his tone sobered. "I hope someday you'll stop being surprised by how much I fucking adore you."

Jeremiah pulled back, his beast calm and satiated under his skin from the closeness of the bond and the coolness of the water. "I don't. It's precious to me. I never, ever want to get complacent."

Remi surged forward and kissed him, his slit spasming around Jeremiah's knot, sending another wave of pleasure through them both. He groaned, which turned into a soft purr, and Remi sagged against him as his spent cock gave a feeble twitch against Jeremiah's stomach.

"Are you happy?" Jeremiah finally asked.

"With you? Or do you mean with… everything?"

"Both. I never want you to feel any kind of regret," he answered.

Remi reached up, absently playing with a wet lock of Jeremiah's hair. "If I hadn't met you yet—like, if it was years before I met you—I think I would have made the same choice to come home. I love my family, and I don't feel as disconnected from Midlona as I did before. I feel… ready. To take on whatever comes next."

Jeremiah just nodded. "We'll take it on together."

"That's my favorite part."

It was clear the royal family adored each other, and although it was less now, Jeremiah still felt a small tendril of envy curling around his stomach for what he'd never been given the chance to have. He looked down at Remi, and he had a sudden vision of their future.

Bonded, happy, maybe even parents.

"Seriously?" Remi asked.

Jeremiah sucked in a breath. It was far too easy to forget Remi could hear his thoughts now when they were particularly strong.

Remi cradled his cheek again. "You seriously want a kid with me?"

Jeremiah's eyes cut to the side, and he shrugged. "Hellhounds are still abandoning their children like they did when I was young, and Demons are a close second. Sometimes I wonder what kind of person I'd be if someone had found me and loved me."

He felt Remi's little pulse of pain in his chest like it were his own. "I hate that you ever went without feeling loved and cared for."

Jeremiah shrugged. "It made me who I am today. It gave me the family I have, and I can't regret that. But yeah. I mean, I've thought about it."

"Someone should do something about that," Remi said after a long beat. He wrapped his arms around Jeremiah and held him close, even as his knot started to deflate and he slipped out. They floated in the water a little farther away from the edge of the pool, and Jeremiah could feel Remi's mind turning through thoughts. "Maybe I could do something like that, you know? Start some sort of organization or charity for those kids."

"An orphanage?" Jeremiah said, his nose wrinkling.

Remi shifted his body and swished his tail through the water. He was so fucking beautiful when he shifted, and Jeremiah wanted to trace the length of him with his tongue. The desire made Remi laugh and splash him. "Insatiable. And also, no. Or, well, yes, I guess? Orphanage just sounds so medieval and cruel. I want a place where these kids can go to feel loved and wanted."

Jeremiah let out a small sigh. "Hellhounds don't breed very often, so there's not, like, hundreds of them wandering the streets or anything. But you need to know that you're not going to be able to find families to take them in. Not unless the stigma changes."

"So maybe we do that too," Remi said. He let go of Jeremiah, turning on his back to float at the top of the water. His eyes were closed, and in the late-afternoon sun, his scales were luminescent. All of him was *breathtaking*. "We do the opposite of what that fucker Thad was doing. I don't want to live in a world where people look at the most amazing man I know like he's worthless."

Jeremiah shrugged. "It's just the way people are."

Remi opened his eyes and held Jeremiah's gaze. "But it doesn't always have to be that way. Just… maybe that's what I was meant to do, you know?"

Jeremiah wanted to keep arguing, but he felt something in the bond—something that told him this was right. Maybe not for him. His job was his calling. But Remi needed something, and he felt settled and sure for the first time since Jeremiah had met him.

"You know the agency is here for whatever you need. All of us are."

Remi looked over and smiled. "I love you so much."

Jeremiah couldn't help but kiss him after that. "I love you too."

Stepping out of the shower later that evening, Jeremiah wrapped a towel around his waist and followed the sound of the TV to the living room, where Remi was sitting on the edge of the couch, his eyes fixed on the screen. Jeremiah glanced over and saw it was a news report of some building, smoke billowing black and heavy toward the sky.

"What's happening?"

"An attack," Remi said, his voice stunned. "In Midlona. But it was a human shop."

Jeremiah's mind immediately went to the cozy little bookstore Priest made any and every excuse to visit whenever he had a chance. Shit. But what were the chances?

He said a small prayer it wasn't Priest's human's place, but then his phone began to ring, and his stomach sank.

Running a hand down Remi's arm as he walked past, he went over to the table where he'd left his phone, and he hated that he wasn't surprised to see Priest's name on the screen. He didn't even get a chance to say anything before Priest started talking.

"I need you," Priest said, his voice thick. "Something happened."

"I saw on the news. Are you there right now?" Jeremiah asked.

"No. But Knight and I are on our way. I… I felt…" He stopped and cleared his throat, but his voice was still unsteady when he said, "Can you meet us there?"

Jeremiah turned to look over at Remi, who was nodding like he knew what Jeremiah was being asked. "Yeah. We're on our way. Hold tight, okay? I'm sure he's fine."

"I don't think he is. And I—" Priest cut himself off with a small, shaky sigh. "Never mind. We'll talk when you get here."

"See you soon." Jeremiah hung up and turned to Remi. "You're coming with me, right?"

"There's no way in hell I'd let you go alone. Is he okay?" Remi asked as he hopped to his feet.

Jeremiah glanced back at the raging fire on the TV, then shrugged. "I don't know. But we're going to figure it out when we get there. I hope you're ready, little princeling. Something tells me this is just the start."

Remi smiled, then kissed him before turning off the news coverage. He tossed the remote onto the couch and cupped Jeremiah's face. "This is the rest of our lives."

Our lives.

Him and his mate.

He liked the sound of that. Jeremiah wrapped his arms around Remi and held him tight, kissing him back deeply. Despite everything else, when he held Remi, the world just felt right for the first time in his life.

And he'd never let that go.

Thank you so much for reading Jeremiah and Remi's story. We really hope you enjoyed it and are excited for more! The Alpha Team of the Trident Agency is back in PRIEST!
Our chaotic sex Demon has to work extra hard to keep his sweet little bookstore human safe. ;-)

(Use the camera on your phone to scan the QR code and jump right to Amazon!)

ALSO BY EM LINDSEY

Kindle Unlimited Books:

Broken Chains

The Carnal Tower

Hit and Run

Irons and Works

The Sin Bin: West Coast

Malicious Compliance

Collaborations with Other Authors

Foreign Translations

AudioBooks

ALSO BY KIKI CLARK

Kincaid Pack

Leather & Chrome

Blue Collar Hearts

Forever Family Trilogy

Audiobooks

ABOUT EM LINDSEY

E.M. Lindsey is a non-binary, MM Romance author who lives on the East Coast of the United States. When they're not working, EM is spending time on the beach, kayaking, swimming, and playing with their dogs.

Ream Stories
Website
Free Short Stories
Amazon
Instagram
BookBub

ABOUT KIKI CLARK

A small-town Michigan girl, Kiki has enjoyed reading since she first picked up a YA fantasy as a child. After that, she devoured everything she could get her hands on and dreamed of one time writing her own books that touched people's hearts.

In 2020, she proudly joined the ranks of authors releasing character-driven, emotionally satisfying books showcasing that everyone deserves to find love.

To keep up-to-date with Kiki, sign up for her newsletter: http://www.kikiclark.com/newsletter.

Keep in touch by following her on any of these platforms:

facebook.com/kikiclarkauthor
instagram.com/kikiclark2017
amazon.com/author/kikiclark
bookbub.com/authors/kiki-clark
goodreads.com/kikiclark

www.ingramcontent.com/pod-product-compliance
Lightning Source LLC
Chambersburg PA
CBHW051535260626
47170CB00003B/953
9798886750102